I0633576

THE LAST ARTIFACT

A TRILOGY BY GILLIAM NESS

Published by POLYMATH PUBLISHING
Toronto, Canada.

POLYMATH PUBLISHING and the portrayal of the letter "P"
within the box are trademarks of Polymath Publishing.

All of the characters and events in this book are fictitious, and any
resemblance they might have to actual persons, living or dead, is
purely coincidental.

ISBN 978-1-988145-00-6

Copyright © 2016 by Gilliam Ness

All rights reserved

January 2016

BOOK THREE
THE SACRED CHAMBER

CHAPTER 1

Los Picos de Europa, Northern Spain.

Isaac passed through a broad set of doors to find himself in a great circular hall of dark and somber stone. Its domed ceiling was soaring and supported by a ring of twelve gothic arches. Enormous stained-glass windows encircled the space, flashing brightly under the light of an electrical storm outside.

At the hall's centre was a heavy round table, and around it were placed twenty-five elaborately carved chairs. All but one were occupied.

Isaac took a deep breath and readied himself. The air smelt of incense and antiquity. Brother Bernardo's whisper sounded hoarse in his ear.

"The Final Council of the Apocatastasis," he said, and just then a succession of flashes sent the stained glass aglow.

Isaac smoothed down his hair and arranged his dark suit as best he could. It was tattered and travel worn and in need of a good cleaning. Studying the faces of those at the table, he counted twelve elders, six male and six female. They were dressed in crimson robes, with the exception of an ancient couple whose gowns were deep blue.

Flanking this couple, and the elders who sat to their left and right, were the twelve armed knights he had seen earlier in the crypt. They were unhelmed now, and he took note of their youthful appearance. The chair that was reserved for him lay directly in their midst.

"You must go and sit down," whispered the hefty monk. "I will be waiting outside."

As Isaac approached, all but the couple in blue rose to their feet. Their smiles of welcome did nothing to mask the deep concern in their eyes.

"Welcome, dear friend," said the seated elder. "I am Alulim, named for the first Sumerian King who came to possess the gnosis of the ancients. This is my wife, Ursula. You are in the house of the Order of St. James the Just, and this special council has been called so that the future glory of the Apocatastasis may be duly preserved."

Isaac bowed low, unsure of what to do. He was still trying to assimilate everything that had happened since he had arrived at the strange monastery. He felt as though he had been transported back in time.

Alulim and Ursula were clearly the leaders here, not only because of their blue robes, but because of the regal way in which they held themselves. Alulim was tall and clean shaven and sat erect despite his advanced years. Ursula possessed an elegance and beauty that defied her age. Her silver hair was long and still thick, her green eyes almond shaped and sparkling with kindness and wisdom.

Isaac could not help but feel like a pauper before monarchs.

"I thank you for the honour of being in attendance here, your Excellencies," he said as formally as he could. "Any help that I can offer is humbly yours."

"Isaac Rodchenko!" cried Alulim officially, rising to his feet. "Do you reject Lucifer and all his works?"

Isaac looked at Alulim with a questioning frown.

"With every fiber of my being, your Worship."

Alulim smiled softly and sat down.

"Be seated then, dear friend. I am convinced of your sincerity. The Final Council of the Apocatastasis can now begin."

Even as everyone sat, one knight remained standing. He appeared to be older than the other knights, perhaps forty. His hair was thick and matted, and his jaw was square and strong. Whereas the other knights wore red over their shirts of mail, his tunic was the same deep blue as Alulim's, and it was clear to Isaac that this man was their captain.

"Our families and friends are dead," he said solemnly, his eyes moving over all those present. "Their bodies are just outside, roaming the streets like rabid dogs. Our once happy village has been destroyed by this plague, and it is clear that the prophecies we have kept in trust for so many centuries have come to pass in ways more horrific than any of us could have imagined."

The knight leaned over the table, planting both of his fists on its dark wood.

"I should like to ask who our guest is," he said bluntly, looking over at Isaac. "And what role he has to play in these events. My men and I are anxious to act!"

Alulim nodded slowly, inviting the knight to sit down with the wave of his hand.

"The souls of our brethren are happily in the beyond, Sir David," he said reassuringly. "We can never allow ourselves to forget this, or despair will surely take us. As far as Mr. Rodchenko is concerned, he is the *Betrayer.*"

No sooner had Alulim uttered these words than all the knights leapt to their feet, their hands moving to their swords. According to the Ascender's Prophecy, the Betrayer was the harbinger of doom; the one who would open the Portal of Ahreimanius and release the demons from the lower spheres. If the truth was being spoken, seated at their table was the very hand of Ahreimanius.

"Please sit down, good knights," said Alulim, turning his gaze to a confused Isaac. "Just as good can come from an act of evil, and evil from an act of goodness, so too is Mr. Rodchenko both the Betrayer and the *Consilio* at once."

The knights took their seats. As opposed to the Betrayer, the Concilio would be a great hero, assisting the Two in their noble mission. That both friend and foe could exist within the same man seemed the greatest contradiction to them, but like many spiritual concepts, the paradoxical was often the crux. It would be as Alulim said.

The council soon fell into discussion, addressing the subject that was the primary reason for the order's existence. Every member present was a humble servant of The Two, and each had sworn to aid them in their mission to release the gnosis that was housed in the Compostela Cube.

Their order constituted the side of the Rex Angelus bloodline that had remained faithful to Jesus Christ. What Isaac did not know, and soon learned, was that he himself was a member of their bloodline, his family belonging to the side that had formed an allegiance with the Luciferic captains at the core of the Vatican; the ones who had called themselves *The Illuminati.*

"You are of unimaginable importance to the great plan of Illac Domus," said Alulim. "Through you, Isaac, shall come the long-awaited reconciliation of the two houses in our bloodline, and the fulfillment of the prophecies."

"I'm afraid I do not understand," said Isaac, more confused than ever.

Alulim smiled kindly.

"In order for you to fully understand your role in all of this, you must hear our story from the very beginning, and the beginning was indeed a very long time ago."

Alulim sat silently for a moment, gathering his thoughts before he spoke.

"If you sincerely consider how ancient this planet is," he said at length, "and how tiny a sliver of time has been occupied by our civilization, it will not appear illogical to you that humanity was not the first civilization to inhabit this world. There were others before us, and their societies were as large and diverse as our own, but these people were not human."

Isaac furrowed his brow in confusion.

What is this man saying?

That a secret society of people should inhabit a village lost in the Cantabrian Mountains was difficult enough to accept. That they had raised their children to be knights, trained in outdated forms of battle, and sworn to protect a pair of saviours spoken of only in obscure prophecy, was even more outlandish.

But to be inferring that another race of beings inhabited the planet before humans did; this was insanity. Even still, Isaac listened politely. Outside, the strange lightning was increasing in frequency and intensity.

"Long ago," began Alulim, "there existed a race of reptilian creatures who possessed the same souls that we possess today, albeit in far less developed states. In essence, we were these creatures, and our primitive souls resided within them as we first incarnated upon this earth."

"If I may ask," interjected Isaac humbly. "How could it be that there are no traces of this civilization?"

Alulim nodded, as if expecting Isaac's skepticism.

"Two hundred and fifty million years will erase many traces, my friend. In the Permian period, life on earth was flourishing, but the planet was an utterly different place. There was but one supercontinent, which geologists have since named *Pangaea*, and it was comprised mostly of desert and savannah. It was within the oceans where the vast majority of life existed, and it was there where the reptilians lived and thrived."

Isaac listened intently as an exceptionally strange story was related to him. Speaking at intervals, the different elders explained that when the first shattered soul fragments of the fallen angels had begun to incarnate on the newly formed earth-sphere, they could do so only in the form of raw minerals and other innate substances.

Slowly, they said, over billions of years of spiritual evolution, these same soul fragments began to unify themselves to the extent that they could now incarnate as plants, and then as brachiopods, arthropods, vertebrates, and so on.

The elders claimed that it was not until much later that the first fully sentient, self-aware beings came to exist on the earth, and that this occurred approximately two hundred and fifty million years before the birth of Jesus Christ.

"Primitive and utterly evil," continued one of the elders, "a race of reptilian beings developed deep on the ocean floor, where the environment was similar in both density and darkness to that of the lower spheres; the spheres from whence they had come.

"Although not human, they were nonetheless manifestations of the countless fallen spirits that longed to return to the world of God. As such they would incarnate again and again, life after life, in the slow process of spiritual purification."

The elder went on to explain that this race of reptiles would continue to evolve over the millennia that followed. Their societies were brutal and merciless, eventually developing sophisticated social structures, and a technology more advanced than our own.

Through the tens of thousands of years of their existence, they came to build vast cities in the deepest regions of the ocean floor, and like humanity, they too warred amongst themselves. Eventually, they developed weapons of enormous power, and the day came when they used these weapons against each other and destroyed themselves as a result.

"Because of the tremendous depths of their cities," said Ursula, "and the tectonic activity that has all but reshaped the ocean floors since their passing, remnants of their civilizations have yet to be discovered. Their skeletons, which were formed mostly of cartilage in order to withstand the tremendous pressures, have left no distinguishable remains either. Bearing in mind these points, you might now understand why no evidence has ever been found to prove their existence."

Isaac listened in amazement.

"Among the many sub-aquatic nations," continued Alulim, "there existed a small and peaceful realm of more evolved reptilians. Their kingdom was ruled by a benevolent King and Queen.

"Through their court oracle, this King and Queen learned that their race would soon perish in a great war and cataclysm, and that every soul but theirs would be taken by Lucifer and imprisoned in the lower spheres."

Isaac listened intently, his amazement transforming into stunned disbelief as he was told of the approaching Dark Rift, and the destruction that would soon befall the earth. It was an event that had happened before, a very long time ago.

"Although they were powerless to avert the cataclysm," said Ursula, "the King and Queen suspected there might be a way to set things right. Their oracle had informed them that it would take hundreds of millions of years of spiritual evolution for the reptilian souls to fully escape their prison in Hades."

"When they finally did accomplish this feat, however," added Alulim, "their souls would be ready to incarnate as a race of human beings that would populate the earth in the distant future. If the King and Queen could save this future race of humans, they would in essence be saving themselves."

"And what was the King and Queen's plan?" asked Isaac.

Alulim exchanged a glance with Ursula and then spoke.

"Using their most advanced technology, they would incorporate all their knowledge and wisdom into a cube-shaped artifact, and build a complex, multi-dimensional labyrinth through which this knowledge might be revealed.

"One galactic year later, when the crossing was once again imminent, the King and Queen would incarnate as two human beings and unlock the gnosis that they had preserved."

"In this way," added Ursula, "they would use the temporal anomalies of the galactic plane to protect humanity from Ahreimanius during the crossing, and give to humanity the knowledge it needed to ascend into the next higher level of spiritual evolution. This would of course bring each of us one step closer to the Apocatastasis."

Isaac struggled to understand.

"But what is this Apocatastasis?" he asked. "I have never heard this word before."

The first to reply was Ursula.

"The Apocatastasis signifies the eventual return of all the fallen angels to their original home in the House of God," she said. "It is our evolutionary fate, and the meaning behind our cyclical life incarnations here on earth.

"The Apocatastasis is the reason why we suffer and die. It is the reason why we learn. The Tree of Life grows towards it, and the wheels of the universe turn solely to arrive there. We are all on a great pilgrimage back to the paradise we left long ago, regardless of whether we know it or not. The Apocatastasis marks our triumphant return."

Alulim leaned forward in his chair.

"The Apocatastasis is Lucifer's bane," he said. "His power is measured solely by the number of souls he holds under his sway. Every soul that ascends into the higher realms weakens Lucifer tremendously and makes it easier for other souls to escape him as well."

Isaac looked up at the towering panels of stained glass, lit as they were by the electrical storm outside. They were in fact a visual representation of what the elders had just described; a complex and brilliantly composed work of art dedicated to what these people claimed to be the meaning of humanity's existence here on earth.

In these panels could be seen many tree-shaped timelines, showing humankind in its various levels of physical and spiritual evolution. Isaac looked at the tunics that the knights wore, understanding now why each was adorned with the image of a tree. They were depictions of the Tree of Life, growing from what appeared to be a single seed. In the hall's central panel, to the right and left of this seed, could be seen images of a King and Queen.

"The Two," said Isaac, at last understanding. "The reptilian King and Queen are the Two."

"Indeed, they are," said Alulim. "And it is our purpose to help them in any way we can."

"But why should they require our help?" asked Isaac. "If they built the Cube and the Labyrinth, they should know exactly what to do."

"There are two reasons," said Ursula. "The first being that the moment any soul is incarnated into the world of matter, all memory of life in the spirit world is lost. Just as we cannot remember our past lives, neither can the Two remember theirs. For this reason, the King and Queen left clues for themselves to follow, and with the help of the divine world, they created institutions such as ours to aid them in their task."

Isaac considered what the elder was telling him. Earlier that day, Brother Bernardo had explained to him that when a soul incarnated, it arrived on the earth anesthetized, the majority of its knowledge being made inaccessible to it. This occurred so that the purification of its lower aspects could take place. The retention of past-life knowledge would make this process impossible.

"And the second reason?" he asked.

Ursula folded her hands and focused her gaze on Isaac.

"After some time, Ahreimanius became aware of the King and Queen's intentions to disseminate the true gnosis to humanity, and he devised a plan to thwart them. He founded a sinister society whose mission it was to not only destroy the Cube, but to infiltrate the Vatican and corrupt the truth behind the meaning of mankind's existence."

Alulim leaned forward in his chair.

"This would be done so that humanity might be in spiritual darkness as we entered into the Dark Rift," he said. "In this way we would be made powerless to escape the trap that he had laid for us there."

"The Two require our help to undermine this sinister plot," added Ursula. "And this is where you play a key role, dear Isaac."

Isaac frowned in confusion.

"But how could I possibly help in this matter?"

"Your father was the leader of the wicked society of which we speak," said Alulim. "It was he who manipulated you so that a hermaphrodite child might be born of your seed. According to the Ascender's Prophecy, your son would be a vile desecration of the Divine Androgyne, conceived through the incestuous union of the Rex Angelus Illuminati bloodline. Only in this way could the Portal of Ahreimanius be opened, and Lucifer's plan be put into action."

Isaac recoiled in shock.

"Incestuous union?" he exclaimed, rising to his feet. "Are you suggesting that my wife was also my sister? Are you mad, sir?!"

As gently as possible, Isaac was told of how Father Adrianus Vanderwerken (or the Nautonnier, as he was also known) had conspired with his father to not only bring about the incestuous birth of the hermaphrodite, but also to groom his younger brother Christian as the new Nautonnier.

Isaac learned that the demons he had released from the Portal of Ahreimanius were none other than the Fourteen Emissaries of Lucifer, and that they would soon captain an immense host of demons due to pass through the Portal at any moment. Their ranks would constitute an army of darkness that, unless stopped, would overrun the entire earth.

Upon hearing these things, Isaac collapsed back into his chair.

"I truly am the Betrayer," he said solemnly. "I am a blight to humanity."

"Not so!" exclaimed Alulim, rising to his feet. "Your actions were extremely necessary! You have drawn out the hidden evil so that it can now be seen in the light."

Ursula came to her feet as well.

"An invisible enemy can never be defeated, dear Isaac," she said gently. "Your purpose as the Betrayer has been fulfilled so that you might now be redeemed as the Consilio."

Isaac brought his hands to his face in frustration.

"I do not understand!" he cried. "How can I be cursed and blessed at once?"

Alulim placed both his hands on the table and spoke with commanding authority.

"Only through you can the *Two* enter into the Labyrinth and release the gnosis held within the Cube!"

"But where are they?" asked Isaac weakly.

Sir David rose to his feet as well.

"They are most likely on their way to the Labyrinth," he said, bending over the table. "It is time to act!"

Isaac looked over at the captain.

"But have any of you ever even met them?" he asked.

The knight shook his head gravely.

"We have not," he said, sitting down. "We know only their names and titles. They are Gabriel, Hero of God, and Natalia, Day of our Saviour's Rebirth."

Isaac locked eyes with the knight.

"Gabriel and Natasha," he said. "I know these names."

He looked back to Alulim.

"Father Franco wrote of them in his diary. They are orphans, children born of unwanted teenage pregnancies."

Alulim nodded knowingly and sat down again. Ursula followed suit.

"*The Two* symbolize a union between the bloodline of Jesus, and the common bloodlines of humanity," she said. "They are not pure Rex Angelus, and for this reason they were given up for adoption."

"The Rex Angelus line does not intermingle with other bloodlines," added Alulim. "They were given up in accordance with our laws."

"But did their families not know of the Ascender's Prophecy?" asked Isaac. "Why would they have given up children who could have potentially been *The Two*?"

"Because the prophecy could not have been fulfilled if they had not done so," said Alulim.

"All this is of no concern!" exclaimed Sir David. "The Portal of Ahreimanius widens with every passing moment! If not stopped, Ahreimanius will use it to draw every human soul into the lower spheres, just as he did with the souls of the reptilians at the time of the last crossing! He endeavors to prevent the Apocatastasis from ever occurring!"

Isaac grew silent as the magnitude of the danger set in. Over the period of the past few minutes the ground beneath their feet had begun to rumble. Outside the undead had begun to respond with horrific, strangled cries. Everyone sat quietly, listening in fear to the unearthly tumult. Alulim was the first to speak, and he did so unfalteringly.

"Know that the dead will not cease their unholy litany until our planet has entered into the Dark Rift," he said. "Nor will the ground stop its quaking until the final tribulation has come to pass. We are arrived at the apocalypse, my brethren. Be stout, and be strong in faith, for God and all his angels are with each and every one of us."

No sooner had Alulim said these words than a ghastly scream was heard, followed by a resounding bark from Shackleton, who had been lying under the table. In an instant every member of the council leapt to their feet. The scream had come from within the monastery itself. A fraction of a second later Brother Bernardo burst into the hall, a bloodied sword in his hand and a frenzied panic in his eyes.

On the floor behind him was the decapitated corpse of the undead child he had just found squatting in the shadows outside the council door. A choking gust of air rushed into the hall, replacing the pleasant scent of incense with the stench of rotting flesh.

"They have breached the walls!" he cried, jerking his head around as yet another horrific scream sounded behind him. "They are everywhere! Hundreds of them!"

At that moment many things happened at once. With a deep and resounding boom, an explosion sounded from within the earth itself, and the ground beneath their feet began to shift so violently that all but the dexterous knights were thrown to the floor. The entire hall was rocking upon itself now, and the mortar between the massive stone blocks was cracking and crumbling before their eyes.

In that instant, each of the towering stained-glass windows exploded into the hall without warning, and hordes of living dead poured in through them like maggots from a bursting corpse. Those in front were being cut to pieces by the heavy shards of falling glass, but even still they continued to advance.

"To the shelter!" cried Alulim. "Brother Bernardo! Instruct all those within to retreat to the shelter!"

The fat monk turned and disappeared through the doors, his sword flashing. The shrieks arising from the undead were deafening, and they sent paralyzing waves of fear through the elders. The latter had gathered together in a tight group now, sheltering behind a line of battling knights.

Like butchers in a slaughterhouse, the swordsmen felled the slow-moving hordes as they poured into the rotunda. With their heads dislodged, the bloodless corpses fell lifelessly to the ground, and it was not long before their gruesome cadavers formed a great mound in front of the knights. It served to slow the advance of the undead that poured in, but the grisly terrain made it even more difficult to fight those that did.

"Go!" ordered Sir David, pointing to four of his men. "Lead the elders to the shelter and secure the entrance!"

He singled out another three knights.

"Keep this horde back until you are called! The rest of you follow me!"

Isaac felt himself being forcibly directed towards the doors and saw four of the knights follow Sir David into the sanctuary, their swords raised and their crimson surcoats flowing. Looking to his left, he saw that Alulim was next to him now. The old man stood tall for his age and not a trace of fear could be seen in his eyes.

"Quickly now!" he said to the other elders. "We must reach the shelter at once!"

CHAPTER 2

Gibraltar.

The underground cavern was holding together remarkably well, given the intensity of the tremors they were experiencing. In its bay, the X-class midget submarine lay safe and undamaged, the seawater rippling around its dark hull.

Gabriel was inspecting the cavernous ceiling for cracks. Unlike the caves they had traversed in St. Michael's Pass, this one was free of stalactites and seemed very solid. Any areas that might have been questionable had long ago been reinforced with concrete.

He thought of Natasha and the others, and hoped they would be faring equally well in the upper galleries. They had taken the service elevator and gone in search of Scotty's Roberts' brother, Major Richard Roberts, in the hopes that he might be able to supply them with the diesel they needed.

Gabriel walked over to where Peralta was sitting. The disheveled engineer was engaged in a flurry of typing, writing computer code with the relish of a concert pianist. He looked up for a second as Gabriel approached.

"The sheer quantity of layers that this artifact is comprised of boggles the mind," he said, shaking his messy white head in amazement. "I've already extracted over ten million of them, and I haven't even penetrated a centimeter into the thing."

The BIRIS had not stopped its scanning since it had begun over five hours earlier, and the data it was amassing was of such an enormous scale that Peralta had been forced to hack into several external data banks to store it. At the sound of an electronic bell, the messy scientist stopped his typing and turned to face one of the dozens of monitors that were positioned around him.

"The results of the tomography are just coming up now."

He squinted at the data.

"Of course," he said in a captivated whisper. "This explains everything. The strange density of the artifact. Its ability to interact with your brain. And its ability to have maintained such an immense quantity of data in such a pristine state for so long..."

He looked around as though searching for something. There was a kind of madness in his eyes.

"It's been regenerating itself the whole time..."

"What do you mean?" asked Gabriel, leaning closer.

Peralta turned to face him with unrestrained urgency. He spoke in a low rasp.

"This artifact is no conventional piece of hardware, Dr. Parker. It's an advanced artificial intelligence. It's made up of densely packed synthetic cells... Living circuits of synthetic DNA. Instead of electricity it uses the equivalent of neurotransmitters to move data around. This is incredible. It's perfect biomimicry."

"Are you saying that the Cube's a synthetic brain?"

"Absolutely," said Peralta. "A super brain. By the looks of how many millions of instructions it's processing every second, it's close to eight billion times more powerful than a human brain."

Peralta paused.

"Wait a minute," he muttered. "What the hell..."

He tapped away at a keyboard, bending closer to one of the monitors as his brow tightened.

"I've never seen anything like this before..."

He scratched his head excitedly and adjusted his glasses.

"It's utterly inconceivable..."

Gabriel turned to face him only to have the lapels of his jacket taken. Peralta pulled him to within an inch of his face, a tiny crumb of hamburger bun still clinging to his white mustache from lunch.

"This artifact exists in many times *at the same time!*" he whispered frantically. "It's not only conscious, it's *interdimensional!*"

He released Gabriel and seated himself in his chair, calming down at once.

Gabriel approached him cautiously.

"If it's alive," he asked, "what does it feed on?"

Peralta seemed lost in thought.

"It feeds on the same thing that gives it its interdimensional properties..." he said to himself, and then looking up at Gabriel he added:

"It feeds on gravity."

Gabriel frowned as he struggled to remember what he had read in a science magazine not so long ago.

"Membrane theory..." he said. "There are four different forms of free energy that we know of. Two are nuclear; strong and weak. Then there is magnetism, and the weakest force of all is gravity. Membrane Theory postulates that gravity is weaker than the other three because it's being spread out over an almost infinite number of adjacent dimensions..."

Gabriel scratched his head before continuing.

"What you're suggesting is that the Cube resides in numerous dimensions simultaneously, and that it's somehow using the force of gravity to fuel itself."

"That is *exactly* what I am suggesting, Dr. Parker!" exclaimed Peralta. "And the really inconceivable thing is that all those infinite dimensions are being processed from the same location inside the Cube; a kind of ethereal mind..."

"What do you mean?" asked Gabriel, confused. "Who's mind?"

Peralta stopped to think.

"Your mind," he said. "My mind. Everyone's mind."

"But how's that possible?"

"Because all consciousness is *One*," whispered Peralta reverently. "And what's more, if this artifact has the power of close to eight billion brains, it's only because it's linked to every brain on the planet. It's like a huge Boink! It's directly hooked up to the collective consciousness!"

Gabriel was silent for a moment before he spoke.

"The gypsy woman in Toledo said that the Cube would communicate to the world through the collective consciousness."

Peralta's eyes opened wide with urgency.

"That's why it's imperative we get to that labyrinth," he exclaimed, "and activate the transponder in this thing! This artifact employs a technology that operates on two metaphysical platforms. The collective consciousness, and the universal field of intelligence."

"What's that?" asked Gabriel.

"I'll tell you in a second," said Peralta, "but first consider this: What if the Cube has been evolving with humanity? What if that was the reason why it's using an ancient Sumerian sexagesimal system to run its internal functions? Why else would it be running website architectures?"

"Hang on a second," said Gabriel, holding up a hand. "Did you just say *website?*"

Peralta nodded rapidly and then removed his glasses to rub his eyes.

"You're not going to believe this," he said, "but ciphered into the outer layers of the Cube is a code that's a dead ringer for XHTML. I couldn't begin to tell you what it's about, but it's definitely a website."

Gabriel was speechless. The idea sounded absurd. Peralta was nodding in silent agreement.

"The only explanation is that the Cube has been evolving with humanity," he said. "That would explain why it's chosen to apply itself through the use of a conventional, twenty-first century website. It must have learned this from us; from humanity. Don't forget. For all intents and purposes this artifact is *conscious.* "

"Tell me about that universal field of intelligence you mentioned," said Gabriel, shaking his head in an attempt to clear it.

Peralta clutched the table as yet another tremor shook the ground.

"Do you know what happens when a man is starving to death?"

"He gets grumpy?" offered Gabriel.

"He also has a very hard time thinking. Ask him what five times five is and he won't be able to tell you. His brain stops working properly."

"And?"

Peralta rose to his feet and moved to one of the neighbouring monitors. He bent over and tapped something into a keyboard before continuing.

"Regardless of how weak he is, that starving man will still know how to tie his shoelaces, even if he doesn't have the strength to actually do it. In short, he will have full unhindered access to all his memories and all his knowledge, right up to the point of brain failure and death."

"So what?"

"So what?" repeated Peralta, frustrated. "Can't you see? If his brain is out of fuel, how can it possibly be accessing and processing all that information? He's dying of starvation, remember? There's no glucose to power the brain's functions anymore, yet somehow, he still manages to know everything. The answer is that our minds are not located in our brains, but rather somewhere else. That's why a guy who's dying from hunger can still access all of his knowledge and memories."

"So our minds reside in the universal field of intelligence."

"Yes," said Peralta, pacing. "It's like cloud computing. Our brains are tuned into it. Synaptic activity is nothing more than a three-dimensional projection of what's happening in that field. And this is the really cool part. Because of the fixed nature of the space-time block, the UFI contains thoughts that haven't even been thought of yet. Ideas from the future. Human growth and learning is all based on our evolving ability to access the UFI. The better we do it, the wiser and more intelligent we become."

"And the Cube's plugged into the UFI," said Gabriel.

Peralta nodded.

"That's why it's been able to evolve with us."

"Let me ask you a question," said Gabriel. "If a certain individual was to uncover knowledge from this field of intelligence, would that knowledge then be propagated to the rest of the world through the collective consciousness?"

Peralta sat down next to Gabriel and let out a long breath.

"Absolutely," he rasped, running both of his hands through his disastrous hair. "The two platforms work together seamlessly. That's why things tend to get invented in different parts of the world at the same time. We're all connected."

Peralta leaned forward.

"Something else occurs that's very fascinating. The greater the number people who acquire a specific piece of knowledge from the field, the easier it gets for others to adopt that same knowledge."

"I've heard of this phenomenon," said Gabriel. "You can see it happening everywhere. Take using electronics for example. The interfaces haven't changed all that much since gadgets started to appear, but whereas only the brainiest types could use them at first, now all kinds of people are using them, even seniors who are supposed to have trouble learning new things."

"That's because a tipping point was reached," said Peralta. "It happens with everything that's learned on a societal level. The mechanism became evident when our species first started using tools, and it's followed us right through to using electronic gadgetry. There comes a point when enough people have adopted something, that it becomes almost second nature for everyone to adopt it."

Gabriel sat up as the realization finally gelled.

"That's what's supposed to happen with the Cube," he said. "Natasha and I are supposed to somehow release the knowledge that's stored in it. That knowledge will then get injected into the collective consciousness. When enough people have worked to assimilate it, larger segments of the population will follow, until a tipping point is reached. After that, everyone will adopt the new knowledge and the world will jump to the next level of societal evolution."

The sound of an opening airlock filled the cavern, and Gabriel and Peralta turned in time to see their friends emerge from the service elevator. First out was Natasha, followed by a hand-cuffed officer with a black hood covering his head. Behind them were Scotty Roberts and the giant Bahadur. Only Miller was missing, having opted to remain in the tunnels above.

"I hope you don't mind a military presence in your laboratory, Peralta my mate," said Scotty, snatching the hood off their captive.

Peralta and Gabriel looked on in surprise. Their prisoner was none other than Major Richard Roberts. The latter was in the process of taking inventory of his new surroundings, an expression of shocked amazement transforming his features. The ground rumbled as if to punctuate his displeasure.

"Scotty," he said calmly to his brother. "I've agreed to your silly games, now get these blasted handcuffs off."

CHAPTER 3

Los Picos de Europa, Northern Spain.

Christian's private jet was making its way eastward over the Cantabrian Mountains when the sun broke the horizon. Its hue was that of blood-soaked crimson, and in the dawning light, the night's strange electrical storms could still be seen flashing through the thick clouds below the plane. High above, like an extended aurora borealis, the entire outer atmosphere was ablaze with ruby and emerald light. A massive, magnetospheric storm was engulfing the planet and it was a sight like no other.

With the galactic plane drawing ever nearer, the intensity of the Dark Rift's gravitational field was playing havoc with the plasma being emitted by the sun. Its solar wind had intensified a hundred-fold, and as such was bombarding the earth's magnetic field with an unprecedented concentration of charged particles.

The result was the appearance of a sky on fire, and this, coupled with the altered hue of the sun itself, made it very clear that there were immense changes taking place, not only on the earth, but in the entire solar system.

Christian wiped his mouth nervously, his face damp with cold sweat. Shortly after takeoff he had been visited by the Zurvanites again. Through the sharp ears of an undead child, the Four had overheard Alulim speaking at the Council of the Apocatastasis and had learned of Isaac's important role in their enemy's plan to activate the Cube.

The destruction of the artifact would no longer be necessary if Isaac Rodchenko were to be eliminated. Without him, the Cube would be unable to disseminate its gnosis and humanity would fall.

To drive the point home, Ahreimanius had shown himself to Christian, manifesting briefly in the horrific form of the hermaphrodite, only to vanish a moment later. His short-lived appearance had been enough to fill Christian with a frenzied urgency to kill his brother. It pressed in on him, causing him to experience uncontrollable jerks and spasms throughout his body.

"Kill him! Kill him! Kill him!"

Christian slapped his face repeatedly, struggling to regain control. Everything was going according to plan. There was no need to panic. The ancient city of Rome would soon be wiped from the face of the earth, and in less than a minute, all of its three-and-a-half million inhabitants would be incinerated instantly. He forced himself to breathe.

"Forty-five seconds to detonation," said the seductive voice of his computer, as if to confirm his thoughts.

Christian produced a pair of protective goggles. As instructed, the pilot was veering the plane northward so as to facilitate a better viewing of the spectacle that would soon be taking place in the eastern sky.

The Vatican was about to offer herself up so that a new "holy institution" could be built from her ashes; an institution that would surpass the church's most monumental achievements and eventually govern the hearts and souls of every man, woman, and child on the planet.

Christian's work was nearing completion. All that remained was that he locate his brother and kill him.

A cold smile of self-satisfaction appeared on Christian's face. The Zurvanites had made it very clear to him that Isaac would be travelling to the Portal of Ahreimanius, and bearing this in mind, Christian had made careful preparations to reach the small island before his brother did. In the back of the plane sat four special forces officers, each being awaited by select units of coalition troops on standby in Santander.

Because of the tempestuous weather, helicopter access to the mountain lake would be impossible. The distance of forty kilometres would need to be covered on all-terrain vehicles, following a footpath belonging to the Camino de Santiago. This trail would take them along an ancient Celtic route, directly to where the Portal lay. It was here where Christian would find his brother and slay him.

"Ten, nine, eight…"

Christian put on his goggles as the AI began its countdown. Even at this distance the light emitted from the blast would damage human retinas through atmospheric focusing.

"Three, two, one, detonation."

Christian's jaw fell open as the blast lit up the horizon, making the rising sun seem pale in comparison. The explosion was over a moment later and Christian was amazed that something so catastrophic could come to pass in such a short period of time.

He removed his goggles, looking down at his computer to study the live feeds coming from cameras along the Italian coast. The mushroom cloud over Rome was gargantuan and still rising, measuring over eighty kilometres in height and fifty in width.

"Taller than Mount Everest," he muttered to himself. "And hotter than the surface of the sun…"

The plane banked sharply to resume its westerly heading, and Christian was suddenly gripped by a crippling pain. It shot through his head and into his eyes. Squinting up from his computer he saw that the four Zurvanites were standing an arm's length away, their grainy forms jerking and twisting in and out of being.

He gripped his head and writhed in agony. Their frenetic chanting was driving the sanity from his mind.

"Kill him! Kill him! Kill him! Kill him!"

CHAPTER 4

Gibraltar.

Major Roberts continued to stare at the monitor even after it had gone black, his right eye twitching and blinking repeatedly. He was still struggling to assimilate everything he had learned.

Earlier on, Cassano had created a video on Peralta's orders, one that explained every aspect of the artifact, and even included a brief interview with Gabriel and Natasha. It was to be sent out to all those friends of Peralta whose assistance was desperately needed, and had proved to be the final piece of information needed to leave the major utterly convinced.

He looked up as his brother struck a match.

"Well?" asked Scotty from his perch on a nearby desk. "See what I mean, bro?"

He exhaled a cloud of smoke.

"It's not just Gib that's in a bind," he added. "It's the whole bleeding world."

Major Roberts was still speechless. He shifted his gaze to Peralta and locked eyes with the rumpled scientist. Yet again the ground shook violently beneath them.

"You can see how urgently we need to get Gabriel and Natasha to the Labyrinth, Major."

Roberts nodded slowly, his expression still blank with shock. He looked over at the old submarine in its berth, as if to confirm that this was all really happening.

"Perpetual darkness," he said dazedly. "That and the complete annihilation of the entire human race..."

Natasha approached and handed him the Cube. He looked up at her and accepted it with hesitation, noting its odd density the moment he had taken hold of it. He peered into its glowing, iridescent depths.

"Incredible…" he mumbled.

In that instant Roberts made up his mind. He looked over at his brother and gave him a single nod. Scotty hopped down from his perch with a grin and gave his brother a heavy pat on the back.

"I knew we could count on you, bro," he said, and then looking to Peralta added:

"You've got your diesel, Captain, but on one condition."

Everyone including Roberts looked at Scotty, curious as to what the stipulation might be. Scotty spit out a shred of tobacco.

"The condition is we pick up Anita and bring her back first," he said. "She's holed up in a cellar, and she's as pregnant as a bloody rabbit."

All looked at the major. His face was chiseled with concern. He gazed back at his brother. There was a deep gratitude in his eyes.

"Thanks, Scotty," he said. "But I'm afraid it's impossible. There's too much radiation out there. Even a few minutes of exposure would be lethal."

"Where is she?" asked Peralta, rising to his feet with sudden concern. "Why didn't you say anything about this?"

The major shook his head, struggling with his emotions.

"What was the point?"

Everyone braced themselves as another tremor shook the cave.

"He's right about the radiation," said Gabriel. "But even still, there's got to be a way to get her out of there."

Peralta took off his glasses, wiped them, and then began to pace.

"The radiation in the first minutes of a detonation will exceed all the accumulated radiation a person could be exposed to in the first week. The first week of exposure exceeds all the radiation that a person could ever be exposed to in a lifetime at the site..."

He looked over at Roberts.

"How pregnant is she?"

The major ran a hand through his short-cropped hair.

"She's due in ten days," he said, frowning. "Maybe less."

"Well then we've got time," said Peralta. "We'll collect her on the way back. By that time the radiation will have dissipated sufficiently."

Everyone looked at the scrappy engineer.

"Look," he said. "We've got to be realistic here. If we fail, we're all dead anyway. If we succeed, we'll have plenty of time to make it back."

Gabriel put a hand on the major's shoulder.

"She could come out just as we arrived and get into the sub before the radiation could harm her."

"It'll be an easy pickup, man!" added Scotty reassuringly. "There's a bloody pier right in front of your place for Christ's sake. Just get her to put on lots of layers. She can strip them off before she gets into the sub."

Roberts' face was alight with hope.

"My God," he said. "Could this really be possible?"

Natasha put her arms around Gabriel.

"It's more than possible," she said. "It's probable. Everything's going to be fine, you'll see."

The major rose to his feet and handed Natasha the Cube.

"You're absolutely right," he said, looking over at his brother. "There's plenty of time, and you guys are going to get the job done!"

He produced his radio.

"Captain Brown. Is the fuel ready?"

"Affirmative, Major," came the response. "It's on the skids and ready to move."

Roberts looked at the others, an excited smile on his face.

"Get it here right away, Captain. There's not a moment to lose. My brother will give you the details."

CHAPTER 5

Los Picos de Europa, Northern Spain.

Isaac squinted up at the bleeding sun, watching it for a moment before it disappeared back into the cauldronous clouds. He was high in the mountains, looking down over the trembling lands. The planet seemed to him like a feverish mother, its curving surface appearing to expand and contract ever so slightly, as though it were struggling to breathe.

"We will rest in the upper gallery!" bellowed Sir David from a raised outcropping of rock.

He was not five meters away, but the wind made his voice barely audible. Isaac turned to look where he was pointing and spotted some fortified walls in amongst the rocky terrain.

He could feel his legs almost giving out with relief. For over three hours now they had climbed, stealthily leaving the monastery behind, along with the teaming hordes of undead who had besieged it. Isaac found comfort in knowing that Alulim and the others were safe inside their shelter.

"You have done well, Consilio," said an approaching knight.

He put a hand on Isaac's shoulder.

"This is a favourite outpost for us. It is equipped with many comforts and will take our minds off our suffering, even if for just a little while."

Isaac tried his best to smile.

"Have you lost many loved ones to the plague?"

The young knight frowned.

"I lost a brother, my lord," he said, "but I am fine. I take courage from our captain. Seeing how he endures brings strength to us all."

Isaac laid a hand on the young knight's arm as they resumed their trek upward.

"Has Sir David lost someone too?"

The youth's eyes were still on his captain. He had stopped atop a steep crag and was pulling up his men as they approached.

"He was our village doctor before all this happened," said the knight, his eyes alight with admiration. "He lost a wife and two daughters to the horde. She was pregnant with a third."

Isaac wanted to say something to show his sympathy, but just then they arrived at the crag. He gave Sir David a nod of thanks and reached up to take hold of his arm.

* * * * * *

The cave proved to be as warm and accommodating as the young knight had promised, resembling more of a clubhouse than a military outpost. It was not long before a fire had been lit in a large stone hearth there, and the strange cataclysmic day was shut out and temporarily forgotten. Only the constant rumbling of the earth gave any reminder of its continued presence.

"Thank you," said Isaac, accepting the piping hot bowl of stew that Brother Bernardo was handing him.

The heavy monk invited him to sit on a sofa by the fire and then fell into a neighbouring armchair. Shackleton, having already eaten, was asleep at their feet.

"We must be well into the rift by now," said Isaac, swallowing a mouthful of food.

"We are merely approaching it," said Sir David.

He was squatting beside the fire.

"Things will get much, much worse."

"Nevertheless, we have nothing to fear," said the monk. "The angels of God are here with us. They will help us succeed in finding and assisting the Two."

"Ours is an ancient plan," added Sir David. "One that the spirit of the Christ himself created."

"In that he came to redeem us," said Isaac, but his words struck an odd chord.

It was as though the monk and the knight knew something he did not.

"Contrary to what the Vatican would have you believe," said Brother Bernardo, "Jesus Christ did not come to redeem, but rather to reveal. He taught an ancient gnosis, the same gnosis that resides in the Cube. It is based on the correlation between personal freedom and personal responsibility."

"I don't understand," said Isaac.

"It means that we are the only ones who can redeem ourselves," said Sir David. "Nobody else can do it for us, no matter how wealthy or powerful their organization happens to be."

The monk took up an iron and poked the fire.

"The Vatican has one central tenant," he said. "It states that Jesus Christ was murdered in order to appease a vengeful, yet somehow compassionate god. They claim that this god willingly allowed the death sacrifice of his only son so that the price for humanity's sins might be paid."

Sir David frowned bitterly.

"This is a reprehensible lie," he said. "The true meaning behind the crucifixion of Jesus' body was to symbolize the crucifixion of the personal ego, with its vanity, neurosis, and selfish will. His life, death, and the resurrection of his spirit, demonstrated the stages of development that each of us must go through in order to regain the kingdom of heaven."

Brother Bernardo nodded knowingly.

"The Vatican's literalist version of the crucifixion metaphor not only misses this point entirely, it also serves to induce a heavy guilt in Christians, along with a feeling of morbid indebtedness to Jesus, and a deep existential fear of God."

Sir David leaned forward in his chair.

"And in order to repay this debt, and assuage the guilt and fear it induces, we are urged to give our wealth and obedience to the Church."

Isaac was taken aback by the knight's words.

"But it was only through Christ's death and resurrection that our salvation was made possible," he said weakly. "Jesus paid the price so that our transgressions might be forgiven..."

"Every one of our sins was forgiven long before Jesus ever incarnated, dear Isaac," said the monk. "Long before they were even committed. Forget your biblical Yahweh for a moment and try to think of God as the ineffable entity he truly is. There is nothing we could possibly do that could offend him, for behind our worst actions lie causes that he fully understands. God wants to help us, not condemn us. He wants us to come home."

Isaac remained silent.

"In the time of Jesus," said Sir David, "the entire Roman Empire was mostly at peace, but this was not the case in Jerusalem. It was a hot bed of insurrection. Early Christianity, with its message of personal empowerment, posed a direct threat to Roman rule. They needed to control this new religion, and the manner in which to do this was given to them by a Pharisee named Saul of Tarsus."

"But Saul of Tarsus was St. Paul," said Isaac. "He was the father of the church. St. Paul could never have been a Pharisee."

"Saul of Tarsus was not only a Pharisee," added Sir David, "he was a cousin of King Herod himself, and as such, a member of the ruling family of Jerusalem. As a young man he had been a member of the temple guard, authorized by the high priests to persecute Christians. He occupied this position even when Jesus was arrested and killed."

Isaac looked at Sir David, unable to respond. St. Paul had freely admitted to persecuting Christians before he had been converted to Christianity.

"Through St. Paul, the Romans would, over time, remove the self-empowering aspects of Jesus' original teachings, and replace them with a dogma that was specially designed to repress and control," continued the knight. "They would equate Jesus with God, making any realistic emulation of him impossible. They would revoke personal responsibility and replace it with blind faith in the church's doctrine. They would take the reincarnation taught by Jesus and replace it with eternal hellfire. Any salvation to be had would come solely through the sanctity of the church, and a sinner's humble adherence to its laws."

"You must forgive us if we appear passionate about this subject," said Brother Bernardo, "but you must try to understand how difficult it has been for our society over the centuries, knowing what we have known about the Vatican, but being sworn to secrecy."

Isaac could not believe what he was hearing.

"But what of all the wonderful things that have been done by the Church?" he asked. "What of all the love that has been spread, and the countless people who have been helped? Surely the Vatican cannot be so evil."

"The blessed things you describe have come from the hearts of individual Christians throughout history," said the monk, "and the incorruptible truth of what Jesus Christ stood for. These blessings did not come from the captains of the Vatican. You must not confuse the government of a nation with its people. A government can be corrupt and vile, while its people remain good and true. It is the Vatican that is evil, not the people who do good work in its name."

Isaac stared into the flames of the fire, reflecting on the early church and its actions to secure power. He knew that in 325 CE the pagan Roman Emperor Constantine had summoned the First Council of Nicaea, where he had made official the doctrine of his new Roman Catholic Church.

With a mighty government to back him, he had proclaimed that any who did not follow the church's new creed would be proclaimed a heretic, and an enemy of Rome. From that council, Constantine had established the papal seat of supreme governance, creating an institution that claimed to be the sole representative of God on this earth. To go against this church was to go against God himself. The power that resulted from the formation of this organization was unimaginable.

Isaac also recalled Theophilus of Alexandria, and the destruction of knowledge and culture that he had reaped throughout the fourth century. He thought of the dark ages that had followed, where the rights of the individual to read and write had been revoked, and given only to those in the clergy, who would in turn perpetuate the repressive dogma, instilling even more fear, more guilt, and more unworthiness into the hearts of men.

He thought of the Crusades, and the slaughter of Muslims, Jews, and Orthodox Christians in the Holy Land, as well as the systematic eradication of the peace-loving Cathars in Europe.

Right into the modern day he saw the damage and destruction that this institution called the church was responsible for. Was this a church of Jesus Christ? How could it possibly be? Jesus Christ stood for freedom and love.

Since its inception, the Catholic Church had perpetuated repression, intolerance, and hatred through its policies, along with guilt, fear, superstition, and unbridled violence in its countless wars. The Vatican was a clear and indisputable distortion of what Jesus Christ had stood for; a complete inversion. It always had been. It was a blasphemous deception, a great and terrible lie.

"If Jesus Christ was not God," asked Isaac suddenly, "then who was he?"

The ground shuddered violently beneath them.

"Just as we are all incarnations of the angels who fell," said Brother Bernardo, "Jesus was an incarnation of the angel of the Christ; the most exalted spirit in all of God's world.

"For thousands of years the Kristos was spoken of in myth. He is the personification of God in the body of a man. He was Horus to the Egyptians, Dionysus to the Greeks, Mithras to the pagans, and known by a hundred different names across the globe. He was, and is, the highest of all the angels and archangels, but he is not God. He is the Christ, and when he incarnated, he was simply Jesus. A man like any other; and not…"

"But how could he be like any other man if his spirit was that of the highest angel?" asked Isaac. "He would have been perfect."

"Yes," said Brother Bernardo, "but he did not know it. You forget the universal law. When incarnated into matter, a being's knowledge of the spirit world is lost, and this applied to the incarnation of the Kristos as well.

"It was for this reason that Jesus struggled like all the rest of us. Much more so, in fact, because Ahreimanius knew who he was, and was bent on defeating him. He desired nothing more than to make Jesus renounce God and join the forces of darkness."

Sir David spoke out.

"Unlike the many sages who have been teachers of the ancient gnosis throughout history, Jesus was the first to successfully apply the teachings in his own life, and gain liberation from the wheel of death and rebirth. Jesus made it to the higher spheres, but the important thing to remember is that he did this as a man, and not as some omnipotent godman, as the Vatican would have you believe. If he could do it, then everyone can do it. It is humanly possible."

Brother Bernardo poked the fire again.

"Jesus introduced a new modality into the collective mind of humanity," he said. "A Christ Consciousness, if you will. This modality or mindset has been spoken of since the time of the ancients. It embraces the fact that God can always be found directly within us, immediately accessible to anyone who cares to make the effort to establish contact.

"Without this contact, one cannot follow the path of gnosis and advance to the higher spheres. It is a paradox. One has to do it by oneself, but one cannot do it without the help of the Divine."

Sir David rose to his feet.

"The Kristos merges with our true self and the two become one," he said. "It is through this merger that liberation from death can be achieved, and the higher realms be entered into. Before Jesus came, this was not possible for us. For this reason, we owe him much gratitude, but it is nothing to feel guilty about. It is only something to be delighted about."

And then placing a hand on the monk's shoulder he said:

"Come, Brother. The Consilio must sleep now."

Brother Bernardo rose to his feet with a groan.

"Rest well, dear Isaac," he said, turning to leave. "You will need all your strength in the coming hours."

CHAPTER 6

Under the Mediterranean Sea.

The midget submarine slipped silently into the dark waters of its secret berth, turning to pass through a short tunnel before entering into the radioactive waters on Gibraltar's eastern face. Echoing through its hull could be heard a strange cacophony of sounds rising from the sea floor. The reverberations lent a surreal quality to the interior of the sub, and reminded its occupants of the tremendous geological stresses that the earth's crust was currently experiencing.

After having removed its weapons systems and installed a new, more efficient engine, Peralta had managed to significantly increase the sub's usable space, improving both its smuggling capacity and its performance. As it was, its contingent of six were finding the quarters ample enough, with only the giant Bahadur having a difficult time moving around.

"Radiation levels are well within limits," said Gabriel, reading a newly added gauge among the high-tech gadgets retrofitted by Peralta. "I've got to say, that was a great idea you had to line the hull with lead."

"A lucky decision," rasped Peralta over his shoulder.

He was busily tapping away at one of several keyboards.

"When I removed the old engines and all the weapons systems, I had to replace the ballast with something that was heavy and took up as little space as possible. Lead sheeting was the best solution. I hid it behind the paneling. I had no idea I'd ever be using it to shield us from beta and gamma radiation."

Gabriel looked around, shaking his head in amazement. Whereas the sub's exterior had been left entirely in its original state, its interior had undergone a complete transformation. Gone were the sweaty steel walls and riveted seams typical to subs of that era. In their place had been installed rich mahogany paneling and buttery leather upholstery, similar to that which could be found in a luxury yacht.

Although nowhere near as extensive as Peralta's laboratory in the underground port, the bridge of the X-Class sub was equipped with many high-resolution monitors, and technologies like those found in the most modern submarines. From his helm, Peralta not only had fly by wire navigation and state of the art communications, but also remote access to his mainframe computers on land, and the many others he had hacked into.

It was for this reason that he had insisted on leaving as soon as Major Roberts had arranged to have their fuel delivered. There was basically no computing that could be done on land that could not also be done at sea.

Gabriel felt a sudden wave of grief come over him and turned in time to see Natasha bring her hands to her face and burst into tears. She was seated before a monitor that showed the face of Bishop Marcus on a live feed from the submarine port. Cassano was standing behind him.

"I am so sorry, my dear child," the old bishop was saying, his face pale with sorrow. "It has only come to our attention at this very moment."

"What is it?" said Gabriel, moving to the monitor with Amir and Scotty bumping in behind.

Natasha stood up and threw her arms around Gabriel, burying her face in his chest.

"Everyone in Rome is dead!" she cried. "All my friends! All their families!"

Gabriel looked to the monitor in shock.

"What happened?"

"Rome has been decimated," came the bishop's frail voice. "There was a massive nuclear strike on Vatican City. There is nothing left. Close to three million people have been incinerated. Many more are wounded and dying in the outskirts."

* * * * * *

The sub's only cabin was located at the very rear of the ship, directly above the engines. Like the rest of the sub, it too had been completely refurbished, its cozy rosewood paneling and amply cushioned interior turning it into a sanctuary of sorts. It was here on a comfortable bed that Gabriel lay with Natasha, her body curled up against his as great sobs of grief escaped her.

Although she had lived in Florence, Rome had been where she had grown up, and the city was not only filled with all the special places of her youth, but also with her closest friends. The event had been devastating, and lying beside her, Gabriel was at a loss as to how to comfort her.

"Why Gabriel?" she sobbed. "Everything I had is gone. They took away Suora and Fra, and now all of my friends. All the people I called my family…"

Gabriel kissed the top of her head and held her close. He could find no explanation for the injustice of the catastrophe and was on the verge of expounding on the meaninglessness of life when a thought occurred to him.

He remembered something he had read in his father's journal; something that seemed to offer an explanation. He ran a hand through his hair.

"It's all about truth," he said, more to himself than to Natasha, but his words caught her interest, and she looked up at him.

"What do you mean?"

"Well," began Gabriel, and the words seemed to come to him as he spoke. "If you keep in mind the truth behind the suffering, it all makes sense."

"But what truth could make sense of millions of people being incinerated, or worse still, being left to die slowly in agony?"

Gabriel tried to be as gentle as possible.

"You know I'm not big on religion, Natasha, but what if the crazy things we've been reading about in the journal are actually true? According to the ancient wisdoms, suffering brings spiritual growth, which eventually leads people to the truth."

"And what's the truth?"

"The truth is that death doesn't exist," he said, surprised to hear himself saying the words. "The physical body dies, but people keep on existing. Come on, Natasha. You know this. You're a theologian."

"But why?" she sobbed. "Why the children?"

"There could be a million reasons. People have been suffering, dying, and being reincarnated for aeons now. It's the way we evolve."

Natasha sniffled through her tears. She understood what Gabriel was saying, but something in her resisted it, nonetheless. The mindset he was describing seemed so cold and so unfeeling, even though she was certain it was based in truth.

She could not be sad for the people who had died, for they, in truth, did not really die. As well, she could not be sad for those who were suffering, because in its ultimate sense, their suffering was a blessing; a way for them to evolve spiritually so that one day suffering and physical death would no longer be necessary.

The only thing she could possibly be sad for was herself, and this amounted to nothing but self-pity, a blight that she had resolved to rid herself of years ago.

"Look," said Gabriel slowly. "I'll be damned if I'm going to acquire all this knowledge about how the universe really works, and then not apply it. If the demons that possessed us were real, then angels and alternate dimensions must be real too. It's getting pretty obvious that an afterlife exists. We need to be able to stand on that truth like it's the solid ground it is, and to do that, we've got to believe in it."

Natasha smiled affectionately. Who was this Gabriel? Surely, he was an angel as well. In the most difficult times, she had never once seen fear in his eyes, only compassion, understanding, and an unwavering resolve to do the right thing. Now she had seen something new in him. A willingness to change his beliefs.

"Knowing the truth really does set you free, doesn't it?"

Gabriel found himself surprised by Natasha's words. He had heard the saying countless times before, but he had never understood its meaning until just now. When one knew the truth about life, death, and suffering, fear lost all its power. He was going to say something when Natasha reached up and put a finger over his lips.

"Make love to me, Gabriel. Make love to me right now."

* * * * * *

The X-class Midget submarine made its way northward along the coast of Portugal, its dark hull slipping silently through cold and lightless waters. In a tiny aft cabin of the boat, Gabriel and Natasha lay entwined in their lovemaking. And whereas most lovers would have been confined to the limited space of the small berth, they had left the world of earthly matter, and through Mithuna, entered into an astral plane that knew no boundaries.

To Gabriel and Natasha, it seemed that they were swimming beneath the surface of a clear and tropical ocean, with soft sunlight filtering down upon them. Here there was no pain or sorrow, only limitless beauty, and an indescribable sense of euphoria.

They could see a shimmering being of translucent light approaching through the waters, and they knew in a moment that it was the same being they had encountered during their first ascension into Mithuna.

"Greetings, my dear friends," it said in the most harmonious voice imaginable. "From the House of God, I bring you many divine blessings."

* * * * * *

Six hours had passed by the time Gabriel and Natasha emerged from the sub's cabin. With over five hundred nautical miles lying between their current location and the north coast of Spain, their journey would still take another eighteen hours to complete, leaving them only six hours to find the Labyrinth of Sarras before the galactic plane was entered into. Even still they were not worried. Their guide had not only revealed to them the exact location of the Labyrinth, but an unexpected route that would carry them there swiftly.

Gabriel and Natasha entered the bridge to find Scotty looking through the periscope. Peralta was busy tapping away at a keyboard, a tiny dragonfly robot perched on his shoulder.

"Hello, Captain Peralta," said Natasha. "When are you going to show us the Cube's website?"

Everyone on the bridge turned to find her and Gabriel standing by the hatch. Amir was about to say something, but Natasha spoke first.

"Don't worry about me," she said, seeing the compassion in their faces. "I'm fine now."

Peralta smiled and nodded, scrubbing at his face and hair in an attempt to revitalize himself.

"Well, now's as good a time as any to show you," he rasped, punching some instructions into the navigation system.

He looked back at Scotty.

"Bring down that periscope. It's time to dive."

All eyes turned to a monitor positioned at the front of the bridge, its large display lighting up to show a forward-facing view. Choppy seawater began to cover the screen as the vessel angled downward into a dive, its twin floodlights probing the murky depths.

"Autohelm is now engaged," announced Peralta, bringing the Cube's website up on a monitor next to him. "Why don't you guys pull up a chair?"

Gabriel and Natasha did as they were asked, with Amir and Scotty filing in behind. Only Bahadur was not present. He was stretched out on the deck at the back of the sub and sound asleep.

"What we've got here is a website with no content," said Peralta in his raspy voice. "Even still, you'll be able to see how it's set up, and what it's capable of doing."

On the lower corner of the screen were two cube icons rotating slowly. Peralta dragged his mouse over one of them and caused it to expand. Each of its six sides moved away from its centre, providing links to six separate areas within the site.

"One cube deals with the practical aspects of life. The other one deals with something spiritual. Let's look at the first one. It serves as a portal to a social networking site. Its purpose is to create governmental directives."

"Like mandates?" asked Gabriel.

Peralta nodded.

"Each of the six sides pertains to a specific category. Government, health and welfare, education, business and trade, environment, and foreign relations. Each of the categories contains local and international forums. It looks like the objective here is to democratically create petitions that can be presented to government officials."

"What is this thing?" asked Gabriel, confused.

"It would appear to be a new form of world governance," said Peralta. "It's a massive content management system that has the ability to process and organize billions of votes in real time, and on any given issue. It uses our existing governments to enact the directives."

"But our governments are a mess," said Natasha.

"Not really," said Peralta. "If you think about it, they coordinate vast arrays of super complex tasks. It's taken centuries for them to evolve. Our governments keep the world running like a well-oiled machine. Problems only exist because of the leaders we put at the controls of that machine. Having democratically generated mandates to tell them what to do would fix things pretty quickly, I would think..."

Gabriel had long been a critic of the current state of democracy in the world, and a fan of the direct democracy that was being implemented in Switzerland. He found the idea fascinating.

"What's stopping politicians from just ignoring the mandates?"

Peralta shrugged.

"I suppose if an official can't execute the directives he's been given by a community, he'll lose their votes. The bigger the communities get, the more he'll have to do what they tell him to do, or he'll be out of a job."

Gabriel looked around the sub. The strange noises consistently emanating from the ocean floor seemed to be intensifying. They were sending strong vibrations through the hull of the boat and felt similar to air turbulence in a plane.

Peralta noticed them as well. He swivelled in his chair to check the sub's navigation system. The minor earthquakes had been continuing unabated for the last twelve hours now, and he was concerned they might be affecting the delicate instrumentation. He spoke over his shoulder as he typed.

"I think this website's capable of ushering in a new age of democracy," he said. "The Cube's a powerful AI. It knows what it's doing. It would probably make all the mundane decisions that nobody wanted to vote on."

"And what about the spiritual cube?" asked Natasha.

Peralta nodded and moved the cursor, expanding the second cube into six different links: Buddhism, Taoism and Confucianism, Hinduism, Islamism, Christianity, and Judaism.

"I can't even guess at what this is about," he rasped.

"It's about the six divine actions…" whispered Natasha, looking at Gabriel as she made the connection. "A spiritual path made up of the wisdoms housed within each of the world's religions…"

"What wisdoms?" asked Amir. "What are you guys talking about?"

Gabriel looked at him for a moment without speaking. The global implications of such a social networking platform were beginning to dawn on him.

"Originally there was only one religion," he said. "If you could even call it a religion. It contained a body of knowledge that eventually became fragmented, with each fragment becoming its own religion.

"If the parts were reassembled again, the original knowledge would be revealed. It could potentially change the way humanity thinks and acts. It looks like this website is where the reunification is supposed to take place."

"Why is that gauge flashing?" came a deep and unexpected voice.

All turned to see Bahadur. He was hunched over and pointing to a blinking gauge on the instrument panel, his shoulders rubbing the ceiling.

"Is that normal?"

"Buoy grid warning!" exclaimed Peralta, jumping from his seat. "Shit! This does not look good! This does not look good at all!"

The scrappy engineer bolted to a different section of the instrument cluster, caressing one of the gauges and muttering words of encouragement as he turned some knobs.

"What is it?" asked Gabriel, coming to his side.

"There's been a massive tectonic shift in the mid-Atlantic ridge!" exclaimed the scrappy engineer, his eyes wide with horror. "It's created an immense shockwave! It's coming directly towards us! We've got to dive as deep as we can! Everybody tie yourselves down! This might get very ugly!"

CHAPTER 7

Santander, Northern Spain.

The plane was rapidly losing altitude as it made its way into Santander. The massive geomagnetic storm was playing havoc with its instrumentation, and while the ride had been relatively smooth in the upper atmosphere, things had changed dramatically as they descended into the churning clouds. The fuselage was shuddering violently, and they had lost all their navigational aids.

"I *will* kill you, brother..." whispered Christian ardently, his face damp with sweat.

The combined influence of the Zurvanites and Ahreimanius was affecting him in ways he could never have imagined. His sanity was slipping away, just as his body was transforming.

Christian looked down at his hands to see them oscillating between ghostliness and solidity. He was becoming reptilian.

He made a concerted effort to regain control of himself and unbuckled his seatbelt, stepping out into the aisle as the plane lurched underfoot. With great difficulty he made his way to the plane's cockpit, bursting in to find both pilots in a state of emergency. A series of alarms were sounding, and the instrumentation was smoking dangerously. Neither of them had even noticed his appearance.

"We've lost control of the rear aileron!" exclaimed the pilot at the yoke. "I'm sending more power to the left engine!"

Christian spotted an unconscious stewardess on the floor and woke suddenly to the gravity of the situation. Her head was gushing blood.

"What's happening?" he demanded.

Only the co-pilot looked back at him.

"Mr. Antov, sir!" he cried, struggling to find something in a manual. "You must return to your seat immediately!"

Christian's eyes opened wide when he saw what lay below them. Stretching out in all directions was a vast body of floodwater, littered with the ruins of the coastal city of Santander. The plane was hurtling towards it at an alarming rate.

"What the hell happened down there?" he cried.

"A tsunami, Mr. Antov!" blurted the pilot.

He was struggling to control the small jet.

"It's wiped out the entire Atlantic coast, sir. The airport's gone! There's nowhere to land!"

The noise in the cabin was rising, and the toxic smoke from the burnt wiring was making Christian's head spin. To make matters worse, the Zurvanites had appeared again.

"Kill your brother! Kill him! Kill him!"

Christian tried frantically to ignore them.

"Go inland!" he cried, shuddering uncontrollably. "Put us down in a field for Christ's sake!"

"I can't keep her up, sir!" exclaimed the pilot, battling with the yoke. "The electrical storm's crippled us. We're going down! There's nothing we can do! Get back to your seat and buckle in, sir! Put on your life jacket! If you stay where you are you'll be killed!"

Christian scanned the ruined city as it sped past below. They were descending far too rapidly, and he knew they would be in the water in a matter of seconds. He turned back into the passenger compartment only to find his four military commanders making their way towards him.

"Get into your seats and tie yourselves in!" he cried. "We're going down!"

They obeyed immediately, and Christian had only managed to secure his own belt when the plane made contact with the water.

In the span of seconds, the luxurious interior had transformed into a living hell, the fuselage screaming as the plane skipped over the treacherous flood water.

Christian shot a glance outside to see that the pilots were bringing them down over what had once been a major avenue. A second later he was thrown forward violently, the door to the cockpit exploding open and sending a deluge of seawater and wreckage into the cabin, along with the bodies of the two dead pilots. The plane began to list.

"Move it! Move it!" came the resounding order from one of the officers.

Christian felt himself being forcibly removed from his seat as the four soldiers burst into action. The plane had come to a standstill now, but the front of it was slipping quickly into the water.

In an instant Christian was being pulled up to the back of the plane and shoved through the service doors into the rear cargo area. After that, things happened very quickly. In a blur of activity, the captains gathered up their gear and ammunition, using their assault rifles to blast away an aluminum hatch as the plane began to sink.

"Get out of the way!" bellowed one of them, and Christian was yanked aside as an officer pushed through with a raft that was already beginning to inflate.

Christian watched as it was thrown from the opening, landing in the water just outside the sinking plane.

"Go! Go!" screamed another, throwing Christian through the opening and into the raft.

In a matter of seconds their escape had been executed, and Christian found himself lying safely in the raft surrounded by three heavily armed soldiers. He watched the twisted fuselage slip under the water and vanish without a trace.

"Wilkinson!" bellowed the captain next to him, his head craning over the side of the raft. "Wilkinson!"

A long minute passed, and then to everyone's surprise the lost officer broke the surface, his resolute face drawing a deep breath of air as he took hold of the raft. Seconds later he was aboard, collapsing back onto the inflated rubber to catch his breath.

"This doesn't look good," said one of the captains, examining the gaping wound on the man's shoulder. "What happened? You were fine on the plane."

"Something was down there," said Wilkinson, his strong jaw trembling. "It grabbed me and took a chunk out of me. I don't know what the hell it was, but there was more than one. If it didn't sound so crazy, I'd say there were people down there."

Christian frowned and scanned the waters. The red light filtering down from above revealed little, but the irregular flashes of lightning told a different story. In the murky depths, Christian could discern movement. And whereas no corpse could be seen anywhere above the water, the same could not be said for what lay below.

"What the hell..." muttered one of the captains, looking overboard.

The undead were clear to see now. They resembled black wraiths in the oily water, slow moving and ghostly.

"What are you doing?" blurted the captain, but Christian had already snatched away his rifle.

Without a word of explanation, he leveled the weapon at Wilkinson and pulled the trigger, releasing it only when the man's head had been reduced to a pulpy mass. The officers recoiled instinctively, a grim spray of brain, blood and bone fragments dripping from their faces.

"You crazy son of a bitch!" screamed one of the soldiers, reaching for his gun.

Christian was faster. He trained the sites of his rifle on him and waited for them to calm down.

"Throw his body overboard!" he ordered, blinking away a shooting pain in his head.

The demons were worming into his brain.

"Kill your brother! Kill him! Kill him!"

Working together, two of the captains took hold of the headless corpse and threw it overboard. The water boiled with a frenzy of motion where it had gone down.

"What the hell's going on?" asked one of them, turning to look at Christian.

"This area's been exposed to an experimental virus," he managed to say.

The screaming whispers in his head were growing louder with every passing second.

"Kill your brother! Kill him! Kill him!"

Christian struggled to speak.

"Your colleague was bitten by one of the infected… He would have killed us all."

The three officers fell silent, trying to understand what Christian was telling them.

"Are you saying there are people down there?"

"Yes!" snapped Christian, a madness in his eyes. "And they are all dead!"

"But we just saw them moving," exclaimed another. "Why haven't they drowned?"

"The dead don't breathe!" barked Christian, snapping his head around. "Don't let them touch you!"

"Ahreimanius! Lucifer! Lucifer!"

Christian battled with his aggressors and managed to regain a semblance of control.

"The water is full of them…" he said, willing himself to grow calmer. "The surrounding hills too. Reanimation can only be prevented by destroying the brain."

He pointed his gun at the captains.

"Two of you pick up those oars and get us to dry land," he said. "You! Shoot at anything that moves. They'll attack when we reach the shallow water."

Christian's prediction proved accurate. No sooner had they reached the shore than the dead began to rise from the floodwater, stumbling slowly and inching ever closer. There were suddenly hundreds of them, and the eerie red light of the aurora filtered down over their ranks.

No sooner had they exited the raft than one of the officers became infected with fear.

"Get away from me you mother fuckers!" he bellowed, and a deafening rattle exploded from his gun.

He was firing directly into the mob, but only the corpses that had received numerous rounds to the head went down. The others were driven back by the force of the bullets, but soon began inching their way forward the moment the firing had stopped.

"For Christ's sake, they don't even bleed!" cried the officer in despair.

Christian turned in his direction, a demonic chorus screeching through his mind.

"Their blood has coagulated," he muttered, wincing under the pain of the icy whispers. "It cannot flow."

Christian let himself be herded to a new position on higher ground. From there the hordes could be seen rising from the waters in their multitudes, illuminated by flickering barrages of lightning. There were tens of thousands of them, all coming towards Christian in twisted, black reverence.

"And the sea gave up the dead which were in it," Christian heard himself say.

He was quoting from the Book of Revelations.

"And death and hell delivered up the dead which were in them…"

"What the fuck are you talking about?" screamed one of the officers.

He jerked around with his rifle only to see they were surrounded.

"Squadron one, squadron one!" barked another into his radio. "Do you read me! This is captain Ronald T. Curtis. We are down. I repeat. We are down! Do you read me!"

"Your troops are all dead," said Christian, a wicked smile of realization suddenly transforming his features.

He threw aside the assault rifle he was holding.

"Everyone here is dead, Captain, including yourself."

And as the ground lurched and shuddered beneath their feet, and as the floodwaters seethed and trembled with the approaching hordes, the soldiers' guns exploded into fire, their bullets vanishing into the throngs like droplets of rain into a jungle, their grenades dismembering corpses that continued forward regardless.

"Die, you bloody sons of bitches!" cried one of them, rushing into the horde in a suicidal rampage of gunfire.

The others watched in dumb horror as he was swallowed up and consumed. Only Christian was without fear. He could see grainy, demonic shadows rising from the floodwaters everywhere now. They were flowing into the undead like black hornets into nests.

Christian watched the corpses transform the moment the demons had taken possession of them, their rotting faces taking on reptilian features, and their movements becoming fiendish and jerky.

No longer were these the thoughtless shells of the undead. They were his subjects now, and he was their lord and master. From every corner they were coming to worship at his feet. This was his army, and they would serve him now and in the future.

Christian saw that the four Zurvanites had appeared around him again, and as always, their frantic desperation was poisoning him to the core. Everything was hinging on his success; an aeon of plotting and conspiring all culminating in a single event. Failure to kill his brother would result in irreversible loss. The Apocatastasis would become unstoppable. Isaac had to die. Failure was not an option.

"Kill your brother! Kill him! Kill him!"

Christian jerked his head around to face the Four. An ocean of dark power was suddenly swelling within him, and his hatred for his brother surged to an unimaginable intensity.

"Feel the Dark Lord within you!" hissed the Zurvanites in unison. *"Your time is at hand. By the fist Ahreimanius will you conquer this world and rule it in darkness!"*

And then, in one instant, the glorious numbness that had always been Christian's fortitude was returned to him. He could feel the strength of Ahreimanius surging in his body, and the panicked screams of the two remaining officers only served to accentuate the majesty of the moment.

With the cartridges of their guns empty, they had gathered closer and closer to Christian, only to be ripped away and devoured by the teeming hordes.

"GET THEE DOWN!" boomed Christian suddenly from his mount, and in that instant every corpse as far away as the distant hills lowered itself before him, writhing and twisting on the ravaged earth like beaten dogs.

High above a single eagle flew, scanning the wasted domain. Under the cataclysmic sky it could see a vast army assembling over the lands, rank upon rank of twisted undead, milling and seething, and armed with a plague that if left unchecked, would devour the entire planet.

CHAPTER 8

Los Picos de Europa, Northern Spain.

Isaac awoke to the clank of armour and the thud of many boots. The knights were preparing to depart. There was an unmistakable haste in their movements and Isaac knew that something must have happened whilst he slept. He rose to his feet, his head still heavy with sleep. He could see Brother Bernardo approaching.

"What's happening?" he asked, rubbing his face awake.

"The demons have taken possession of the dead," said the monk in a low voice. "They are reptilian now, just as the Ascender's Prophecy foretold. They use their hands and feet to propel themselves and they are fiendishly fast. A rogue group of them attacked the knights on watch. They were destroyed, but not without cost. We lost two of our men."

He threw Isaac his pack.

"The scouts have spotted a horde behind us. They are approaching fast."

Sir David burst into the cave just then, his sword drawn and bloodied.

"We move now!" he barked, vanishing a second later.

In the space of a minute Isaac found himself rushing along a narrow mountain pass, with Shackleton at last appearing at his side. The state of the planet's surface had worsened considerably over the time they had been in the cave. Its atmosphere was now heavy with the toxic expulsions of recently formed volcanoes, and in the blood red sky could be seen great blankets of gaseous green fires.

The relentless barrage of charged solar particles was breaking down atmospheric water molecules into oxygen and hydrogen, only to be ignited by the sheets of lightning. The result was the birth of a cataclysmic world that no longer even resembled Earth, but rather a strange and foreign planet in some cursed region of space.

"The horde is upon us!" cried a knight suddenly.

He had been on the rear guard but had run up to warn his captain.

"Three hundred strong! Perhaps more!"

Sir David wasted no time, ordering the party to gain higher ground immediately. To their good fortune, the path at this point ran along an almost sheer precipice. The rocky terrain above the trail would at least slow the attackers.

"God help us," he said, taking a last look over his shoulder before following the others up.

He had witnessed firsthand the metamorphosis that had taken place in the undead. They could travel over the rocky terrain with freakish speed now, and he knew there would be little they could do to defend themselves against such a mob, regardless of their strategic position above the path.

"Form a ring around our charge!" he cried, and his knights scrambled to obey, their shields interlocking to form a formidable barrier bristling with the blades of their swords.

In the blink of an eye, Isaac, the monk, and Shackleton found themselves completely enclosed. It was not long before they felt a strange rumbling in the ground. It rode atop the regular churning of the earth's crust.

Moments later the horde came into view, a macabre mass of shadowy grey corpses leaping like rabid animals along the narrow path below them. Through the gaps and spaces between the knights, Isaac could see them passing. There was a cold malevolence in their lizard-like eyes, but they were all looking eastward, never once glancing up.

Isaac felt a hand on his shoulder. It forced him down behind the boulders. The defensive ring of knights was breaking apart, and he turned to see Sir David's face only inches from his own.

"Stay down!" he whispered, his eyes alight with hope. "They have not seen us!"

Isaac swallowed hard, fighting back the urge to bolt. Brother Bernardo had not been exaggerating. The undead were truly reptilian now, and it seemed to him that a horrific nightmare was playing out before him.

Many of them were plunging from the cliff's edge as they stampeded past, only to rise from wherever they fell to continue their maddened flight into the east. In this way the mighty horde came and went in the space of just a few minutes.

"Where are they going?" asked Isaac, struggling to compose himself.

He had come down to join the knights on the path and was having to step around the fetid gore that covered the earth. Amid the sludge of clotted blood, bile and excrement could be seen grey swaths of skin, severed digits, and grisly sections of tooth and gum.

"They go to the Portal," said Sir David, grimacing. "Just as the Ascender's Prophecy foretells. There will be no stopping them until the demons have been exorcized and forced to descend again."

Isaac let his head fall, knowing that it was he who was responsible for this. In that instant, however, he felt a comforting hand on his shoulder, and looking over saw that Brother Bernardo had come to join them.

"For a large wound to be healed," said the monk softly, "it sometimes requires that a smaller wound be inflicted first. Do not regret your actions, dear Isaac. In opening the portal, you also made it possible for *The Two* to descend into it. Therein lies our only hope."

Isaac turned to face the monk. In the eastern sky behind him a funnel of churning clouds had amassed. It loomed black over their destination, a sinister finger pointing to the very same island where he had committed his atrocities.

Isaac felt his eyes burning with tears as he gazed out over the tortured lands. It was a panorama of oblivion, writhing under the force of an ever-worsening cataclysm. Despite the brother's kind words, he could not shake the feeling that he was responsible for all this, and it weighed on him heavily.

"I had a dream whilst I slept..." he said quietly, his gaze lingering in the east.

Brother Bernardo drew close, his eyes solemn but compassionate.

"What did you dream, dear Isaac?"

"I dreamed of a shadowy emperor," he said. "Attended to by the Fourteen Emissaries of Lucifer. They were at the head of an army that covered the earth like a blanket of cinder."

Isaac looked down to find Shackleton loyally by his side. He fell to one knee and ruffled the fur atop his head.

"The emperor was my brother," he continued, squinting up at the monk through the stinging rain. "He's coming to kill me."

CHAPTER 9

Somewhere under the Atlantic Ocean.

"This is unbelievable!" exclaimed Amir.

His eyes were wide with surprise as he gazed into the monitor. Peralta looked up from his work at the control panel, wondering what all the fuss was about.

After having been hit by the underwater shockwave, the small sub had tumbled to depths that had threatened its structural integrity. It was only by a miracle that they were still alive. As it was, many systems on the boat had been damaged as a result, and repairing them was proving to be no small task.

"What is it?" asked Peralta, looking up from his calculations.

He had only just managed to get the internet systems online again, but there was still a long list of configurations that needed to be made. Amir looked over at him, his face beaming with excitement.

"You're gonna love this."

Peralta rose groaning from his seat. A stretch would do him good. He hobbled over to Amir's station and peered into the monitor. The video Cassano had made was online and streaming. Gabriel and Natasha were presenting the three-dimensional scans and describing the Cube's ability to interface with their brains.

"All right," said Peralta, yawning. "He did a great job on the video. What's the big deal?"

"You haven't looked closely enough," said Amir, chewing on one of his cinnamon toothpicks. "Look at the number of views it's had."

He watched Peralta's eyes shift.

"What the hell…"

In a split-second Peralta's sleepy expression had transformed into utter surprise. He craned his neck forward to be absolutely certain he was reading it correctly.

"That's right," said Amir proudly. "Over twenty million hits and counting!"

"But how?" stammered Peralta.

"It's gone viral, my friend," said Amir, sitting back and crossing his arms. "We've already got over six hundred thousand people hooked up to our Boink worldwide. As soon as you get your systems working, I think you're going to be seeing some crazy amounts of fully extracted algorithms in your data banks."

Peralta stood in silent amazement, his arms dangling at his sides as his mind struggled to understand.

"But what could have been in the video that made the world embrace it like this?"

"Hope," came Natasha's voice from behind.

Peralta turned to see her smiling happily.

"Just when the planet's lost all hope, the Compostela Cube comes along."

Amir nodded in agreement, his dreadlocks swaying.

"A communications artifact created by an advanced civilization that lived on earth two hundred and fifty million years ago," he said merrily. "That's pretty big news, especially if it's holding a secret that's going to solve all our problems, man.

"I'm sure people are thinking if this isn't a hoax, it's the biggest discovery ever made. And the fact that there's a mysterious website you can interact with just makes it even more exciting."

"But there's no content on the website," said Peralta, scrubbing at his messy head in an effort to get the blood flowing.

"Maybe that's where the hope comes in," said Natasha, turning to see Gabriel entering the bridge.

To their relief his thumbs were both held up in a gesture of success. Behind him came Bahadur, bending low to squeeze in through the small hatch. The two of them were drenched from head to foot, having been outside repairing the communications antenna while the sub continued its race northward.

Given the turbulent state of the ocean, making the repairs had not been an easy task. Peralta wasted no time in darting to his workstation to reactivate the central telemetry. In an instant the old bishop's face had appeared on the main monitor as the connection was made, his eyes alight with relief and happiness.

"Thanks be to God," prayed the bishop, and then turning his head he exclaimed:

"Cassano! You must come at once, my son! We have re-established contact! They appear to be safe and sound!"

"Uncle Marcus!" exclaimed Natasha, delighted to see the old man's face. "We're all fine! We were hit by a tsunami."

"I know, child, I know!" came his reply, beaming with joy.

"Good God," exclaimed Cassano, his face appearing behind the bishop's. "I've just had a look at your transponder. How did you cover so much distance?"

"The tsunami must have sucked us northward," said Peralta, "We lost our positioning system when the initial shockwave hit. Where exactly are we?"

"You're at the top of Spain, Captain," said Cassano. "You'll be able to take up an easterly heading within the hour. I'll send you the data so you can recalibrate."

"Much has happened since you lost contact," said the bishop as Cassano disappeared to do his work. "Your video has circled the globe."

Peralta was nodding in amazement.

"I still can't believe it..."

"Well, that is not all," said the bishop. "It would appear that leaders from the six world religions have also joined our cause."

"What do you mean, Uncle?" asked Natasha.

The old bishop shrugged.

"An official World Religion Consortium has been formed. It is momentous, my child. Planet Earth has risen to its feet and is rallying behind the Cube!"

"But that's crazy," said Gabriel, waking from his initial shock. "There's no real proof out there that the Cube even exists. How could all this come from a single video?"

"The video represents something that the world hungers for," said the bishop. "It represents democracy and solidarity. The Cube has six equal sides, my son. One for every religion. Its very existence sings of unity.

"Just as people are drawn together by crisis, so has the entire world been drawn together by this cataclysm. You do not fully understand. You have been out of touch with the world for the past ten hours. Everything has changed. As far as proof of the existence of the Cube is concerned, there is a substantial amount readily available."

"What proof?" asked Gabriel.

"Why, the social networking platform," said the old bishop matter-of-factly. "Already there are millions of citizens interacting on it. Word is spreading like wildfire. There are democratic forums already planning cease fires in numerous countries worldwide."

Peralta darted back to his workstation and brought up the Cube's website.

"Twenty-two thousand forums in attendance…" he said over his shoulder, still having difficulty believing what he was seeing.

"Response has been overwhelming!" exclaimed the bishop. "And it is only natural given the circumstances. Everyone is locked in their homes as a result of the tempestuous weather and curfews. They are glued to the internet. People want to resolve this crisis, and the website is giving them a way to do it."

Peralta returned his attention to the monitor, an expression of concern coming over his features.

"It'll all be for nothing if we can't locate that labyrinth and activate the Cube…"

"For nothing?" said Amir, "I hardly think so. The new directives they're formulating could end this stupid war."

"Sure, but it won't make a difference," said Peralta.

"What do you mean?"

Peralta took a deep breath and centred himself.

"When we cross the galactic plane, the gravitational field is going to do a lot more than move some tectonic plates around. It's going to affect our *brains*. Our sense of perception will be shifted and distorted. Time will literally be warped. It'll be as though everyone in the world's been given a massive dose of LSD for God's sake! It's going to be disastrous…"

Amir held Peralta's gaze without saying a word. He himself had experimented with psychotropic substances in university and knew what it was to have one's mind enter into such altered states. If Peralta was right, it would be the final blow to end society.

Gabriel had assisted Amir in the experiments, and his attention was fixed on Peralta as well.

"Of course," he said slowly. "That's how the whole thing works. That's why the Cube is the way it is."

"What do you mean?" asked Natasha. "What do psychotropic drugs have to do with the Cube?"

Gabriel turned to face her.

"The effects of any mind-altering drug are directly related to the participant's state of mind," he said slowly. "In other words, after consuming a psychotropic substance, the ensuing experience will be positive or negative, euphoric or hellish, depending on what one's mental attitude was before the drug was ingested."

"It's the difference between a good trip, and a bad trip," said Amir with a shrug.

"Exactly," rasped Peralta. "And the present state of the global consciousness pretty much guarantees a bad trip. The world population is currently experiencing an unprecedented level of fear and anxiety, as well as bitterness, hopelessness, and doubt. A crossing of the galactic plane under these conditions would have a devastating effect on the minds of every person on this planet. We'd be plunged into despair and come out of the crossing in a state of general insanity."

Gabriel interjected immediately.

"But just as with all psychotropic hallucinogens," he said, holding up a hand, "the mind-altering effects could also be a profoundly positive and deeply spiritual experience."

Gabriel paused for a moment before continuing.

"Speaking for myself, my limited experiments with peyote and hallucinogenic mushrooms were enlightening, but my mental state was healthy and peaceful going into them. I can see what you're saying, Captain, but perhaps this is where the Cube can make a difference."

"Which is exactly my point!" rasped Peralta. "The Cube is plugged into the collective consciousness, and it has been for the past quarter of a billion years. If we can get to the Labyrinth on time, and you two can activate the Cube's systems, it's very likely that something beneficial will occur."

"Like what?" asked Amir.

"I have no idea!" said Peralta, frustrated. "All I can tell you is what I know from the numbers we've decrypted.

Some kind of data pattern will be injected into the universal field of intelligence at the time of the crossing."

"Peace," said Natasha softly.

She had suddenly recalled Suora's last words.

Bring peace to the hearts of all those who will make the crossing.

She looked at the two rotating cube icons on the monitor.

"It's going to be a profound feeling of peace and serenity that'll get injected into the collective consciousness," she said quietly. "Like the warm fuzzy feeling you get on Christmas Eve. Do you know the one I mean?"

Everyone turned to face Natasha. Her words had struck a chord. From the outset, they had all known that the Cube's purpose was to usher the world into a new and better age, but it was not until this very moment that they fully understood how the artifact was going to accomplish this feat.

The Cube would first endow humanity with the peace of mind needed to survive the crossing, and it would then imbue humanity with the wisdom it needed to socially evolve after the crossing had been made.

Now, more than ever, an urgency to complete the mission surged within each of them. Locked in this Cube lay a gift so wonderful, so benevolent, that they could not even begin to imagine the benefits it would bestow upon humanity. They simply had to find the Labyrinth of Sarras, and as quickly as possible. Time was running out.

Peralta was the first to break from the silence that had come in the wake of Natasha's realization.

"Cassano," he said. "I just looked at the data you sent me."

While the others had been lost in thought, the scruffy engineer had returned to his workstation and got down to the more practical matters at hand.

"Our position is good," he rasped, "but we're still approximately six hours from Santander. Less than eight hours remain before we cross the galactic plane. How are we supposed to locate this labyrinth in two hours, especially if we don't know where it is?"

Gabriel rose to his feet. Because of the tsunami crisis, he had not yet had a chance to share what he and Natasha had learned of in their trance.

"Where exactly are we?" he asked, moving to Peralta's side.

"Approaching the northern tip of Spain. We've just got to head west along the coast, and we'll be on our way to Santander."

Gabriel looked back at Natasha.

"We forgot to mention something," he said. "We don't need to go to Santander anymore."

"What do you mean?" asked Peralta. "If not Santander, then where?"

"Do you know a village called Finisterre?" asked Natasha, stepping closer.

Peralta checked his navigation system.

"Finisterre is on the west coast, directly east of our present location," he said, frowning. "I could have us there in twenty minutes. But if the Labyrinth is south of Santander, it would be way faster for us to travel there by sea rather than over land."

Peralta saw Gabriel and Natasha exchange a knowing glance, a smile appearing on both of their faces. He stood up, his fists propped on his plump hips.

"Perhaps you might like to share your little secret with us now?" he said, clearly annoyed. "What's it going to be? Over sea, or over land?"

"Neither," said Gabriel with a wink. "Take us into Finisterre and we'll show you how to get us to the Labyrinth on time."

CHAPTER 10

Los Picos de Europa, Northern Spain.

Christian moved forward like someone passing through a dense and viscous liquid, his concentration bent solely on putting one foot in front of the other. Blanketing the lands around him was a host of undead so large that its numbers were uncountable, and still more came with every passing minute.

Christian was encased in them as he stumbled forward, held aloft by fetid reptilian arms, with each frenzied corpse herding him to the place where all would be decided. His body was jerking and trembling uncontrollably now, his advance resembling less the procession of a powerful emperor, and more the parade of a captured lunatic.

For over eight hours he had travelled in this way. Overhead the sky bled and boiled, lit by fires of molten gas, and expanding sheets of verdigris lightning. With the Dark Rift now only hours from being crossed, the planet was shuddering fitfully, its crust expanding and contracting with the force of falling mountains; enraging the sea and the air, and all that was ever once calm.

Christian squinted up into the acid rain, his eyes burning and his lungs on fire. For hours now he had been accompanied by the silent ghost of Dr. Bennington, conjured by his unconscious mind in an attempt to regain the confidence he had exhibited while under the doctor's care.

"As you can see, my good Doctor," muttered Christian, stumbling over a rock made slippery with gore. "Everything is moving according to plan. Soon all of humanity shall bend to my will."

But whereas the doctor had always been kind and patient with him in life, his specter had been made cruel and wicked by the tremendous guilt that Christian harboured.

"Your will means nothing!" hissed Bennington, his eyes glowing red. *"You are a piece of refuse, adequate only to be used as a vessel for the sexual gratification of your superiors."*

Bennington's words cut Christian to the bone, reopening the wounds that lay at the root of his torment. His body fell into uncontrollable spasms and seizures, and soon after, everything went black.

* * * * * *

Christian awoke to find himself lying on the rocky ground, surrounded by a frenzied mob of demonically possessed corpses. The stench of them was outlandish, and as he rose unsteadily to his feet, he realized that his numbness had once again been revoked. It had been replaced by a seething, baleful force that wormed through his mind like a nest of maggots.

He could hear his father's hissing voice in his head, and whereas before it had been a great torment to him, it was now almost comforting, reminding him of a time when he had been impervious to pain.

All power is based in fear. Fear in the masses must be maintained at all costs.

Christian pushed his fingers into his eyes, straining to regain his mind and set straight something that was driving him into madness.

In times such as these, when his reptilian self prevailed, he experienced strange sounds and visions. They were brief glimpses of scenes, where he found himself in other parts of the mountains, but always among the undead.

The visions were becoming clearer to him now, and in that moment, he understood that he was seeing through the eyes of the undead themselves. The demonic corpses were a part of him now, and along with this new understanding came a sudden realization. He now possessed tens of thousands of eyes through which to look for his brother. It would only be a matter of time before he found him.

Christian made his way to the edge of a high precipice, the undead hordes clearing a path before him. From here the earth could be seen writhing in agony, the expulsions of newly formed volcanoes belching poison into the toxic air. The ground was shaking and lurching constantly now, and Christian had to make an effort to stay on his feet.

Far below him lay a small mountain lake, its surface black like carbon. Even the burning sky, with its fiery clouds and rippling sheets of lightning could do nothing to illuminate it. Only a tiny island was visible there, its burnt trunks rising from it like charred fingers from a shallow grave.

Christian passed his hands over his face in an attempt to revitalize himself. He had at last arrived at the Portal of Ahreimanius. Here, with the help of his army, he would find his brother and kill him.

CHAPTER 11

Isaac looked down at the lake from his elevated perch. His arrival had coincided perfectly with Christian's, but he and his knights were on the western side, directly opposite his brother, and considerably closer to the island.

Christian's army of corpses could be seen on the eastern shore, a gargantuan host of seething cinder-grey shadows amassed on the hilly terrain. Shackleton was at Isaac's side, and the fat monk behind him. In their worst nightmares they had never foreseen such a large force opposing them. Their numbers were literally in the millions.

"What do we do now?" asked Isaac, turning to see that the knights had grouped to form a protective barrier behind him.

"We wait," said Brother Bernardo. "We wait and we hope."

"But we have no boat. How will we reach the island?"

Sir David approached just then.

"Our way into the City of Sarras will be shown to us when the Two arrive, just as it is written in the Ascender's Prophecy."

Isaac was perplexed.

"What city? There is only a tiny island here."

"We will wait, and we will see," said the captain. "In the meantime, we shall rest. My men are tired, as must you be, dear Isaac. Sit and eat. We are safe here for the time being."

CHAPTER 12

Finisterre, Northern Spain.

All eyes scanned the images being shown on the bridge's main monitor. Having arrived at Finisterre, Peralta had followed Gabriel's directions and turned the sub into the sheltered port. Using what he proudly referred to as his Synthetic Aperture Sonar, Peralta had located some unique rock formations about thirty meters below sea level.

"Could that be it?" asked Natasha, pointing to the monitor. "The dark section there, next to that big rock."

Peralta used the joystick to nudge the sub a few degrees starboard until its lights fell on the feature that Natasha had pointed out.

"That's definitely a cave," he rasped. "By the looks of it, I'd say it was big enough to steer this boat into as well."

A tremor shook the submarine and he turned to exchange a worried glance with Gabriel.

"Are you sure about this, Dr. Parker?"

Peralta rubbed his temples when he saw Gabriel nod. He was still having difficulty believing what he had been told. He made some adjustments to the navigation system.

"A two-hundred-and-fifty-million-year-old tunnel," he said, shaking his head. "Built by an ancient race of hyper-intelligent reptilians. All so they could get to an underground city they built in the middle of the mountains…"

He swiveled in his chair and adjusted some knobs.

"A tunnel that has not only survived countless geological events, but one that also travels horizontally for approximately three hundred kilometres."

He finished his preparations and looked over at Natasha. "Forgive me if I'm a little skeptical."

All eyes were glued to the monitor as Peralta eased the submarine into the cave. It did not take long before it became obvious that they had found what they were looking for. The sonar showed a long and spacious tunnel heading due east, its trajectory perfectly level. A moment later Peralta was increasing the sub's speed.

"Well then," he said, shaking his head again, but this time in amazement. "This tunnel is definitely not a natural formation. Those reptilians knew what they were doing. It's perfectly straight."

Gabriel's eyes met with Natasha's. The tunnel seemed familiar to them, and not just because they had seen it while in Mithuna. There was something remotely familiar about this place, as though they had been here many times before.

"Captain Peralta," said Natasha on an impulse. "Do you think you could turn off the headlights for a moment?"

The messy engineer raised an eyebrow at her odd request, and then flipped a few toggle switches on the instrument panel. The exterior monitor went black.

"Well I'll be damned…" whispered Peralta.

The tunnel had begun to glow with iridescent blue light. He bent to tap on a keyboard and adjust a few knobs.

"We're definitely going to need to find out what's causing this…"

Scotty and Amir entered the bridge as Peralta went about his work. They had been in the engine room with Bahadur.

"What the bloody hell…?" said Scotty, his attention fixed on the sub's main monitor. "Don't tell me that's the tunnel you were talking about. That's a video game you're playing, right, mate?"

Peralta's face wore a mask of astonishment.

"Judging by these scans, it would appear that the walls are lined with the same material that the Cube's made of. They're synthetically alive… And flexible…"

"That'll do it," said Gabriel. "Couple that with the fact that the Precambrian rock formations here are over two billion years old, and we can see how this tunnel's stood the test of time."

Amir was shaking his head in disbelief.

"You'd think that would surprise me, but it doesn't."

He paused to scratch behind an ear, thinking.

"What I don't get is why they would have to build the Labyrinth so far inland... Why not just build it on the coast and save themselves all the trouble of having to dig such a long tunnel?"

"The Labyrinth had to be built where the portal was located," explained Gabriel. "From what I gather, the portal's some kind of wormhole located in outer space. It's in a very specific location that our planet actually moves through as our solar system orbits the centre of the galaxy."

Peralta turned to look at Gabriel.

"A wormhole?"

"I think so," said Gabriel, frowning. "It's located directly on the galactic plane. I guess it just so happened that these mountains are the place on the planet where it all lines up."

Peralta held up his hand, wanting to be absolutely sure he understood what Gabriel had said.

"Bear with me, please," he rasped. "The Labyrinth is built precisely on the point of land that will align itself with a wormhole, just as we pass through the galactic plane."

"That's right," said Gabriel. "That specific place happens to be located deep underground, directly beneath that island we keep talking about. That's where they built the City of Sarras."

"Of course..." said Peralta. "That explains everything. The natural place for a wormhole to form would be in an ultrahigh gravitational field, just like the one in the galactic plane..."

A shadow of fear passed over his face.

"What the hell are we heading for?" he whispered, peering into the depths of iridescent blue tunnel as it sped past. "Going through the galactic plane is going to be crazy enough, but to do it right beside a wormhole? Have you any idea what we're in for? Wormholes are very enigmatic things, Dr. Parker. They're suspected of connecting utterly different dimensions outside of space and time. We could be lost forever!"

"I guess that's why they call it a labyrinth," said Gabriel, cocking an eyebrow. "This location seems to be some kind of a gateway. One that runs in two very different directions."

"One gate goes to heaven," said Natasha slowly, "but the other one goes to hell."

Peralta swallowed hard, recalling what the bishop had spoken of earlier that day. There had been very disconcerting reports coming from the Cantabrian Mountains. The area had been quarantined by the military, but news of the atrocities that had befallen the people living there was still leaking out.

Unbelievable as it sounded, the dead were said to be walking, their corpses infected with a strange experimental virus that was highly communicable. If this were not bad enough, Natasha had earlier informed him that Professor Metrovich had written of these evils in his journal, stating that the victims would soon be possessed by demons from hell, and that the only way to destroy them would be through decapitation.

Peralta removed his glasses and rubbed his weary eyes.

What are we driving into?

CHAPTER 13

Six hours had passed when they finally reached the end of the tunnel, leaving only two hours before the earth began its descent into the gravitational field of the galactic plane. Despite the heightened seismic activity in the earth's crust, the small sub had smoothly navigated the tunnel, reaching an enormous underwater cavern beneath the island. It was perfectly spherical in shape.

"This is unbelievable," whispered Peralta in awe, looking at a three-dimensional sonar-generated image of the space.

On the sub's main monitor was the section that lay directly before them, its entire surface aglow in the same blue light as the tunnel.

"What's that over there?" asked Natasha, gesturing to the corner of the monitor. "It looks like a flight of steps."

Peralta manoeuvred the sub to face where she had pointed.

"That's exactly what it is," said Gabriel, taking hold of the control panel as yet another tremor shook the boat. "It's just like it was in our trance."

The image became clear as the sub approached. Before them was a wide platform, with a broad flight of steps glowing in phosphorescent blue. It led up to a raised portico.

"Why would aquatic reptilians need to build steps?" asked Amir. "Couldn't they have just swam up there?"

Natasha scanned the image.

"Nothing was underwater when we visited this place in our trance. We were walking around."

She looked at Gabriel.

"There was a slot at the top of the steps where we inserted the Cube. Do you remember?"

"I do," he said. "The doors opened right after that."

"So what are we supposed to do now?" asked Amir. "How are we supposed to get to those doors if everything's underwater?"

"This sub is equipped with an access hatch," rasped Peralta. "It's down below. The trouble is there's only one diving suit."

"That's all we'll need," said Gabriel. "How much time have we got?"

"Just a little under two hours."

The submarine lurched violently as another tremor shook the tunnel.

"Then we'll have to hurry," said Gabriel. "We're running out of time."

* * * * * *

Gabriel made his way through the frigid water, turning to see the little submarine floating in the centre of a colossal chamber shimmering with blue light. What had been an impressive glow through the sub's external camera was in fact an awe-inspiring iridescent splendor. He had been diving since he was a boy, and seen incredible things, but this literally took his breath away.

Turning to face forward, Gabriel could see an enormous wall comprised of gigantic stone pilasters. It measured at least thirty meters in both height and width and had a broad flight of steps leading to a massive portico at its top.

"This is unbelievable..." he stammered, swimming forward.

Peralta's raspy voice sounded in his helmet.

"How close are you to the entrance?"

"I'm here. I can see the slot."

Gabriel approached an enormous pair of doors that looked to be ten meters in height. They were adorned with an intricately carved image of the Tree of Life. Next to the doors was a small, square-shaped indentation. He produced the Cube.

"I'm inserting it now," he said. "Here goes nothing."

Natasha looked intently at Gabriel's grainy silhouette, dwarfed as it was against the massive entrance. She gasped in alarm. The submarine had begun to shake violently.

"Something's happening!" came Gabriel's crackling voice. "There's a loud rumbling coming through the water. It started as soon as I put the Cube in the slot. It sounds mechanical. Something big's going down. Can you feel that?"

"Affirmative!" said Peralta, taking hold of the control panel to stabilize himself. "Now get back to the sub!"

"But the door hasn't opened!" cried Gabriel amid the rising tumult. "I'll try something else!"

"Gabriel!" barked Natasha, her hands making fists. "Get back to this submarine right now!"

Gabriel turned to face her.

"All right, all right," he said, putting away the Cube. "I'm on my way. Jeez, you'd think it was the end of the world or something."

CHAPTER 14

Shackleton rose swiftly, protectively moving to Isaac's side moments before the strange rumbling began. An instant later everyone could feel it too. Unlike the irregular shuddering of the earth's crust, this was a steady, mechanical vibration, accompanied by a deep, chest shaking hum.

"What is this?" asked Isaac, standing up.

He saw the knights jump to attention around him.

"Something is happening to the lake!" hollered Brother Bernardo over a clap of thunder. "Look at the island! The water level is dropping!"

The monk was not mistaken. In the few minutes that had passed since the mechanical rumbling had begun, the lake's waterline had already dropped considerably.

It was not long before they saw that the island was in fact the tip of an enormous pyramid-shaped structure that had been hidden beneath the waters. It was covered in dark green algae, and intricately adorned with a latticework of strange and complex architectural details.

"The ancient city of Sarras!" cried Sir David, amidst a barrage of thunderclaps. "Make ready to descend!"

Isaac looked back to see the knights assembling themselves. Far below, massive vortexes had appeared on the lake's surface, and as the water level continued to drop, a way down opened up before them. Sir David wasted no time leading them into the valley. They were soon making their way along a treacherous path, slippery with mud and algae.

"Where are we going?" cried Isaac over the roaring thunder and tumult.

"An opening will soon be revealed!" bellowed Sir David. "We must get to the city before the hordes, and then seal the entrance behind us!"

With the lake almost entirely drained now, Isaac could see the colossal structure in its entirety as they descended. He estimated it to be at least three hundred meters in height, twice the size of the Great Pyramid of Giza. He was amazed that such an awesome thing could have remained hidden for so long.

Its builders must have diverted rivers to fill this valley.

The pyramid was now towering ominously above them, its ancient surface lit by pulsating sheets of verdigris lightning. Underfoot, the earth was lurching violently. It took the ground suddenly from beneath Isaac and were it not for the stout knight who caught him, he would have fallen to his death.

No sooner had they reached the valley floor than they were made aware of a new and pressing danger. Something, it seemed, had alerted the undead to their presence. What had once been a dense body of milling corpses had now formed into a single, coherent mass; one that was rushing towards them in a maddened frenzy.

"Make haste!" bellowed Sir David over the din. "The entrance to the city is there!"

Isaac followed the captain's pointing finger to see a tiny opening at the base of the structure. A narrow flight of stone steps wound precariously up to it. It would have been indistinguishable amid the countless niches and alcoves, were it not for the strange blue light that emanated from it.

"Move!" bellowed Sir David, turning to look again at the advancing hordes. "We must secure that entrance!"

Having reached the floor of the valley, only a level stretch of land now separated them from the base of the pyramid, and the stairway leading to its entrance. It was not a hundred meters away but with the lake now drained, a thick and slippery silt coated the ground, making their progress slow and treacherous. Looking back, Isaac could see that the charging undead were unaffected by the sludge. They were gaining on them rapidly.

The company arrived panting at the stairway just as the first wave of undead arrived, their twisted corpses frantic and filled with indescribable hatred. The shields of the knights strained under their onslaught, and Isaac gasped as strong arms hauled him up the steps. Two knights had remained below while the rest of them sprinted upwards to establish a defensive position above.

Fortunately for them, the thick algae covering the pyramid was thwarting the attempts of the undead to scale the structure, making the steps the only means of ascent. Their narrowness, in turn, was limiting the frontal attack to no more than two or three undead at a time, and in this way, fighting side by side, the two knights who remained below were able to hold back the advance. Even still, it would only be a matter of time before the horde overwhelmed them.

"Hurry!" bellowed Sir David. "Move! Move!"

They were almost at the entrance now.

"Good God…" muttered Isaac, aghast.

Having reached the top, he had turned to look out onto the lakebed below. That such an immense army could have amassed there so quickly seemed impossible. A sea of teaming undead was now covering the entire valley floor; hundreds of thousands strong, each one ravenous and frenzied, and lit by the burning sky. Their ranks swayed with the lurching earth like black weeds in a festering sea.

Isaac glanced down the steps in time to see the knights of the front guard falling. Seconds later a densely packed host of savage undead were leaping and bounding up the steps towards the next line of defence. There, another two knights held them back with flashing swords and straining shields.

This was no longer the slaying of slow-moving zombies. Being possessed by demons, their assailants were now as quick as cobras, and more frenzied than rabid beasts. It would only be a matter of time before this next bastion fell as well. Already two more knights had filed in behind them, waiting for their turn to die in the service of the Two.

"We must not linger here!" said Sir David to Isaac, bellowing so as to be heard over the unearthly cries. "I will escort you into the city whilst our brothers hold back the dead!"

But even as Sir David spoke these words, there came crashing down from above a group of seven undead who had managed to scale the slippery walls. It was all the knights could do to cut them down as they moved past Isaac. Even still, four managed to escape into the city entrance, their dark forms hurtling down a long, glowing tunnel that plunged into the depths of the pyramid.

Glancing down, Isaac could see that Shackleton was in a dilemma, shifting his attention between him and the fleeing undead. In a second the dog had made up his mind, sounding a resounding bark and darting off into the tunnel after his prey.

"Shackleton!" cried Isaac, feeling a sharp pain in his neck just as the words left his mouth.

He brought a hand to the spot and when he pulled it away, it was covered in blood.

"No!" gasped Brother Bernardo, tearing open Isaac's collar to examine his neck. "This cannot be!"

Isaac said nothing. His eyes were wide with surprise as the scene replayed itself. A filthy hand had slashed at him when the corpses had passed, its blackened nails carving a deep gouge in his neck. Almost instantly he began to feel engulfed by a cold fog as the virus made its way into his system.

Isaac slumped to the ground and let out a shuddering breath. The clangor of the attacking hordes was merging with the laboured beats of his heart. He was beginning to lose consciousness.

CHAPTER 15

Natasha turned and looked down to see Peralta standing atop the submarine. She was climbing the ancient steps with Gabriel at her side, the very same steps he had been swimming above a few minutes earlier. Behind them was Amir, with Bahadur and Scotty Roberts following up the rear, their assault rifles poised.

Shortly after his return to the sub, Gabriel and the others had watched in amazement as the chamber emptied itself of over half its water, becoming a massive subterranean port in the space of ten minutes. With the platform now serving as a dock for the sub to berth at, it was becoming increasingly obvious that the edifice had been built for humans.

As it was, the small party now found themselves before two massive doors leading into the mysterious city, their surface still wet from waters that had covered them for the past quarter of a billion years.

"Let's try this again," said Gabriel, producing the glowing Cube and inserting it once again into the slot.

Shortly after, a loud boom reverberated through the chamber and the massive doors swung silently inward. Gabriel spun to face the sub. He could see it floating far below, dwarfed under the chamber's enormous, towering dome. The ground was shaking incessantly now. The planet was just one hour away from entering the Dark Rift.

"How's the signal?" he said into his radio, peering down at Peralta's tiny form.

"It couldn't be better," came the response. "Good luck!"

After collecting a sample of the glowing bio-synthetic substance that coated the chamber's walls, Peralta had found that it was an excellent transmitter of radio waves. By reconfiguring their communications devices, he had not only managed to sync their radios through it, but also re-establish a perfect connection with the satellite feed that kept them linked to their base in Gibraltar.

"The reptilians must have used this blue goo to communicate with their underwater cities," he had explained. "It's faster than fibreoptics and its constantly emitting the axiomatic codes I need to decrypt the Cube's data streams. We shouldn't have any problems with communication as long as things continue to glow blue, no matter how deep you go."

Gabriel took a breath and stepped through the ancient threshold, his trained eye scanning his surroundings as he proceeded. The others followed close behind. In the iridescent blue light, the strange organic quality of the architecture was easy to see.

Carved from the living rock, their surroundings took on the nature of having been constructed by insects, the rounded edges and curving walls expressing proportions characteristic to all naturally occurring structures.

"This place is a testament to the Fibonacci sequence," said Gabriel, looking around in awe. "The proportions are perfect."

The chambers they passed through were exceedingly beautiful, but it was not long before they had left them behind. They were traversing a long glowing passageway now. It ascended at an even incline and brought them to a junction where another passage led off into the centre of the structure.

"There's a good chance this could be the entrance to the Labyrinth," said Gabriel, pointing down the passageway.

"From the configuration of these tunnels, I'd say we were in the descending passage of a pyramid, and if that's the case, the central chamber should be right down there."

He dug into his pack and produced the Cube, exchanging a glance with Natasha to set it aglow.

"I think we should be keeping an eye on this from now on," he said. "Peralta mentioned there'd be some kind of transponder near the entrance that would communicate with it."

Gabriel stopped short. A mass of fetid air had suddenly engulfed them. It was thick with the putrid reek of rotting flesh.

"What the hell is that stench?" asked Scotty, grasping the wall to balance himself during a particularly aggressive tremor.

Gabriel frowned.

"It's coming from an exit up there."

"Something is not right," said Bahadur, peering up the tunnel.

It was at that very moment that they saw four dark shapes hurtling towards them.

"What the hell are those things?" cried Gabriel.

Bahadur wasted no time finding out. In a matter of seconds, he had leveled his assault rifle and opened fire.

"Scotty!" he bellowed, and in a second the smuggler's gun was sounding as well.

The effects of their salvo seemed to have only a moderate effect on the advancing beasts, serving to slow their advance but not stop them. Bahadur suddenly remembered what the old bishop had said earlier that day.

"Aim for their heads!" he bellowed.

The frenetic corpses were almost upon them now, and with them came an indescribable sensation of evil. Natasha felt herself shuddering with fear. It was the same paranormal force she had encountered in the storeroom that day, only much more potent.

It was as though the beasts had tentacles that were reaching into her. She fought them back with all her strength. Something demonic was attempting to take her. She jerked herself around to face Gabriel, only to see that he was engaged in a similar battle.

"What the hell is this?" he grunted; his fists clenched as he fought off the invisible enemy. "Get the hell out of me, you sons of bitches!"

The assault ended as suddenly as it had begun, coinciding with the empty clicking of the assault rifle cartridges. Four corpses lay on the tunnel floor, their heads reduced to lumps of grey flesh.

Bahadur and Scotty turned to look at the others. The last of the undead was not two meters from where they stood. They were lucky to be alive.

"Got any more ammo, mate?" asked Scotty, looking over to Bahadur.

The fearless smuggler was clearly shaken.

"I do not," he said, his voice deep with concern.

Natasha was still trembling.

"What just happened, Gabriel?" she asked. "There were demons in those people. They tried to come into me…"

Gabriel took her into his arms.

"It's all right," he said, gathering himself. "They can't get into you if you fight them."

He lifted her chin and looked into her eyes.

"Don't ever let yourself be scared of them, Natasha," he said, remembering something he had read in his father's journal. "Demons are pathetic cowards. Fear's their only weapon, and the minute you call them on it, they scatter and run."

Natasha nodded with resolve. Behind Gabriel she could see Bahadur examining the crumpled bodies, a large combat knife in his hand. It was at that moment that one of the corpses began to shake violently. It launched itself at his back before she could cry out in warning.

It would have reached him were it not for a blurry form that appeared out of the glowing tunnel. It leapt through the air to impede the attack, taking the corpse by the neck and ripping off what was left of its head. Bahadur turned instinctively, ready to do battle with the new assailant.

"Don't hurt him!" cried Natasha. "We know that dog!"

Bahadur shot his head around, surprised to see the brown dog bound past him and into her arms.

"Shackleton!" exclaimed Natasha. "I can't believe you just did that!"

Bahadur frowned in confusion, walking cautiously up to the fallen corpses, and bending to sever what remained of their heads. As grisly as the task proved to be, he wanted no more surprises.

He returned to the group with a scowl on his face. Never before had he been required to do anything even remotely similar, and it was comforting for him to see Natasha smiling happily. Shackleton was attempting to nuzzle his head into her lap as she repeatedly pushed him away.

"No, Shackleton!" she said, laughing. "You're covered in zombie gore. Get away from me!"

Scotty was squatting on the floor next to his pack. He looked over at the corpses and then up at Bahadur.

"That was a little too close for comfort, mate," he said, snapping a cartridge into his gun and tossing the weapon up to the giant.

Bahadur snatched it out of the air and looked down at the smuggler, a puzzled expression on his face.

"I fixed a jammed cartridge that was in my pack. It's half empty so use it sparingly."

Amir put up a hand in a plea for silence. Footsteps were approaching from the passage above them. Bahadur spun instantly, levelling the gun. He had spotted several figures approaching.

"Who goes there?" he bellowed. "Stop or you will be shot!"

The figures came to a standstill at once, swaying as the earth shifted under foot. There were four of them in total. One of them was wounded and being held erect by two figures.

Oddly enough, they appeared to be dressed in medieval armour. Bahadur could see shields slung over their backs and drawn swords in their hands. The fourth figure wore the robes of a monk, and it was he who called out to them.

"Do not fire!" he cried. "We are friends of the Two!"

CHAPTER 16

Christian made his way along a route that cut through the last of the throngs. Almost an hour had passed since he first saw the great pyramid begin to emerge from the water. He had been high on a cliff then, and the way down had been fraught with danger. In some places he had been forced to call upon his servants for assistance, letting himself be lifted and carried by their festering hands.

Now he had arrived at last, and amid the panicked demonic whispering in his head he could see that only two knights remained to defend his brother's position. They were perched high atop a narrow flight of steps, their swords flashing as they held back the unrelenting hosts. Christian made his way towards them, the frantic hissing in his mind blotting out all other sounds.

He had seen his traitorous brother only moments before through the eyes of the undead, and watched in frustration as a group of his minions disobeyed his orders to kill him. Instead, they had charged down a long, glowing tunnel, overwhelmed by their frenzied attraction to the Two, and their insatiable desire to possess them.

Before the four renegade minions had fallen however, Christian had caught a glimpse of the Cube in Gabriel's hands. The Two were on the verge of finding the entrance to the Labyrinth. They had to be stopped immediately, but the last remaining knights still stood in his way.

"Kill your brother!" hissed the demons in his head. *"Kill him now!"*

At that moment one of the knights fell, leaving only one to defend the entrance.

"I am coming, dear brother," said Christian, his body shifting in and out of its reptilian state. "I am coming to destroy you."

CHAPTER 17

"He is the Consilio!" exclaimed the sturdy monk, gesturing to the unconscious Isaac. "Without him you cannot gain entry into the Great Labyrinth!"

Gabriel and Natasha looked at each other.

"Peralta," said Gabriel into his radio. "Did you just hear that?"

"I did," came the engineer's raspy reply. "He's got to be the missing alpha-wave sequence! You've got to get him to the entrance right away!"

"Boss!" said Amir suddenly, brandishing the timer.

Gabriel's eyes opened wide at the sight of it. Less than fifteen minutes remained.

My God... We're running out of time...

In a matter of seconds all were sprinting up the tunnel. Sir David and the remaining knight were carrying Isaac, with the bulky monk following close behind. He was last to arrive at a towering chamber located directly in the centre of the pyramid. Like everything else, its walls were organically shaped and glowing blue, its soaring ceiling held aloft by arching columns fashioned to resemble trees.

On a swelling mound in the centre of the chamber sat a dais. Three sculpted thrones were set upon it, each carved from stone and made to look as though they were comprised of tangled boughs.

At the foot of the thrones were two stone sarcophagi of simple design. A waist-high obelisk rose between them, emerging from a circular slab of black stone that measured a metre in diameter.

Brother Bernardo approached, pointing to the thrones as he struggled to keep his balance. The ground was shifting violently now, and a deep groaning sound came from it, ever-increasing in volume.

"The King must sit to the right of the Consilio!" he cried. "The Queen to his left!"

"We're not the King and Queen!" cried Gabriel over the tumult. "We're the Two!"

"They are one in the same, my liege!" hollered the monk. "Your souls are those of the ancient King and Queen, the builders of the Great Labyrinth!"

The tremors in the earth were becoming deafening now, and the sound of cracking stone and volcanic explosions filled the air.

"Only the two of you can help humanity survive this crossing! Only the two of you can open the way of Illac Domus, so that all may follow you into the higher spheres!"

Gabriel glanced over at Natasha.

"Ready?"

Natasha gave a decisive nod and Gabriel shot a glance at the knights. They acted immediately, carrying Isaac up the steps to the dais and placing him on the central throne. Brother Bernardo approached, bending next to him.

"Isaac," he said softly. "Wake up, dear friend. You must focus all your thoughts on the Cube."

Isaac opened his eyes and smiled weakly.

"I am ready," he whispered.

He was shuddering violently now, and his face was ghastly pale.

Gabriel looked at Natasha and then sat down in his throne.

"Let's do this."

Natasha followed suit, holding the Cube aloft as she did so. Nothing was happening. All eyes fell on Brother Bernardo. He was still kneeling beside Isaac. He looked up to face them, his brow knotted with grief and fear.

"The virus has taken him!" he cried. "The Consilio is dead!"

Gabriel rushed over and put two fingers on Isaac's neck, looking for a pulse.

"Amir!" he called back. "How much time have we got?"

"Eleven minutes, boss!"

"He's just unconscious!" cried Gabriel, his eyes alight with hope. "We've got to wake him up!"

Gabriel's eyes scanned Isaac's face in desperation. Natasha brought her hands to her head.

"What's happening?"

The room around her was warping and distorting in a manner that she could not understand. Peralta's raspy voice sounded suddenly over their radios. It was barely audible over the tumult.

"I'm totally feeling the gravitational effects on my brain!"

"Is that what this is?" cried Natasha.

"It's going to get way worse!" said Peralta. "It's not your sanity! It's just the Rift!"

Gabriel was battling with the effects as well. A desperation was taking him. He simply had to revive Isaac. There was no other option.

Acting on an impulse, he pulled him from the throne and laid him down on the shifting ground. The noise in the chamber was deafening.

"Breathe!" he cried, pumping his chest rhythmically.

When no response came, he increased his efforts and shot a glance over at Amir. The fate of the world was at stake, and they were almost out of time.

"Breathe, you stupid son of a bitch!"

"Gabriel!" screamed Natasha. "Gabriel!"

Gabriel stopped what he was doing and looked up at her, his eyes vacant. He could see her, but she seemed so distorted, so out of context. It was only then that he began to recall his experiences ingesting peyote cactus.

He had been assisting Amir with a university project on the Yaqui Indians of North-Western Mexico. They had experimented with the plants and herbs used in their shamanistic rituals. The symptoms he was experiencing now were almost identical, and the knowledge of the fact made everything change. He looked up at Natasha, a strange lucidity encompassing him.

"I'm sorry," he said, his anxiety slipping away. "I lost it there for a second..."

He rose unsteadily to his feet and took her hands into his. The ground was shaking violently.

"We're in big trouble, baby," he said. "The clock's running out."

The bishop's voice sounded suddenly over their radios. Peralta had patched him through from Gibraltar.

"All hope is not lost, my children!" he cried, and his voice showed signs that he too was experiencing the same mental distortions. "Remember that only truth and love will serve you now!"

"Gabriel," said Natasha, glancing down at Isaac. "The Cube can bring him back."

Gabriel looked deeply into her eyes.

"Of course it can," he said, nodding slowly. "We've still got nine minutes. We've still got a chance."

Natasha held out the Cube only to see it warping and shifting before her.

"We'll heal him just like we healed Amir."

The explosive rattle of Bahadur's assault rifle called everyone to attention. A mob of undead had just arrived at the chamber's entrance.

In a matter of seconds one had already fallen, its head turned to pulp by the last of Bahadur's bullets. Three more crumpled to the ground as Sir David and the other knight lopped off their heads. Even still the situation was deteriorating rapidly.

Unlike the narrow stairway they had earlier defended, the wide opening into the tunnel allowed for dozens of undead to attack simultaneously. The knights could do nothing to prevent them from entering into their midst.

"Dear God!" gasped Brother Bernardo.

A crippling force of the purest evil had entered into the hall now. Combined with the mind-altering effects of the Dark Rift, the demonic presence was paralyzing.

Strangled and discordant screeches were filling the space, and Brother Bernardo moved his hands to his ears instinctively, his eyes gaping in terror when he saw the younger knight fall. The chamber was teaming with undead now. It was only a matter of seconds before they arrived at the dais. After that, death would come quickly.

Only Gabriel and Natasha were unaffected by the attack. The chamber was shifting and lurching around them, but their minds were focused on something else; something not of this earth.

The demons had come to accost them with their age-old weapons of doubt and fear. They had filled the chamber with a coursing evil designed to distract them from their purpose, but Gabriel and Natasha were fully aware of their tactics. They negated the illusory darkness with ease, and in that instant the Cube exploded with blinding light. It was so intense that everyone in the chamber was forced to shield their eyes, and the undead recoiled from it in excruciating pain.

Outside the earth fell into its final cataclysmic seizures; its crust cracking, its mountains tumbling, and its oceans exploding. All around the planet those who were not perishing in horrific natural disasters were one by one falling into a void of dark insanity.

A paralyzing fear and confusion was taking root in the very soul of humanity, and like a spreading virus, it infested every living person, driving any hope of salvation from their twisting and contorting minds.

CHAPTER 18

Christian made his way down the glowing passage, consumed by his desire to end this insurrection, and secure his reign as emperor once and for all. A frantic mob of undead was flowing past him, rushing to replace those who had been felled by the knights.

Before their heads had been hewn from their bodies, Christian had seen his brother through their eyes. He had been unconscious at the time, with a gaping wound on his neck.

Christian scanned the twisted reptilian faces that surrounded him. He would have no shortage of help to destroy his enemies, but if his brother was still alive when he got to him, he would slaughter him with his own hands.

The ground lurched underfoot as he moved forward. He could sense the mind-warping effects of the Dark Rift but compared to the ordeals he had suffered at the hands of the Zurvanites, the mental distortions were inconsequential. Instead, he channeled his murderous rage to remain focused, ensuring he never lost sight of his objective.

"Kill your brother!" hissed the Zurvanites. *"Kill him! Kill him!"*

It took Christian longer than expected to arrive at the central chamber, and frustration was consuming him as he approached it at last. Near the halfway point the undead had begun to fall to the ground, shrieking in agony for some unknown reason. He had been forced to clamber over their ranks to complete the route.

Now, with the mind-contorting effects of the rift subsided, his purpose rang as clear as his wrath. He would kill his brother. He would bathe in his blood.

Christian scrambled over the last of the cowering undead to stagger out onto the hall's expansive threshold. What he saw before him made the Zurvanites in his mind explode with fury.

The Two were already sitting on their thrones, and his brother was occupying a smaller throne between them, his eyes open and impossibly alert. The sight of him well again transformed Christian's rage into turmoil and confusion. The wound on his brother's neck had completely vanished.

To make matters worse, in Natasha's upraised hand he could see the Compostela Cube, but its light was now white and blindingly intense. It was this that his army of undead were cowering from. By the intensity of their torment, he knew that the demons infesting them could not bear the Cube's emissions. Their wailing was ear-splitting.

Christian looked down at the beasts that trembled at his feet and pointed to the dais.

"Kill them!" he bellowed, but his voice was inaudible over their shrieks.

He looked up in time to see the Cube's energy suddenly double in intensity. It became so bright that he was forced to shield his eyes. Through his fingers he could see the lids of the two sarcophagi slowly opening, and at that moment a radiant sphere of blazing light exploded from within the stone arches above. What followed left Christian swaying dizzily on his feet, his jaw slack with disbelief.

A glowing procession of what could only be described as angelic warriors was swooping down towards him. They were comprised of translucent light and possessed of mighty wings and fiery swords. They were a thousand strong at least, and in the blink of an eye their multitudes were rushing past him like a coursing river, disappearing into the glowing tunnel that led to the lands outside.

Their effect on the demons was instantaneous. Not just in the great hall, but across the surrounding mountains and valleys as well. These angels constituted the most potent army ever assembled, and they attacked the undead everywhere they stood, their blazing white broadswords slicing through dozens of them at a time, leaving the corpses untouched but vanquishing the dark entities that resided within them.

Everywhere demons were exploding from their hosts like swarms of black hornets from their nests. An even louder wailing ensued just then, and these cries only subsided when all the unholy entities had plunged into the ground to disappear forever.

"Behold the glory of the higher spheres!" cried an elated Brother Bernardo, rising to his feet. "The angels of heaven have come to our rescue! The Cube of Compostela has been restored!"

It was at that moment that Christian locked eyes with Isaac. His brother was sitting on the central throne, his face alight with love and compassion directed solely at him.

"My little brother," said Isaac softly, and impossibly, Christian could hear his words. "My dear sweet brother. What have they done to you?"

Christian ground his teeth until they cracked, his features twisting into a mask of hatred and violence. It was because of Isaac that all this had come to pass. Every torment and degradation he had been made to endure throughout his life, had now been for nothing. His brother's love felt like a dagger in his back.

It was only then that the dark self in Christian reacted, and its wrath was unimaginably potent. It brought with it that final burst of vigour that comes to every entity on the threshold of death, and it served to detonate a conflagration of such hatred in Christian, that his sense of identity was stripped away. All that remained was pure destruction, and the desire to bring to oblivion anyone or anything he could drag down with him.

In the Cube's white light, the recently exorcized undead could now be seen stirring from their stunned positions. They were everywhere in the chamber, but they were moving slowly now, as they had done before they had become possessed.

Thankful of the reprieve, an exhausted Sir David had lowered his sword to catch his breath. Bahadur and Amir had done the same with their weapons. Christian saw this and blinked in disbelief as he scanned his surroundings.

Nothing lay between him and his brother except Natasha and the upraised Cube. Everyone in the chamber was staring at the artifact in amazement, and no one but his brother had seen him enter the hall.

Christian could feel his heart pounding in his chest. Out of nowhere a newfound hope had been given to him. It was still not too late. He would tear the life from Natasha and his brother and stop the Apocatastasis from ever happening. The Cube might have been reawakened, but victory was still within reach.

It was in the wake of this realization that an unexpected change began to take place in Christian. Black acid vitriol was pounding through his veins now. His slitted pupils had begun to dilate, and his scalp was tightening as the skin on the back of his neck began to thicken. He could feel the intoxicating power of Ahreimanius swelling in him like a cancer, and the metamorphosis it brought was almost orgasmic. The bones in his body creaked and snapped as they altered in size and shape, his joints popping as his muscles became imbued with outlandish strength.

Isaac's eyes were still locked with Christian's as the transformation took place, and his rapturous expression soon gave way to one of horror. What he saw across the chamber was no longer a man, but rather a venomous reptile, jerking in and out of existence like a phantom or wraith.

Gripped by shock, Isaac could only manage to point a finger and sound a muted cry as he saw the beast leap towards him. Natasha noticed his gesture and shot a glance over in time to see the creature advancing, her eyes going wide with fear.

With unimaginable strength and agility Christian was rapidly closing the gap between them. His hands and feet had grown talons, and he was clawing over the awakening dead like a lizard over loose rubble.

Sir David spotted him coming as well but could do nothing. Christian was moving too quickly, and his bloodied sword came up a fraction of a second too late. As it was, the knight had been the only line of defence between Natasha and Christian. The others could only look on in stunned disbelief. It would only be a matter of seconds before the beast reached her. Soon everything would be lost.

Christian's dark self watched as the space between him and his first victim closed. He could already feel his clawed fingers tearing her eyes from her face. He could already taste her blood. He would extinguish her pathetic life, and then he would take his brother's as well. He would eat their flesh. He would drink their blood. He would crush the Cube underfoot and cast the angels of God to hell.

For Natasha, everything had slowed into a lucid frame by frame succession. She watched dumbly as Gabriel leapt over Isaac but knew he would never get to her in time. His cry hung heavy in the air around her, and there was a desperation in it that confirmed what she already knew.

The beast that barrelled towards her carried with it too much speed and momentum. When it reached her it would be unstoppable. There was nobody close enough to save her. Natasha swallowed hard. The hour of her death had come.

How can this be? How could we fail now?

It was only when Christian was on the verge of bounding up the final steps to the dais and taking into his hands that which he had sought to destroy for so long, that he felt something snag his foot. His momentum allowed him to jerk free of it, but when his other leg became entangled, he felt himself being pulled to a stop.

In fury he looked down to see a slow-moving corpse grasping his ankle. Pain shot up his other leg a moment later, and he jerked around to see the bloodied teeth of an adolescent boy sinking into his thigh.

Christian bellowed in rage. All his will was bent on conjuring the wrath of his dark self again, but this time it did not respond. Ahreimanius had abandoned him, leaving him weaker and more vulnerable than ever before. It was only then that Christian lost his balance.

All watched as he toppled backwards into the hungry mob. Natasha's fate had seemed sealed, and now her assailant lay at their feet, prey to the beasts he had once commanded. Christian's reptilian state was collapsing rapidly as well, and in the space of a few seconds he had reverted to his pale self again.

A pressure of unspeakable magnitude was weighing down on him now, and he brought both his hands to his head in an effort to stave it off. Not only were the Zurvanites and the Fourteen Emissaries accosting him, but the Dark Lord Ahreimanius as well.

"You will pay dearly for this failure!"

Christian writhed in agony. His ears were bleeding from the mounting pressure, and his leg was exploding with pain as it was masticated and consumed. He looked around in horror. More and more of the undead were converging on him now, their distended jaws snapping hungrily, and their arms outstretched and grasping.

In one desperate attempt he kicked frantically at the corpse that was feeding on him. It recoiled from his repeated blows and chewed ravenously on the piece of flesh it had managed to tear free. A moment later Christian was back on his feet, limping towards the mouth of the tunnel. He was bleeding badly, and desperately fighting off the groping hands that sought to pull him down.

"I am your master!" he bellowed in desperation. "You will do as I bid! GET THEE DOWN!"

Christian was surrounded on all sides now. He scanned the hideous faces. These were no longer his reptilian servants. They had reverted back into mindless human cadavers again, and they were following the single, primordial instruction that had been programmed into the virus that infected them: A genetically imbued compulsion to feed.

He screamed in fury when a hungry mouth found his kidney. Everyone in the chamber was looking at him now, and his broken pride pained him more than all his wounds combined. He could see Natasha safe in Gabriel's arms, and his hatred of them felt as though it would consume him. He could see the gossamer angels, and his brother looking at him from the central throne above. He could feel their pity. He could sense their love. His humiliation burned like a white-hot furnace.

Christian screamed in rage and just then felt another jolt of pain. He jerked his head around to see the twisted visage of an old woman clamping her teeth into his shoulder.

More undead were latching onto him with every passing second now. One of them had succeeded in tearing the fingers from his hand, but Christian's attention was bent on something even more horrifying. In amongst the throngs, he could see the ghost of Dr. Bennington, its eyes glowing red.

"This was your doing, Christian," it hissed. *"You have no one to blame but yourself…"*

Christian felt his knees buckling under him. The doctor's eyes had suddenly burst into flames. His voice was like a surgical probe, stabbing into his brain without mercy.

"Now you will know the torment of the dungeons of Hades…"

Christian recoiled and crumpled to the ground. The grim irony of the situation was penetrating into him like a fast-moving poison. His organization had developed this virus. He himself had loosed it upon the world. The weapon designed to imprison humanity would instead imprison him. The horde closed in. He could see nothing but distended jaws and bloodied teeth now.

"In the name of Lucifer!" he screeched. "I order you to release me!"

But the teeming undead pressed down upon him nonetheless, feeding upon the flesh of what would have otherwise been their lord and master in another, darker world.

CHAPTER 19

Isaac looked at Gabriel and Natasha in turn, his eyes wide with wonder. The fourteen angel-warriors who had remained in the hall were gathering around them now, their gossamer forms indescribably beautiful and comprised solely of translucent light. Their presence had also purified the air, restoring the great hall to its former glory.

"Dear Father in heaven," whispered Isaac fervently. "How wonderful…"

The noble angels were radiating so great a peace that even the lurching earth had been temporarily stilled. Only a tranquil serenity remained. It was felt by everyone in the chamber, including Sir David and Bahadur, who were still engaged in the slaying of the slow-moving dead.

They had already decapitated the group of corpses that had taken Christian's life, and left their cadavers piled over his remains in a kind of macabre burial mound.

"It is the Two who have called this peace upon us," announced Brother Bernardo, looking at Gabriel and Natasha in turn. "In saving the life of the Consilio, they have not only opened their way into the Labyrinth but completed the primary part of their mission."

Natasha was the first to register his words.

"To bring peace to the hearts of those who will make the crossing…" she said, remembering what Suora had told her. "Only through an act of love could it have been accomplished..."

She looked down at the Cube in her lap, recalling the power that she and Gabriel had conjured in order that Isaac might be healed. By leveraging the gravitational energy of the galactic plane, the Cube had propagated their harmonious alpha-wave pattern to the entire collective consciousness, in effect, reaching and penetrating every sentient mind on the planet.

The results had been dramatic to say the least, awakening a peaceful, psychotropic bliss in the world's population. Across the planet, all traces of anxiety had given way to a state of pure rapture. In every region, every man, woman, and child had seen their terror transform instantly to serenity; every plant, animal, fish, and insect becoming peaceful and silent as the planet itself grew calm.

This reprieve had stretched on for a timeless moment, and when the earth finally did begin its quaking again, the peace and serenity of its inhabitants remained intact. Amir approached the dais with a profound calmness in his eyes. He was holding the timer out for everyone to see.

"Our alignment with the wormhole's getting close."

"Five minutes," said Natasha, her eyes focusing on the clock.

Brother Bernardo was first to awaken to the reality of the situation. The grinding sounds of shifting tectonic plates were once again filling the hall, and they were growing louder with every passing second. He had to holler in order to be heard.

"The Two must descend!" he cried. "They must find the entrance to the Labyrinth!"

"I thought *this* was the entrance!" cried Gabriel.

"The Labyrinth lies in the lowest sphere of Hades!" bellowed the monk.

Gabriel and Natasha exchanged a concerned glance and then looked back at Brother Bernardo.

"You will become separated!" he continued. "Only to be reunited at its entrance! You must open the Seals of Gnosis and enter into the Ostium Sanctus! All this must be done before the portal moves out of the Dark Rift!"

"And how long will that be?" cried Gabriel.

Brother Bernardo furrowed his brow.

"I do not know!"

"Well I do!" came the voice of Peralta from their radios. "If the vertical velocity of the solar system remains constant, it'll take precisely seventy-two hours to pass through the galactic plane! But that's of little use for the two of you! Time has no meaning where you're going!"

The chamber shook so violently that it seemed on the verge of collapse. The angels began to rise and exit the hall. The tumult was deafening.

"Hey!" cried Scotty, looking up as their translucent forms vanished into the ceiling. "Where are they going? Even they don't want to be in here!"

Brother Bernardo was also watching them depart.

"The Emissaries of the Kristos are ascending! Sarras will soon be destroyed! Every living person on Earth will be made to lose consciousness! Only when the first seal has been opened will the Cube reawaken the world!"

Amir was the first to do the math.

"Are you saying we're going to be unconscious for three days?"

Gabriel locked eyes with Natasha.

"Peralta!" he bellowed. "You guys have to leave right now!"

"I'm programming the navigation system to take us home!" hollered Peralta from the sub's helm.

He was tapping away at his keyboard furiously.

"Whoever's coming had better hurry up! Even that blue goo can't hold up the weight of a collapsing mountain, and that wormhole is right on top of us!"

Gabriel looked for Bahadur and found him standing with Scotty and Sir David. They were near the entrance of the chamber. All of the undead had either wandered off or been hewn down.

"Bahadur!" he bellowed. "Get everyone back to the sub!"

Bahadur turned to face him, with Scotty Roberts following suit. Amir was the first to voice what each of them was thinking.

"But what about you guys?" he asked. "How the hell are you going to get out of here?"

"We will be leaving this sphere," said Brother Bernardo, looking over at Isaac.

The latter was ruffling the fur atop Shackleton's head.

"You mean you're all going to die!" screamed Amir. "Boss! We're in a pyramid for Christ's sake. This is a tomb! There's no labyrinth in sight! Just two coffins with your names on them!"

"Amir's right!" said Peralta over the radio. "There's no labyrinth here! It's a dead end! You've got to come with us! The world will make the transition in peace now! Your job's done! There'll be another way to release the gnosis!"

"No, Mr. Peralta!" cried Natasha, looking with resolve at Gabriel. "You're wrong! There *is* a labyrinth, and we know the way into it!"

Gabriel nodded in agreement.

"We've got to do this!" he cried. "We're just going to be going somewhere else, that's all! We'll be fine!"

A deafening crash sounded suddenly from above, only to be followed by massive shards of falling stone. Amir looked down at the clock. Only a few minutes remained until the rift was entered into. When this happened, the poles of the planet would shift, and the real destruction would begin. Even with the sub's autopilot engaged, there no guarantee they would survive the trip home.

"All right, boss!" hollered Amir reluctantly, pushing back his dreadlocks. "You've managed to slip out of every mess you've ever been in! I can't see why this one should be any different!"

Gabriel gave Amir a confident wink and then looked over to Bahadur.

"You've got three minutes!" he bellowed.

In a split-second Bahadur had burst into action, gathering the company together and herding them into the shifting tunnel outside. Only Brother Bernardo refused to leave.

"My place is with the Consilio, and with the Two!"

Isaac put his arm around the fat monk and smiled.

"We go to inner sanctum!" he cried, and then giving Shackleton a slap in the rump he bellowed:

"Go home, you silly dog!"

Shackleton darted to Natasha's side.

"You heard what Isaac said!" she hollered, pushing him away. "Go with Amir!"

Gabriel watched as a reluctant Shackleton joined the others.

"Now all of you get the hell out of here!" he cried over the tumult. "Now!"

In a matter of seconds all had evacuated the chamber, leaving the four of them standing in the midst of the towering hall. The tree-like columns were swaying above them as though they were being blown by some invisible wind.

"The Cube must be placed upon the gate!" cried the monk, pointing to the top of the waist-high obelisk that was positioned between the two sarcophagi.

Gabriel and Natasha hurriedly approached, inserting the Cube into a square-shaped slot at its top. The column sank quickly into the slab of black stone at its base, leaving only the top surface of the glowing Cube visible at its centre.

"This gate will mark the entrance to the Labyrinth in the lower spheres," cried the monk, pointing to the black slab. "The Consilio must now stand upon it!"

Brother Bernardo bowed to Gabriel and Natasha and gestured towards their sarcophagi, inviting them to enter.

"*To transcend the Cube is to see it in all things!*" he cried.

Gabriel took Natasha's hands in his. The chamber was literally collapsing around them.

"Ready?" he asked, trying to be heard over the clamour.

Natasha smiled bravely and nodded, giving him a quick kiss on the lips.

"Scared?"

"Very!" cried Natasha. "But nobody ever gets off the rollercoaster when it's about to go over the top!"

* * * * * *

Natasha was lying on her back in the sarcophagus. The clamour in the hall was deafening. To her right she could see Isaac standing fearlessly on the stone slab, the top surface of the Cube still glowing white at its centre. Brother Bernardo was standing at his side.

Natasha swallowed hard. The lid to her coffin was closing slowly on its hinges above her. She kept her eyes fixed on Isaac. He was standing erect in his tattered suit, his arms hanging loosely at his sides as he swayed with the lurching chamber. Around them, more and more debris was falling, and Natasha thought it remarkable that no one had been struck.

"Only by finding himself shall the King lose himself!" bellowed Brother Bernardo over the din. "And only by losing herself shall the Queen find herself! This is the way of the universe! For Truth is Love! And Love is Truth! And they are both the same!"

Natasha screamed in horror. A massive section of stone had come down on both him and Isaac as his words ended, obliterating them instantly. A split second later the lid to her sarcophagus began to seal itself shut. It closed with a stony thump and Natasha's cry was swallowed by the darkness.

All became still and icily cold, and Natasha began to shiver uncontrollably. Something was very wrong. A complex, stereoscopic pulsing sound was filling her ears now, and from within the tight confines of that lightless sarcophagus, the same demonic force that had accosted her and Gabriel not fifteen minutes before, was once again attempting to gain entry into her. Like a poisonous fog it twisted and pitched around her, and it was all she could do to keep it at bay.

A moment later she was falling, as though from a great height, and with her descent there came upon her a terrible and pressing weight. It was as though a great ocean of liquid density had enveloped her. It threatened to crush her, and it filled her head and body with excruciating pain.

In that moment Gabriel and Natasha were swallowed body and soul; sucked into the lightless void of the lower spheres as the planet slipped at last into the time-warping gravitational field of the galaxy's equatorial plane.

CHAPTER 20

When Natasha regained consciousness, she was enveloped in a pale fog. She was no longer in her sarcophagus but rather walking alone at night. A frigid gust broke the mist into tattered patches around her. Through bare and tangled boughs, she could see a waxing moon above. It cast a cold pallor on everything.

"My God…" she whispered, shivering with cold. "Where am I? Where's Gabriel?"

Around her lay groupings of crooked and ancient tombstones. She was standing in a neglected graveyard, its terrain disappearing into the gloom. She scanned the shadows, her eyes probing the crumbling graves.

The hissing whispers that had plagued her throughout her descent still echoed in her head. If what Brother Bernardo had said was true, she was now in the lowest sphere of hell. A cold shiver ran up her neck and along her scalp. There were shadowy, robed figures walking among the tombs. She could sense their evil.

They can't get into you if you fight them.

It was Gabriel's voice in her mind and Natasha found strength in it as she picked through the gravestones. Just then an iron gate emerged from the fog, with a gravedigger's cottage appearing behind it a moment later. It was a blackened dwelling, surrounded by thick briar, all dry and brittle and twisting. A path of greasy flagstones carved its way through to its door. Next to it was a tiny window glowing orange and warm.

Natasha looked up to see that the moon was no longer visible, and in the growing darkness the cozy window became impossible to ignore. It was not long before she found herself beside it, her hand reaching out to sound the knocker. The door began to open.

"My child," said the old woman before her.

"Suora?" whispered Natasha. "Is it really you?"

The old nun turned to open the way for Natasha to enter. The cottage had a low ceiling and a crude wooden floor, with two of its walls comprised entirely of packed earth. It was furnished with nothing but a single chair.

"Sit down, my child."

Natasha did as she was instructed. Outside a storm was approaching, and in a sudden flash of lightning she saw Suora's face change and distort unexpectedly. Her features were reptilian.

Natasha's eyes went wide with fear. Seven lightless figures were suddenly emerging from the earthen walls, their twisted bodies repugnant, and comprised of densely packed cinder. The whispering in her head was growing louder. These were the demons who had possessed her as an infant. She was sure of it. Seven of the Fourteen Emissaries of Lucifer. Of all the demonic entities in existence, they were the most powerful.

Natasha tried to move but found her body paralyzed with fear. The demons were gathering around her now, and each was pressing itself into her. She battled to keep them out, only to find that she was lying in a sumptuous bed now, in a dark and frigid room. Bending over her were Father Franco and Bishop Marcus. They were chanting in an ancient tongue, but their faces were twisted and evil, and their eyes glowed red.

Natasha jerked her head around to see an open window beside her. Its diaphanous curtains were billowing in the night wind. Outside, amidst twisted boughs and tombstones, a pyramid-shaped mausoleum was coming into view. It seemed to Natasha that blue light was emitting from the cracks around its door.

"The Labyrinth..." she thought frantically, her wide eyes darting from demon to demon as they pressed into her. "I'm forgetting why I'm here..."

Natasha knew she had to escape at once, but her fear was still too great. Try as she might she could not make her body move. It was like being in a nightmare.

The emissaries were sending their tentacles into her now, attempting to gain entry to her soul. It was taking everything she had to keep them out.

"You belong to Ahreimanius," hissed the demon who had taken the shape of Father Franco. *"Who do you think you are, coming into our realm as you have done? What did you expect would happen? You are Lucifer's now."*

It was only then that Brother Bernardo's final words came to her mind.

Only by losing herself shall the Queen find herself.

Natasha closed her eyes and focused her thoughts. The solution to her dilemma lay in those words. She was sure of it.

Losing and finding...

With a flash of insight, the answer came to her.

Negative and Positive. Feminine and Masculine.

Ancient wisdom postulated that the human psyche was comprised of two halves: Two divine modes of being. The divine female was inward moving. Receptive, passive, negative. The divine masculine was outward moving. Creative, assertive, positive.

Her salvation lay in her ability to contact that part of her which was masculine. It was there where she would find the strength she needed to oust the demons. This was what Brother Bernardo had meant by the Queen finding herself.

Natasha struggled to think clearly. To lose herself was to do something inherently feminine. The riddle was suggesting that only by doing something feminine, could she gain access to the masculine part of her.

I need to let go... I need to let go now!

With all the will she could muster, Natasha did precisely what her instincts screamed she should never do. She let go of all her defences and became vulnerable to the demonic tentacles. She opened the doors of her soul to them.

No sooner had she done this than there appeared behind her a great void, and taking a leap of faith, Natasha let herself fall back into it, finding to her great relief that she did not fall at all, but rather floated safely above it, completely unharmed.

A great strength was pouring into Natasha now. It was masculine, assertive, and extremely proactive. When she opened her eyes, she could see that the demons had already withdrawn.

CHAPTER 21

Gabriel made his way through dark labyrinthine tunnels, their tangled paths plunging him deeper and deeper into the bowels of the earth. He was already being forced to walk in a stooped position, and the ceiling was becoming progressively lower as he advanced.

It seemed to him that he had been lost for hours, although it was difficult to be sure. Just as Peralta had predicted, time seemed to be distorted here, and his malfunctioning wristwatch only served to confirm this. To make matters worse, the batteries in his flashlight were beginning to show signs of expiring. His situation did not look good.

Gabriel stopped to make another addition to a rough map he had been drafting. By pacing off the distances and keeping note of all the turns and divergences, he hoped to at least not have to revisit the places he had already been.

He wiped the sweat from his brow. The winding passages had stripped him of all his confidence. He felt hopelessly lost and on the verge of panic. The earthen walls were closing in.

I'll never get out of here…

Gabriel scanned his surroundings. The beam of his flashlight had just fallen on yet another demon lurking in the shadows. He had counted seven of them so far, and although he tried his best to ignore them, he knew they would not be going away. They were poisoning his thoughts. It was only a matter of time before they began their attempts to possess him.

Gabriel pushed a hand through his messy hair and struggled to clear his mind. Natasha was surely in need of him, and he was of no use to her lost in this maze. He remembered how Brother Bernardo had warned them that they would become separated, only to meet again at the entrance to the Labyrinth. What if she were there already? What if she were in danger?

Gabriel plodded onward as quickly as he could, counting each pace and adding the data to his map. The ceiling height had been dropping consistently for the last while, and it was not long before he found himself navigating the passages on his hands and knees. A short while later he found himself gripped by a frantic desperation. Ashy black forms were emerging from the earth all around him now, whispering in cold, nefarious voices.

"We are the Emissaries of Lucifer."

Gabriel could feel himself starting to panic. He knew that these were the same demons that had possessed him as an infant, and this only made matters worse.

He battled forward in vain. He could see that not only was the way before him constricting, but the way behind him as well. It was only then that his flashlight failed, and an inky blackness enveloped him. The demons began their assault. He fought them with all his strength.

Get away from me you sons of bitches!

The air was becoming thick and difficult to breath now, as though he were running out of oxygen. Gabriel rolled onto his back and reached into his pocket, producing a half-used book of matches. He gasped aloud as he struck one to life. The earth had entirely closed in around him. He was in a grave, buried alive with seven twisting demons. He could feel them clawing at him. Their filthy nails were cutting into his skin.

Gabriel tried desperately to pull himself together. Something in him was insisting that this was not really happening. It was a dream. It had to be.

Only by finding himself shall the King lose himself.

They were Brother Bernardo's words, and Gabriel understood them at once. Finding himself meant making contact with his inner core. He pushed aside his fear and centred himself, feeling the tormenting demons recede almost instantly. Even still, he suspected that the full resolution of his dilemma lay in the second half of the riddle.

Why would the King need to lose himself?

Gabriel lit another match and forced his body to relax.

This isn't just about the King and the Queen. It's about the masculine and the feminine...

He looked down at the match. Its flame was brighter. There was more oxygen in the air.

Losing yourself. What could that mean?

A sudden thought came to his mind, and he spoke it aloud.

"Losing yourself is just another way of describing the act of letting go, of letting yourself be vulnerable."

Gabriel's voice was muffled by the proximity of the earth, but the sound of it was also sobering. It helped him to concentrate.

"Letting go is a psychological prototype of femininity," he said. "Discipline is a prototype of masculinity. Both of them exist within the human psyche."

The concept had been introduced to Gabriel in the Cube diary. His father had transcribed an ancient text into the journal. In his side notes he had written about masculine and feminine powers. True mastery over oneself, he had explained, could never be obtained unless the two forces were in perfect balance.

With sudden clarity, Gabriel recalled every word of the ancient text.

When the initiates fear their sexuality, the men let go when they should be exercising discipline, and the women exercise discipline when they should be letting go. Only by finding himself shall the King lose himself. And only by losing herself shall the Queen find herself. This is the way of the universe.

Gabriel struggled with the words. He could still not fully understand. If he were the King, why would he want to let go of himself in this of all places? Surely remaining in disciplined control here would be the best thing to do. Now more than ever, he had to be in contact with his masculine core; his inner King.

Gabriel noticed that the spaces around him were slowly increasing in size, as though the earth itself were pulling away. He lit another match and looked down at his feet. The tunnel was opening there as well.

It was not long before he could sit up, and just then he remembered the spare batteries in his pack. In his panic, he had completely forgotten about them.

Gabriel rose to his feet. The passages of the catacombs could now be seen branching off in all directions. He had followed the monk's advice and found himself. Because of this he had pulled himself out of danger, but now what? He was back where he had started.

Why would the King want to lose himself?

He produced his map and was about to resume his work when a complete understanding came flooding into him.

Up to this point, he had been relying on his masculine faculties to find a way out of the maze. He had kept a disciplined record of all his movements, but this was the last thing he should have done. The monk's words made this explicitly clear.

"What an idiot I've been!" he said, stuffing the map into his pocket. "My God, I hope it's not too late."

A second later Gabriel was speeding through the tunnels, listening into himself for directions at every branch he came to. Natasha had led them out of the catacombs in Rome by following her intuition, and intuition could only be accessed by letting go of the need to be in control. It was a feminine thing, and it was precisely what Gabriel would need to do if he ever wanted to find Natasha again.

He needed to contact his feminine core, but in order to do this, he first needed to be in complete control of himself, and this could only happen by contacting his masculine core first.

Only by finding himself, shall the King lose himself.

Gabriel sped through the tangled passages at full speed, putting all his faith in his gut. He could distinctly feel directions being called out to him as he ran.

Right, straight, right, left, straight.

The passages were becoming broader now, and in a few moments he came to single wooden door. He threw open the latch only to find himself in what looked to be a pyramid-shaped burial chamber. Everything was glowing in the familiar iridescent blue.

He sprinted across the room, passing a central tomb to arrive at a broad door in the opposite wall. He opened it to find Natasha standing directly before him. She looked radiantly beautiful.

"Natasha," he said, catching her as she fell into his arms. "How long have you been waiting here?"

She was beaming with joy.

"About ten seconds," she said, covering his face with kisses. "What took you so long?"

CHAPTER 22

Somewhere under the ocean.

Bahadur was the first to stir. He opened his eyes to find they were all well, and safely strapped into their makeshift harnesses. It had been a precaution that Peralta had insisted on, and Bahadur saw what a good idea it had been. Evidence of their tempestuous voyage could be found everywhere, yet apart from the general disarray, the bridge seemed undamaged.

"Bloody hell, mate…" came Scotty's groan.

Bahadur turned to see the smuggler untie himself and rise to his feet. He was rubbing a bump on the side of his head.

"That autopilot ought to have its license revoked."

"At least we're still alive," said a waking Peralta, his voice particularly hoarse. "And that's more than I expected. I wonder how Gabriel and Natasha are faring…"

"Are we receiving any communications from them?" asked Bahadur. "If we are awake, it must mean that the first seal has been opened."

"All our systems are down," said Peralta. "We have no way of knowing if they're trying to contact us."

"I feel like I spent the night drinking bad tequila," groaned Amir, rubbing his temples.

They heard a bark and then Shackleton burst onto the bridge with tail wagging. Sir David followed behind. They had been in the rear cabin during the voyage. Peralta rose from his seat and made his way to the back of the sub.

"Where are you going?" asked Amir.

"To find out why we're only running on emergency power," he said. "I'll be right back."

Not ten minutes passed before Peralta returned. He was muttering to himself, his hand scrubbing absently at his messy white hair.

"What's wrong?" asked Amir, slipping a cinnamon toothpick into his mouth. "Are we out of fuel?"

Peralta looked at him intently.

"The little diesel we have left is all gummed up. I'm polishing it right now, but it's going to take some time."

He returned to his control panel and began bringing the systems back online.

"It's really strange," he rasped. "I'd swear that fuel was ten years old. It's a good thing the emergency generator runs on butane, or we'd be in the dark right now."

Moments later, the bridge was aglow with the light of electronic gadgetry again. Peralta scrutinized one of the monitors before him, shaking his head.

"Amazing," he said. "There isn't a single satellite in the sky, or at least none that are functioning. It's a good thing I programmed the navigation system to use our topographical scans to get us out to sea. If I'd used the compass or GPS we would have probably run aground. As it is I have no idea where we are. It looks like the earth's poles really did shift."

Bahadur looked down at him.

"What exactly does that mean?"

Peralta took hold of the ballast controls.

"It means the earth's equator is in a completely different place than it used to be. If we're going to find out where we are, it's going to have to be the old-fashioned way."

Everyone watched the main monitor as Peralta brought the sub to the surface, their eyes opening with surprise at what they saw. There before them, shining in the sunlight, was the Rock of Gibraltar in all its glory.

"You did it, Captain!" said Scotty, slapping him hard on the back. "You brought us home, mate!"

Peralta shook his head in disbelief. Although he had programmed the navigation system to bring them back, with the tectonic shifting of the ocean floor, the chances of it succeeding had been a hundred to one at best.

"It looks beautiful out there," said Amir. "I thought I'd never see the sun again."

"We must not forget the radiation," warned Bahadur morosely. "The planet is poisoned and will remain so for many decades to come."

The giant smuggler turned to Peralta, only to find that the messy engineer was shaking his head, his white eyebrows gathered in confusion. Behind his thick glasses his eyes were darting between several gauges on the control panel, his fingers tapping away at two different keyboards simultaneously.

"I've triple checked these readings," he muttered. "There's no doubting they're correct..."

He sat back in his chair, scratching his head in confusion.

"What?" said Amir, coming to Peralta's side. "What are you looking at?"

In a moment Amir had himself spotted the strange anomaly on the control panel.

"What is wrong?" asked Bahadur, stepping closer,

Peralta swiveled in his chair.

"There would appear to be no significant levels of radiation outside," he said, shrugging with amazement. "Only trace amounts."

"How can this be possible?" asked Bahadur.

Peralta produced a pad of paper and began making hurried calculations.

"I'd need more time to really figure this out," he said, scribbling, "but the dissipation of radiation would appear to be directly related to the gravitational forces in the galactic plane."

He scribbled a bit more.

"It looks like a form of accelerated quantum tunnelling, just like in the Schrödinger equation... Beta particles, antineutrino's, gamma rays, they're all barely traceable. It's as though the detonation happened more than two hundred years ago."

"Are you suggesting that it's safe to go outside?" asked Amir, dumbfounded.

"Not only safe," said Peralta, moving back to the sub's controls. "Highly advisable. I didn't want to say anything before but we're running dangerously low on oxygen. If it weren't for the fact that we've been comatose for the last three days, we would have all suffocated in here."

"Well then let's get the hell out!" said Amir, smiling suddenly. "I don't know about you guys but I'm dying for some fresh air and sunshine."

He swung open the main hatch and everyone looked up to see a clear blue sky. A warm gust of air flooded the bridge.

"Something is not right," said Sir David as Amir climbed out. "It is still December. The air is much too warm."

Amir called down.

"You guys should really get up here," he said. "You're not going to believe this."

Peralta was last to emerge, poking his messy head out of the hatch in time to see a strange tropical seabird flying past. The others looked down at him, their faces alight with happiness. Surrounding the submarine were waters typical of the South Pacific, the air carrying a fragrant scent foreign to that of the Mediterranean Sea. Behind them the Rock of Gibraltar was covered in lush vegetation.

"My God," whispered Peralta in awe. "Look at all this plant growth. The galactic plane must have spit us out a couple of centuries into the future... I suspected we would be experiencing some distortions in time, but nothing like this..."

He scratched the back of his head.

"What I can't understand is why we haven't aged when everything else has. We should all be skeletons by now."

"It is as the Ascender's Prophecy foretold," said Sir David, a serene smile on his face. "The world has been born anew."

Scotty struck a match to light his cigarillo.

"We'd best fetch Anita then, mates," he said, exhaling a cloud of smoke. "The world ain't the only thing being born. She's probably ready to pop by now."

CHAPTER 23

Deep in Hades.

"There was a tomb in the centre of the mausoleum. It consisted of two sarcophagi. Natasha moved towards them.

"The gateway to the Labyrinth has to be around here," she said. "Brother Bernardo said we'd be reunited at its entrance."

Gabriel followed, noting the circular slab of black stone lying between the stone caskets. It was the same one that Isaac had stood on before they had descended, and at its centre, resting in the slot where they had placed it, was the Compostela Cube, glowing in iridescent blue again.

Gabriel looked over at Natasha to find that her attention was still focused on the sarcophagi.

"They're so beautiful…" she said, dazedly.

The stone caskets were identical to the ones they themselves had lain in, and there was something about them that demanded all their attention. Gabriel shook his head in trepidation.

"Those things are really creeping me out," he said. "Let's get out of here."

No sooner had he said this than their stone lids began to open. They both gasped in horror. Within the coffins were decomposing replicas of their own bodies, with sinister black vapours curling around them.

"What the hell is that?" stammered Gabriel.

He bent to get a closer look, but the toxic gasses had already engulfed the corpses. The mists cleared a moment later to reveal the mummified remains of two reptilian humanoids lying where the corpses had been. Each was arrayed in rich clothing and adorned with strange and beautiful jewelry.

Resting upon the body of the male reptilian was an elaborate shield, its surface adorned with the image of an elegant tree growing from a single seed. At his side was a beautiful lance, its shining blade engraved with the image of intertwining boughs. Gabriel was captivated.

"The Reptilian King and Queen..." he whispered in awe, "According to Brother Bernardo, we're looking at the remains of our own bodies from a previous life..."

He glanced over at Natasha and then back to the sarcophagi.

"Do you realize that these tombs are two hundred and fifty million years old?"

Natasha, who had initially turned away in horror, was now peering into the stone casket as well.

"I don't understand..." she said, her eyes wide with fear. "Why did we just see our own dead bodies in there?"

Gabriel looked at her but said nothing. There was a distinctly sinister presence in the chamber now. He tried to ignore it. He wanted nothing to distract him from the splendor of the archaeological find. The mummified bodies were irresistible to him. He bent closer to examine the spearhead. It was glowing in a ghostly hue of blue.

"Gabriel!" gasped Natasha, grabbing his arm.

He looked up to see that four robed figures had appeared immediately around them. Their forms were grainy and oscillating, and they exuded an air of icy wickedness. They were jerking violently from side to side, their robes grey and shadowy. Unlike the other demons, these figures had bodies similar to men, and they were soon reaching up to pull back their dark hoods.

Their voices were like venom.

"Insolent fools. You will bow to Lucifer at once!"

Gabriel and Natasha gasped when they saw their faces. Similar to the mummified remains, they too were reptilian, but still living, and looking older than anything could possibly be. A moment later Gabriel and Natasha were under attack, but this was like nothing they had ever experienced before. The assault was entirely psychic.

For Gabriel it came as an irrepressible urge to climb into the king's tomb, and he knew that Natasha was being manipulated in the same way. He could see her inching towards the queen's sarcophagus, her face growing more and more pale as the psychic assault continued. He made a concerted effort to speak. It took everything he had.

"Natasha…" he grunted through clenched teeth. "Stay away… from that coffin…"

But even as he said these words, he could see that he himself was climbing into his own sarcophagus. With all the strength he could muster he forced himself to look over at Natasha again. She was already settling herself down onto the mummified body, its brittle bones crackling beneath her.

Gabriel was mortified. Natasha's face was as white as parchment, and around her a black vapor was rising. The oscillating forms of the Zurvanites were so close they were almost touching him now. Gabriel heard himself trying to speak. It was like somebody else was saying the words.

"Let go… of her…"

He knew he had to act now or never. With desperate resolve he summoned all his strength and broke from the spell. In one swift motion he took up the king's lance and plunged it into the nearest Zurvanite. No sooner had he done so than all four ceased to flicker in and out of existence. They had suddenly become solid in form.

"What have you done?" hissed the Zurvanite who had been pierced, its reptilian eyes wide with surprise as it looked down at the spear in its chest. *"This is impossible… We are immortal…"*

The Four fell to the ground as one, and their tortured screeches were deafening. Gabriel watched in amazement as a flurry of insect-like particles exploded from their midst. Their ancient reptilian bodies were disintegrating before his eyes.

He looked at the spear in his hands, noticing only then that its head was glowing in the same blue as the Cube. He rushed to Natasha's side and lifted her out of the coffin.

"It's all right, baby. It's over."

She smiled weakly and Gabriel kissed her gently.

"Are you in pain?"

Natasha shook her head.

"I just feel tired…" she whispered, her eyes closing. "I need to sleep…"

Gabriel laid her down beside the circular slab in the floor. As they neared it, the Cube rose up from its slot and hovered an inch above it, as though it were being supported by a magnetic field.

"We'll use the Cube to make you better," he said.

No sooner had Gabriel taken hold of the artifact than the stone slab beneath it dissolved with a hiss, revealing a spiralling flight of stairs leading down into a chamber of glowing blue.

Gabriel wasted no time. He picked up Natasha and in a matter of seconds was laying her down on the floor of a cube-shaped room below, folding his jacket and placing it under her head. He looked up in time to see both the entrance and the flight of stairs melt into the glowing walls. The chamber had no exits now.

Gabriel took Natasha's hand in his. It was icy cold.

"Hey," he said, patting it gently. "You need to wake up."

He looked down at the Cube. It was beginning to grow dim.

"Ok," he said to her. "I want you to focus your thoughts on me. We're going to light up this Cube and use it to make you better again. Got it?"

Gabriel closed his eyes and concentrated, but no matter how hard he tried, he could not get the Cube to glow any brighter. On the contrary, in the ten minutes he had been trying it had grown even dimmer. Knowing that the Cube needed both of them in order to glow made it easy to see what was happening. He was losing Natasha.

Gabriel shot a worried glance over his shoulder. A circular pool had appeared in the centre of the room and water from it was already beginning to fill the chamber. When he turned back to Natasha, he saw that the liquid was already lapping around her head. There would be nowhere to escape if it continued to rise.

It was not long before Gabriel was treading water and trying to keep Natasha afloat on her back. He had searched desperately for a way out of the chamber but found nothing. He could only watch in horror as the last of the space filled. He took one last breath from the disappearing gap of air at the chamber's ceiling and let himself sink to the floor with Natasha in his arms.

My God, can it be that they really have won?

He looked down at her, his heart surging with grief and love, and the panic of approaching death. How could this have happened? They had come so far and at such great odds...

A deep serenity was coming over Gabriel now. They would at least die here together. He embraced the fact bravely. But just as Gabriel felt his lungs begin to spasm, he saw something that he could not understand. Natasha's chest was rising and falling rhythmically. She was breathing.

This is impossible...

Gabriel summoned all his courage and emptied his lungs, feeling his body inhale by reflex. He felt a burning pain as his lungs filled with water, only to be followed by the immediate relief of oxygen rushing through his system.

Within seconds he had grown accustomed to the strange feeling, and he recalled, as though from a long-forgotten dream, a distant memory of having breathed water before.

We were once reptilian....

Gabriel's eyes fell on the opening where the water had originated and swam towards it with Natasha in tow. He saw that it was in fact the mouth of a cave, one that led straight into the depths below them. Like the chamber, it too was covered in the glowing blue goo.

Gabriel descended into it with Natasha in his arms and soon found himself in an enormous underwater expanse. He looked down at Natasha and saw that she was opening her eyes.

"Gabriel," she said through unmoving lips.

She was smiling warmly now, but her voice seemed to be coming to him telepathically.

"What happened?" she asked. "I was in a dark prison, and then the water came to free me... Was I dreaming?"

Gabriel was smiling from ear to ear. He hugged her tightly.

"You gave me quite a scare, kid," he said without speaking. "From now on, no more sleeping on the job, OK?"

A formless being of translucent light approached them just then.

"Greetings, my dear friends," it said in the most harmonious voice imaginable. "From the House of God, I bring you many divine blessings. Follow me and I will take you to the Oracle. He will be the one to guide you through the seals."

CHAPTER 24

Gibraltar.

Peralta eased the submarine into its secret military port, steering the boat towards its berth on the south side of the cave. Amir opened the main hatch as soon as its hull broke the surface. He jumped onto the dock and secured the sub to its moorings, noticing just then that everything in the cave was covered in a thin layer of dust.

It's been two hundred years since we've been here…

He attached the gangway to the submarine and stood by while Bahadur and Sir David carried Anita out.

"Easy does it," said Peralta coming up behind them. "She might still be asleep, but she's also on the verge of giving birth. The last thing we want is to induce labour."

It was not long before everyone had settled into the familiar surroundings of the secret cave, with Peralta administering immediately to the old bishop and Cassano. They had found them lying unconscious on sofas in the common room, and just as he had done with Anita, Peralta administered intravenous drips, though he was unsure they would help. Anita's blood pressure had continued to drop regardless of the hydration she had received. Something more was at play here, something metaphysical.

Sir David squatted next to her, noticing the concern on Peralta's face.

"Before the apocalypse, I was the village doctor," he said. "No medical treatment will save our friends, Mr. Peralta. It is clear that the Two have not yet opened the first seal. Humanity will remain unconscious until they do."

"What I can't figure out is why *we* woke up," said Peralta. "It must have had something to do with our proximity to the wormhole when we made the crossing..."

Amir poked his head into the room. There was a lit chillum pipe in his hand. Peralta frowned.

"I see you found my stash in the cryogenic freezer."

Amir flashed an impish smile and exhaled a billowing cloud of smoke.

"You'd both had better come out here and take a look at this."

With their patients now cared for, Peralta and Sir David followed Amir into the main area, only to find Scotty and Bahadur waiting there with Shackleton at their side. Peralta sat down at his workstation and examined the monitor that Amir was pointing to.

"A trailer's appeared on the Cube's website," said Amir, exhaling another cloud of smoke.

He bent over and tapped a key to start the video. Bahadur came up next to him.

"It is called *Apocatastasis,*" said the brown giant, frowning down at Peralta. "It appears to be based on a creation myth called *The Fall of the Angels.*"

Peralta glanced up at him and then looked back in time to see a line of blood-red text fade up on the monitor.

TO TRANSCEND THE CUBE
IS TO SEE IT IN ALL THINGS.

Moments later the trailer began, its dramatic computer-generated cinematography setting the stage. It told the story of how the earth had been formed as a means for the fallen angels to return to heaven, and how their lost souls had congregated here to evolve both physically and spiritually.

The migration back to heaven would take hundreds of millions of years to complete.

The video played on. The reptilian race was at war and destroying itself with advanced weapons, all while the solar system plunged into the galactic plane. The ensuing cataclysm was absolute, and the destruction of the earth complete. Everything grew silent and faded to black.

An ancient rain forest appeared. Two hundred and fifty million years had passed now, and out of the primordial mists came the first human beings. They were the highest incarnations of the fallen angels yet; crude and primitive, but capable of greatness. A female human appeared superimposed over the scene. She stood floating in the centre of the screen, rotating slowly. Everything dissolved to white.

"That's where it ends," said Amir, looking over at Peralta. "Any idea why it's there?"

The scrappy engineer rolled his chair up to a keyboard and started to type.

"Go and get yourselves something to eat," he said, engrossed by the discovery. "I'm going to need some time to figure this out."

* * * * * *

Three hours passed before Peralta summoned them back. Several times they had gone to check on him, but they had always found him either bent in concentration or lying back in his chair with his eyes closed and his headphones on. This time he was fully present.

"All right," he rasped, gathering his thoughts. "I know this is going to sound crazy, but it appears that the Cube has created a video game."

"A video game?" asked Scotty, puzzled.

"The Cube's an advanced AI," said Amir. "Anything's possible, but why a game?"

Peralta rose to his feet and began rummaging through cluttered drawers while the others looked at him in bewilderment. He did not stop until he had produced four sets of earbuds and given them each a pair.

"This isn't your conventional video game," he said, inviting them all to sit down. "You don't play it by looking at a monitor. The technology uses binaural frequencies to stimulate the brain. Each ear gets its own set of frequencies, and the interference pattern in your head makes your brain think it's asleep and dreaming. The simulation's very convincing."

"How do you interact with it?" asked Amir.

"Just as you would interact if you were really dreaming," said Peralta, picking up a wireless tablet and plugging his headphones into it. "The Cube knows what you're thinking, and it knows what you want to do."

"How can it know that?" asked Amir.

"Because it's connected to every brain in the collective consciousness, remember? It knows what *everyone* is thinking."

"But why a game, mate?" said Scotty.

"I'll tell you inside."

Peralta tapped the screen of his tablet. After a few moments spent listening to a series of complex, stereoscopic pulses, they all fell asleep, only to awaken in a dark and densely populated city. The illusion was as real as waking life.

"Where are we?" asked Amir in awe.

The air was heavily polluted, and a bleak drizzle was falling. Amir looked over and found Peralta standing beside him.

"This is what is referred to as *Outer World*," he said, looking up at the jagged skyscrapers. "It's where the game begins."

"And who are all these people?" asked Scotty, looking at the dense throngs that filled the streets.

"Simulants," said Peralta. "If you told them they lived in a computer-generated world they'd say you were crazy. It's like the Matrix in here."

"Why are there so many people?" asked Bahadur.

"So they can be interacted with," said Peralta. "An avatar advances in levels through his or her interaction with people and events."

"I do not understand," said Sir David.

"The objective of the game is to find the *Seven Seals of Gnosis* and pass through each of them. It's all about going deeper and deeper into the game, but it's not as easy as it sounds."

"And why's that?" asked Amir.

Peralta paused to collect his thoughts.

"Seals are personal," he said, recalling everything he had learned. "They're unique to each avatar. They could be hidden anywhere on the planet, or even on other planets. To find them, you ask questions and get involved. You keep an eye out for clues that the Cube sends you. You follow your gut, and you watch your back. There are evil forces that are constantly working to stop you from finding the seals."

Everyone looked at Peralta, trying to understand.

"Moving through the game is like moving through life," he said with a shrug. "It's all about learning and evolving. The gnosis for the first seal isn't unlocked yet, but if it were, a player could study that gnosis, think about it, and then apply it to everything his avatar did in the game.

"Once you've amassed enough experience points and fully assimilated that seal's gnosis, you can pass through it and move into the next inner level. The Cube's constantly scoring you on your avatar's reactions to the tests and trials it sends."

"Tests and trials?" asked the smuggler.

"They're designed to bring out your weak points so that you can eventually learn the skills you need to get through your seal. Finding each seal and passing through it is the objective. I can't begin to describe how brilliant this game is. Apocatastasis is the most awesome MMORPG imaginable."

"What's a MMORPG?" asked Scotty, cocking an eyebrow.

Amir was shaking his head in disbelief.

"It's an acronym that computer geeks use. It stands for *Massively Multiplayer Online Role-Playing Game*."

Peralta manipulated his tablet, and they appeared in a circular room of grey, polished stone. At its centre was the shell of an avatar in the process of being formed. It was hovering weightlessly over a stone dais and connected to dozens of liquid-filled tubes that emerged from the ceiling above.

"Bloody hell," muttered Scotty, scrutinizing the body.

Its skin was still only partially formed.

"Every player gets to build his or her own avatar," said Peralta. "It's really cool."

"When can we start playing?" asked Amir.

Peralta shrugged and tapped the tablet to terminate the simulation. They awoke simultaneously a moment later, as though from a deep sleep. Peralta yawned.

"I think we'll be able to create our avatars once Gabriel and Natasha open the first seal and wake up humanity."

He looked over at the bishop and Anita as they slept.

"I just wish they'd hurry up…"

CHAPTER 25

Deep in Hades.

Gabriel and Natasha broke the surface of the water to find themselves close to a tiny beach. Behind them a half moon was hanging over a mist enshrouded lake. They swam forward and made their way onto the sand, doubling over in fits of coughing as the water left their lungs. Their angelic guide had just disappeared.

"That was a very strange experience," said Natasha, gulping in the air.

Gabriel was looking around and shaking his head in disbelief.

"This has got to be some kind of a lucid dream..."

It was only when he had fully come to his feet that he noticed a hermit's cabin not a stone's throw away. He turned to see that Natasha had spotted it as well.

"Shall we go?"

Natasha took Gabriel's hand and pulled him forward.

They arrived to find a crude image painted on the cabin's door. It consisted of a seven-pointed star, with the bearded face of a man crudely drawn at its centre. Behind the star was an inverted triangle, its outer points holding a sun and moon, with the image of a cube at its bottom-most point. Natasha recognized the icon immediately.

"This is an alchemy mandala," she said, looking over at Gabriel. "It was used by ancient alchemists to illustrate the seven operations of the Philosopher's stone; a method for turning lead into gold."

"And what's with the cube at the bottom?"

"It represents the physical body, or matter," said Natasha, pointing out various parts of the drawing. "The Sun represents the soul; the moon represents the spirit. If you notice, there's a second upside-down triangle drawn over the bearded face in the middle. That's a symbol of cosmic consciousness, or the Christ consciousness."

Gabriel scanned the cabin's facade.

"Let's see if there's anyone inside."

He had no sooner knocked on the door than it opened instantly.

"I have been expecting you, my Lords," came a voice from within.

They entered to find a black-robed priest standing in what could only be described as an alchemist's den. It was a cluttered, smoky chamber crammed with overflowing bookshelves, half walls of scrolls, and rough-hewn worktables laden with bubbling beakers and primitive laboratory equipment.

The man appeared to be in his sixties, with a full beard and raven black hair. On his breast hung the same Tree of Life symbol that they had seen engraved on the reptilian king's shield, as well as on the massive doors that had led into the City of Sarras. He gave a low bow.

"Dear King and Queen," he said reverently.

Gabriel shot a puzzled glance at Natasha.

"We're looking for the oracle," she said. "Can you help us?"

The man bowed low again.

"You have grown into a beautiful woman, my Queen."

"Thank you," said Natasha with a smile. "Have we met?"

"But of course," he said. "The two of you helped me find the tomb of James the Just, and with it, the Compostela Cube."

Natasha tore her eyes from the priest and glanced over at Gabriel.

"You're Gutierrez de la Cruz?" she asked, looking back at the man.

"That is I," he said. "Come in. You are both cold and wet. I will light a fire so that you might dry yourselves."

Gabriel and Natasha were just finishing the soup they had been given when Gutierrez emerged from an adjoining room. He came and sat down near them, moving aside a pile of scrolls.

"Thank you," said Natasha, laying down the empty bowl. "Will you be taking us to see the oracle now?"

"I am the oracle," said Gutierrez, turning to gaze into the crackling fire, his eyes distant. "Long ago I stood at your side and assisted you with your great plan."

He paused for a moment and then added, "Life is a labyrinth and truth is its only exit."

Gabriel exchanged another confused glance with Natasha.

"You said you were expecting us."

Gutierrez's eyes returned to the flames.

"I foresaw this meeting."

Gabriel looked around at the cluttered laboratory.

"What year is it?"

"It is the year of our Lord, eight hundred and ninety-eight," said the priest. "It was thirty-three years ago to this day that you both visited me in a dream. It was also the day I landed on this island."

He turned to look at Gabriel and Natasha over his shoulder.

"You are much more than you think you are, my King and Queen. It will be my task to help each of you regain the knowledge that you once possessed."

Gabriel rose and moved to the window. Over the last few minutes, a thick fog had engulfed the cottage.

"Is this the island of Sarras?"

The alchemist rose to his feet with groan.

"It is, my liege."

"Above the reptilian city," ventured Natasha. "By the Portal of Ahreimanius."

Gutierrez gave a nod.

"You must never forget that your physical bodies are not present here, my Queen," he said, "but rather your ethereal bodies. You are experiencing an altered state of consciousness; a simulation created by an ancient technology. It is similar to a dream, but unlike a dream, there is little difference between it and waking life. Harm can befall you here. You remain mortal."

Natasha looked at Gabriel and then back to the priest.

"Are you saying that our real bodies are still inside those coffins?"

Gutierrez remained silent.

"But what will happen to them?" she asked. "The chamber we were in was collapsing all around us. We'll be buried alive."

"If you do not find the Ostium Sanctus," said Gutierrez, looking back into the flames, "your fate will be much worse than that."

He snapped from his reverie and made his way briskly to the door. The night fog spilled over the threshold as he opened it.

"We have spoken enough, my lords," he said. "You must begin your final quest. I will take you to the first Seal."

CHAPTER 26

Gabriel and Natasha followed Gutierrez through foggy woods until they arrived at a circle of standing stones. The place was unsettlingly familiar to them both, and a dim recollection of having once been here surfaced in each of their minds.

At the centre of the clearing, where the large monolith had been, could now be seen a jagged pit, with a flight of crudely hewn steps descending into it. A viscous fog spilled down over them, sinking into the depths.

"I cannot instruct you as to how to navigate this labyrinth," said Gutierrez. "My role is solely to help you remember what you have forgotten."

Gabriel peered into the gloom and reached into his pack for his flashlight. Gutierrez put a hand on his shoulder.

"Let the Cube light your way, my King."

Gabriel gave a nod of understanding and brought out the glowing artifact instead. He looked over at Natasha to find her smiling back at him.

"Stay close," he said, stepping into the pit.

It seemed that more than an hour had passed before the narrow tunnel they had been traversing arrived at a chamber at last. It was circular in shape, and barely three meters in diameter. Seven blazing furnaces lit the space, and their rounded openings were spaced evenly around the room. At the centre of the floor was a flat, golden disc about the size of a manhole cover. Cast into its surface was the image of a four-petaled lotus flower.

"That's the symbol of the *Muladhara*," said Natasha, wincing at the heat from the surrounding furnaces. "It's the Hindu *root chakra.*"

Gabriel wiped the sweat from his brow.

"That means we're here. This is the first seal. What do you know about the Muladhara chakra?"

"It sits at the base of the spine," said Natasha. "We both have a scar there."

Gabriel nodded and squatted next to the seal.

"What else?"

"It's associated with calcination," she said. "The first of the Seven Stages of Alchemy."

Natasha passed her hands lightly over her face and sat down next to Gabriel. She tried to forget the heat and think clearly.

"What exactly is calcination?" asked Gabriel.

"It is the fire of introspection," announced Gutierrez from the entrance of the chamber.

"Why fire?" asked Gabriel.

Gutierrez raised an eyebrow.

"Pride is always the biggest hindrance to spiritual evolution," he said. "It must be recognized and eliminated so that the ego might be ousted from its customary seat of power. The humbling of the ego is an uncomfortable process. It feels to the initiate like a kind of burning."

Natasha pulled the Book of Khalifah from its watertight bag in Gabriel's pack. It was heavy from the abundance of gold leaf on its pages. She laid it down on the stone floor.

"This seal is paired with Prajñā," she said, opening the gem encrusted book. "Prajñā is the first Divine Action."

Gabriel nodded.

"The Buddhist contribution to the Cube."

"It's the first stage of *The Noble Eightfold Path*," said Natasha as she scanned the page. "It says here that Prajñā means Wisdom, or Discernment. It's about seeing things the way they truly are, as opposed to the way you think they are, or the way you'd like them to be.

"Once you've learned how to apply Prajñā to yourself, it becomes possible to apply it to life, and to other people, but it always begins with the self. Know yourself, and you will know the world."

Natasha turned the page and read aloud a riddle that was written there.

The eyes of the mind are many.
The truth is always illusive.
An infant's vision is nearsighted.
Its conclusions must always be questioned.

In the Royal Palace,
Bejeweled curtains are never hung where there are no windows.
Therefore, the Two say:
Better an ugly hole in the wall
And self-loathing.

To seek perfection is noble.
To embrace imperfection is majestic.

Natasha looked up from the book, her face lit by the fiery furnaces.

"What do you think?"

Gabriel frowned.

"I think self-truth is a monster nobody wants to look at."

He studied the seal and noticed a square indentation at its centre.

"It seems about the right size, doesn't it…"

Natasha watched as he inserted the Cube into the indented slot. In that instant the artifact began to glow in a deep crimson, and both she and Gabriel clasped their heads in pain.

"Ouch!" exclaimed Natasha. "Did you feel that?"

Gabriel nodded. No sooner had the Cube changed its colour than they had experienced a brief, stabbing pain in their temples.

"The discomfort arises as your temporal lobes are synchronized to the Cube," said Gutierrez. "When you fully understand the wisdom the riddle is relating, your brains will generate the correct alpha wave sequence and the seal will be opened to you. Do not dally, the heat in this chamber will soon become lethal."

Natasha wiped the perspiration from her face, noticing only then that the entrance to the chamber had completely vanished. The only way out was through the seal. She began to feel claustrophobic.

"The first two lines are easy," she said. "There are so many different ways to look at something, that it's always hard to know what the truth is."

Gabriel nodded in agreement.

"The next two lines struck a chord in me," he said, thinking. "Babies are all born nearsighted. Taken as a metaphor, it could mean that as children, our understanding of things is limited."

"And?" asked Natasha.

Gabriel shrugged.

"A few years back it occurred to me that many of the opinions I had about myself had been formulated when I was a kid, using childish logic. They weren't true at all, but I'd had them so long I never thought of questioning them."

"I understand," said Natasha. "And if this Divine Action is about seeing yourself as you really are, what better place to start than with your childhood images?"

Gabriel nodded.

"The trouble is they're really hard to find. They operate like subroutines in your mind."

Natasha chewed her lip and then drew the connection.

"If traumatic circumstances in a person's childhood made them form the opinion they were inadequate, then they're always going to believe they're inadequate, until they realize that it was just a childish conclusion they made, and that they're really not inadequate at all. Until the person does this, they'll always be trying to act in ways to counter their perceived inadequacy."

Gabriel nodded.

"And those counter measures will literally make them inadequate. When you try to fix a problem that doesn't exist, you're bound to create a real problem."

Natasha's eyes opened wide as the realization struck her.

"The result is that you become what you're struggling not to be," she said. "It's a vicious circle. The more a person tries to act in ways that counter an imaginary problem, the bigger the problem gets, and the more he or she has to try to act in ways to counter it.

"It goes round and round. The only way to break the cycle is to fully understand that the original problem was based on a childhood image, and that the image was false. The truth is there's no problem."

Gabriel nodded.

"So, the first part of the riddle is all about questioning the things you've always believed to be true about yourself."

Natasha read the second stanza aloud. It was getting unbearably hot.

In the Royal Palace,
Bejeweled curtains are never hung where there are no windows.
Therefore, the Two say:
Better an ugly hole in the wall
And self-loathing.

"This is all about seeing yourself for what you truly are," she said, looking up from the book. "And not trying to cover up the ugly things with pretenses or shifting the blame away from yourself."

"All self-deception has got to be eradicated," said Gabriel, amazed by his deep understanding. "The truth about yourself has to be relentlessly searched for at all costs, even if it makes you hate yourself when you find it. *Better an ugly hole in the wall, and self-loathing.*"

"Calcination is the most unpleasant of all the alchemical stages," said Natasha. "It's a direct attack on personal pride, and it truly does feel like burning."

"As you can now see, my Lords," said Gutierrez, bowing. "You are already in possession of the gnosis. You acquired it when you were King and Queen, long ago. All that is required is that you remember it."

Natasha looked up at the priest. He was right. She knew these things, even if she could not recall where she had learned them.

"And the last two lines?" asked Gabriel.

"That's easy," said Natasha. "The key to true self-honesty is your willingness to embrace your imperfection. As long as your ego is fixated on being perfect, you'll never be able to walk the path of Illac Domus. Your pride won't let you."

Gabriel nodded as a full recollection of the first stage of the gnosis flooded into him.

"Prajñā's all about striving to be perfectly imperfect..."

"Look!" exclaimed Natasha. "It's dissolving!"

Gabriel snatched the Cube from its slot just as the seal disappeared beneath it. It left a dark hole in the ground with a ladder descending into it.

"Come on," said Gabriel, rising to his feet and shouldering his pack. "Let's get out of this oven."

CHAPTER 27

Gibraltar.

Major Richard Roberts awoke on a sofa just outside the governor's chambers. His head was aching, and his mouth was parched. He sat up and looked around, waiting for the fog in his mind to dissipate. It took a while before he could remember what had happened.

His eyes fell on the coffee table before him, and he spotted a copy of the emergency bulletin he had circulated after Bishop Marcus had given him the news about the galactic plane.

The Governor of Gibraltar has issued an
EMERGENCY NOTICE
Please be advised of the possibility of dizziness and temporary loss of consciousness occurring as the result of a rare cosmological event to take place at precisely 11:11am on Dec. 21st. You are advised to find a comfortable place to sit or lie and remain there until the event has completed
its natural course.

What had occurred just prior to this event, however, had been completely unexpected. Roberts could still feel evidence of the profound euphoria that had overcome him just before the crossing had taken place, and apart from his tremendous thirst and aching head, a happy excitement still seemed to be surging in his heart; one that was completely at odds with the gravity of the situation.

This is ridiculous. Why do I feel so merry?

Roberts sat up and looked around to make some very peculiar observations. He reached over and picked up the bulletin, only to find that the paper it had been printed on was yellow and brittle, as though it were very old.

What was more, everything in the room, including himself, was covered in a fine layer of dust. Studying his surroundings, the major noticed that all the plants in the room were missing. Only the soil in their pots remained. He rubbed his face in an attempt to fully awaken.

I saw those plants being brought in from the Convent only the day before yesterday. What the hell is going on?

Just then the governor's nurse entered the room. She was carrying a tray with a pitcher of water and some glasses. She seemed dazed, but like the major, she was at peace. In her eyes was a glimmer of the same excitement that Roberts was feeling.

"Hello, Clara," he heard himself saying. "Is everything all right?"

She stopped and gave him a smile, her pretty eyes sparkling.

"I think so," she said. "But I must say, sir, everything seems rather odd today. I think that cosmological event left me a little out of sorts. I woke up so thirsty… I thought I'd check on the governor and see how he was doing. Would you like a glass of water, sir?"

Roberts took the proffered glass and drained it in a single draught.

"Thank you, Clara," he said. "I was parched as well."

She walked to the door of the governor's chambers, but stopped and turned to face him before entering, her hand still on the knob.

"Why is everything covered in dust, sir?"

The major held her gaze, his brow furrowing ever so slightly.

"I'm not really sure," he said, and then he looked down at himself. "Tell me, Clara. Do you find that your clothes feel," he searched for the right word but drew a blank, "…funny?"

"Why, yes, sir," she said, nodding in earnest. "I do. They seem almost brittle. It's quite strange."

She gave a shrug and then followed it immediately with a cheerful smile, disappearing into the governor's bedroom.

Roberts rose to his feet, his head finally clearing. He produced his mobile phone but found it was not working, only to check his two-way radio and discover the same.

"Faulty batteries…?" he muttered to himself. "Very strange…"

He shot a glance at the phone behind the receptionist's desk and walked over to pick up the receiver.

"This is Major Roberts," he said after dialing. "Get me Captain Brown, please."

There was a pause.

"Captain," he said, his right eye twitching. "Can you give me a status report?"

"Yes, sir," replied the officer happily. "And it's good to hear from you, sir. Happy Christmas!"

"Thank you, Captain," said Roberts, cocking an eyebrow. "But Christmas isn't until the day after tomorrow."

"I'm afraid that's not the case, sir. It would appear that we've been asleep for quite some time. It's Christmas morning, sir. We only just checked our clocks with Geneva."

For a moment Roberts was speechless.

Three days. That's why I feel so groggy.

As odd as it seemed, it truly did feel like Christmas morning, and his heart was happy, though he could not understand why. There had been a nuclear strike in the Strait. Tens of thousands were dead. The world was at war, and Anita and his unborn child were still trapped in a cellar with supplies running low. He had absolutely no cause to be happy, yet he was, and this confused him more than anything else.

"There's something else, sir," continued Brown over the phone. "It's difficult to explain."

"Well spit it out, Captain," said Roberts, emerging from his thoughts.

Brown cleared his throat.

"For starters, sir, almost everything is offline," he said. "The only thing that's still working is our geo-thermal generator, and even that's shown signs of exceptionally heavy wear, sir. It's on the final redundancy system, and the electrode clusters are on the verge of failure. The technicians are amazed that they can still be producing hydrogen and oxygen in the state they're in. If they go, we're as good as dead, sir."

"I'm well aware of that..." said Roberts. "What do they think the cause is?"

"Entropy, Major," said Brown. "It would seem that all our systems have experienced substantial amounts of decay over the last three days."

Roberts thought about the batteries in his phone and the yellowed quality of the bulletin paper.

"What's the life span of an electrode cluster under continuous use, Captain?"

"Just a minute, sir," said Brown. "I'll find out."

There was a brief pause.

"Fifteen to twenty years, sir, maybe longer. There's no reason why we should have gone through all ten clusters."

The nurse emerged from the governor's suite.

"Major," she said quietly, her eyes filled with tears. "The governor wants to see you."

Roberts gave her a concerned nod.

"Captain," he said. "What the hell's going on?"

"We're not entirely sure, sir."

Roberts turned to look at the nurse, doing the math in his head. If the clusters were any indication, two hundred years could have passed in the space of three days.

"I'm going in to see the governor now," he said, moving to hang up the phone. "I'll be in the control centre as soon as I'm done. Get a team on the redundancy electrode clusters right away. We can't afford to run out of power."

Roberts entered the governor's chamber to find the room dimly lit. The nurse approached and clung to his arm. Her face was wet with tears, and she was smiling sadly.

"What's wrong, Clara?" whispered Roberts, trying to comfort her.

The nurse shook her head. She was unable to speak, and Roberts knew why. The old Duke was dying. He made his way to the bedside and laid a hand on the governor's shoulder.

"I'm here, sir," he said gently. "You wanted to see me."

The governor opened his eyes and smiled tenderly.

"My faithful Aide de Camp," he said weakly. "Give me a status report. What is the condition of the Rock?"

"It took us three days to pass through the galactic plane, sir," said Roberts. "We've suffered some damage. It would appear that the increased gravity has not only affected our instrumentation and mechanical systems. It appears to have also altered the way time has passed, sir, as odd as that might sound. Our technicians are looking into it as we speak. Many of the systems are showing signs of severe entropy. It's as though a couple of centuries have passed in the period of three days."

The old knight nodded slowly and then smiled.

"That would make me very old indeed, now wouldn't it, Major," he said with a weak smile. "I needn't feel bad about moving on."

The governor pointed feebly to his night table and Roberts saw an envelope there. He picked it up. It was yellow and brittle, just like the bulletin.

"Open it," whispered the governor, smiling softly.

Roberts obeyed. Within was a document announcing his official appointment as the new governor of the now independent Gibraltar. Along with this was the duke's last will and testament.

"Everything I have shall be passed on to you, Richard," he said weakly. "You are the son I never had."

"But, sir," said Roberts. "There's no need for any of this. You'll soon be well."

The old governor smiled affectionately.

"Tell me about Anita," he managed to say.

Roberts could see that the life was beginning to leave the old duke.

"She's still locked up in the cellar, sir," he said, looking down.

"All will soon be well, young man," came the weak reply. "Do not fret..."

The governor released a long breath and then closed his eyes. Roberts bent closer, his gaze glassy and sad.

"Watch over Gibraltar..." whispered the dying knight. "Keep her safe..."

With these words the governor passed away, his face a mask of serenity. Roberts lowered himself to his knees next to the bed. He had loved the old man like a father.

Goodbye old friend...

Five minutes had not passed when Roberts heard the door opening slowly behind him. He glanced over his shoulder with tear-filled eyes, amazed to see his brother Scotty enter the room.

"I always liked that old bloke," said the latter, nodding sadly. "Even though the bastard would have locked me up without a second thought."

Roberts' heart was pounding in his chest upon seeing his brother, but he would not allow himself to rejoice just yet; not until he was certain. His words came out in a choked whisper.

"Did you bring her back?"

Scotty's smile was warm.

"Just like I promised, big brother. She's waiting to see you."

CHAPTER 28

In the Labyrinth of Sarras.

Gabriel and Natasha pushed their way through tangled and encroaching passages. They had been doing this for more than an hour now and Gutierrez was nowhere to be seen. They needed to find the seal that would take them into the next inner level of the Labyrinth, but there had been no trace of it anywhere.

"We've got to be getting close," said Gabriel, holding out the Cube to light their way.

The tunnels they traversed burrowed their way into the densely packed earth, moving within what Gabriel and Natasha knew was a cube-shaped structure. Forks in the warren appeared constantly, and their intuition always told them which path to take. It was as though they knew the way.

"I think it's here," said Natasha, wiping her brow with the back of her hand.

A low breach had appeared suddenly to their left. It opened into a somber, cavernous hall. There was a black pool at its centre, echoing the chamber's oval shape. There was something out of context in the space as well.

"Are those what I think they are?" asked Gabriel, cocking an eyebrow.

"I don't get it..." said Natasha.

Oddly enough, the dark pool was encircled by dressing mirrors, each as tall as a man and numbering fourteen in total. As they approached them, they could see a flight of concentric steps leading down into the pool's opaque, black water.

Natasha opened Gabriel's pack and removed the Book of Khalifah while he scanned the chamber for Gutierrez. The alchemist was nowhere to be seen.

"Which seal are we looking for?"

"Taoism and Confucianism," said Natasha, sitting down cross-legged and opening the book on her lap. "The Divine Action for this seal is called *P'u*."

Gabriel frowned.

"What does that mean?"

Natasha looked up at him from the book.

"Roughly translated it means, *The Uncarved Block*."

Gabriel held her gaze.

"It's a symbol for an unbiased state of awareness," she explained. "In the state of P'u, nothing is good or bad, there's only what is, without judgment. The metaphor of an uncarved block describes an object or an event in its original state, before the mind has been able to shape it into something with its judgments and labels."

Gabriel nodded.

"And how does the second stage of alchemy fit into this?"

"That would be Dissolution," she said. "It refers to the dissolving of the constructs that make us want to judge and classify things. It opens the initiate's mind so that he can adopt new vistas and re-evaluate his opinions."

Gabriel understood at once.

"So basically, the ugly character traits that were found and calcified in the last stage, are now dissolved into a new substance that's neither good nor bad."

Natasha nodded and looked down at the pool.

"There's something symbolic about those mirrors, Gabriel."

Gabriel moved away from Natasha and approached one of them. They were supported by armatures that allowed them to be angled upwards or downwards, but unlike regular mirrors, these had warped surfaces that offered severely distorted reflections. The pool itself was no less mysterious. Its water was as black as a void and seemed to be warning them that its surface should in no way be disturbed.

Gabriel walked back to where Natasha was sitting and squatted down behind her, looking at the book over her shoulder.

"Could we go so far as to say that P'u is the absolute positive state of anything that can be? Good or bad, beautiful or ugly; it's positive simply because it exists?"

Natasha looked up from the book and paused to think.

"I think that would be correct," she said.

Gabriel nodded and sat down next to her.

"What does the riddle say?"

Natasha read it aloud.

When searching for something that is lost,
One first finds the places where it is not.
In a bowl of bitter salt crystals lies a diamond in the rough.
Each piece is tasted until the treasure is found.
Therefore, not finding leads to finding,
And bitterness becomes sweet.
The Two find the One by finding the places where it is not.
They look to the left and to the right,
And loath not the seven sins that lie there.
Although veiled in darkness, the sins are a blessing,
For they point to the Kingdom that was lost.

Gabriel considered the mirrors grouped on either side of the pool.

"The Two," he said, pointing to each side. "Male and female. Left and right."

Natasha pondered on the observation.

"What are the seven deadly sins?" asked Gabriel. "Can you remember them?"

Natasha smiled.

"That's easy. There's pride, covetousness, lust, anger, gluttony, envy, and sloth."

"Can sins have male and female aspects?"

"A sin committed inwardly would be its feminine expression, and one committed outwardly would be its masculine."

Gabriel rubbed the stubble on his face.

"What if the mirrors represented the seven deadly sins?"

"That would explain their distorted reflections," said Natasha. "If you think about it, a sin is nothing but distorted behavior; a misconception that's acted upon."

Gabriel got up and began to pace.

"The riddle says that the Two find the One in the places where it is not. In other words, they find the truth by finding the misconceptions first; by being aware of them."

"That's what we learned to do in the last seal," said Natasha.

Gabriel shook his head.

"None of this tells us where the next seal is."

"If these mirrors represent the seven sins, then the next seal should be in the pool."

"How's that?"

Natasha turned to face Gabriel.

"Because the mirrors would be *veiled in darkness* if we angled them down towards the pool."

"Why would they be veiled in darkness?"

"Because they'd reflect the black water."

Gabriel nodded slowly. He was beginning to see where Natasha was going with this line of thinking.

"If we pivoted them to face the pool, that would mean they'd be pointing to the *Kingdom that was lost*, which is just another name for the higher spheres…"

Natasha smiled.

"And because the seal is a door to the higher spheres, it has to be in the pool."

Gabriel pointed a finger at her.

"You think you're pretty smart, don't you..."

Natasha beamed.

"I'll do the ones on the left. You do the ones on the right."

Moving to their respective sides, Gabriel and Natasha angled the mirrors downward so they would point to the pool. They did so in unison, one at a time, until only one set remained unchanged.

"All right," said Gabriel. "Let's do it on the count of three. One, two, three—"

Natasha gasped aloud. No sooner had the mirrors been aligned, than the black water became suddenly clear. She could see the second seal at the bottom of the pool, glimmering in solid gold. Moments later the water began to drain away, leaving the manhole-sized portal readily accessible.

Gabriel wasted no time, carefully making his way down the concentric steps towards it. Natasha followed close behind.

"This is the symbol for the *Swadhisthana* chakra," she said, kneeling beside the seal. "It's the second chakra, located in the genital area."

"Marked by the scars below our bellybuttons," said Gabriel.

Natasha nodded.

"It's the centre of unconscious emotions and sexual desires."

Gabriel studied the golden disc. The image of a six-petaled lotus flower covered its surface in bas-relief, with a square indentation for the Cube at its centre.

"Are you ready?" he said, holding the Cube over its slot. "This is probably going to hurt again."

Natasha nodded and Gabriel lowered the Cube into place. They immediately felt a spasm of pain in their heads.

With the connection now made, the Cube began to change in colour, this time turning from crimson into a rich orange.

Natasha moved to sit on the steps, carefully placing the Book of Khalifah down beside her.

"I can understand how the seven sins represent the destructive aspects that were unearthed in the first seal, but how could any of them possibly be good, as the Divine Action of P'u would suggest?"

"Because, my Queen," said Gutierrez, appearing suddenly above them at the top of the steps, "when we use denial and self-deception to hide our *destructiveness*, we bury much of our *constructiveness* along with it. Because of this fact, the bad things actually become good things when they are exposed and removed. The process of purification releases vast amounts of creative power."

"Bitterness becomes sweet," said Gabriel, looking up at the alchemist. "Tasting each bitter salt crystal is like finding each misconception. It brings you one step closer to finding the hidden diamond of creative power. If you don't expose the bad, you'll never find the good. In that way the bad becomes good. *Not finding leads to finding.*"

"Provided the initiate does not identify with the evil that he unearths in himself," said Gutierrez, holding up a finger. "There is always that danger."

Natasha nodded in agreement.

"The initiate needs to realize that the dark things are only a small part of him. They're not the whole of him. He can never let himself forget that he's an evolving person, prone to mistakes and misconceptions."

"That's easy to say," said Gabriel, "but harder to do when real, justified guilt is involved."

"It is simply a matter of applying the Divine Action of P'u," said Gutierrez. "In their ultimate sense, good and evil are both good. If a person does or says something that causes harm to another, to that same degree, he does the other person a great service."

Gabriel cocked an eyebrow.

"How can that be?" he asked. "That sounds completely illogical."

"It's not illogical at all," said Natasha, turning away from Gutierrez to look at Gabriel. "But first you have to understand this concept: A person can do the same bad thing to two different people, perhaps say something offensive, and one person will be harmed, while the other will just let it slide. In other words, it's not the person's action that hurts us, but our reaction to it that causes the harm."

Gabriel considered what Natasha was saying. It was an odd concept, but he could see some truth in it. He nodded slowly.

"I think I understand," he said. "If we're ever hurt, it's only because there's something in us that makes us susceptible to being hurt. It's always due to some kind of misconception that we house.

"By hurting us, the perpetrator is actually aggravating our misconception, and giving us a chance to become aware of it. You can't get rid of something if you're not aware that it exists."

"Yes," said Natasha, "but the gift is lost when we try to blame the person who inflicted the harm on us, instead of taking full responsibility for our reaction to their act. It works the same in the opposite direction too. Any harm that we might have inflicted on others in the past was also a gift to them, no matter how horribly we acted."

"We can never know what the other soul needs in order to evolve," said Gutierrez, "but there is comfort in knowing that the universal laws will never allow anything to befall anyone that is not in strict accordance with universal justice."

"But what about innocent victims?" asked Gabriel. "What about the child who's been murdered? How could that possibly be a gift to the child, or its parents for that matter?"

"As long as you continue believing in death, my King," said Gutierrez, "you will never acquire this wisdom. The child's soul is very old and is in need of experience regardless of its bodily age. Its particular incarnation might appear to have been cut short by human standards, but this is not so on a larger scale.

"We do not know the workings of the universal intelligence, but if such a seemingly unjust things occurs, it is certain that both the souls of the child, and its parents, were in need of the experience in order to advance and evolve.

"There is a positive evolutionary reason behind all human suffering. That is why suffering must be respected, and never pitied; why it must be embraced and never rejected."

Natasha was nodding in agreement.

"Nothing can ever happen to us that we don't need to happen to us," she said. "There are no victims."

"Suffering occurs because of misconception," said Gutierrez. "It occurs because of untruth. A mind must be fully in truth if it is to create a heavenly world in which to abide."

"Heaven's a state of mind..." said Gabriel pensively, recalling what Bishop Marcus had once said.

Gutierrez smiled and nodded.

"For this reason alone, suffering is a blessing, my Liege," he said. "It creates pain in the areas where we are not seeing things clearly. Were it not for the pain of suffering, we would never be motivated to address the problems within us, and as such, we would never be able to create the mindset needed to return home.

"The prideful ego does not want to accept this. It becomes outraged and insulted when things do not go its way. As a result, it makes every effort to skirt the truth, and project the blame outside of itself."

Natasha rose to her feet.

"The fact is we all have a choice," she said. "We can take responsibility for everything bad that happens to us and know that it's what our soul needs to evolve, or we can decide to be powerless victims. The choice is ours, and I choose power over helplessness."

"Agreed," said Gabriel. "And because of the inherently positive nature of suffering, we can forgive ourselves for the harm we might have done to other people in the past, as well as to ourselves. It was all part of our individual and collective evolution."

"Yes, my King," said Gutierrez. "But that is not to say that we should go out and purposely try to harm other people, in order that we might help them. We would only end up hurting ourselves if we were to do this. What one does always comes back to oneself."

Gabriel rose to his feet.

"True, and that's why the next time somebody wrongs me, I'll know that I had it coming, and I'll try to figure out which of my past thoughts or actions brought it on, instead of just blaming the perpetrator, or life in general."

"Good is positive," said Natasha. "But evil is also positive in the long run. Both opposites make up the Uncarved Block."

Gutierrez pointed to the golden seal. It was quickly vanishing.

"The Divine Action of P'u has now been unlocked to the world."

CHAPTER 29

Gibraltar.

Major Richard Roberts arrived at the submarine port just minutes after his son had been born. He was in the company of Scotty Roberts, and the two medics they had brought along. Anita had gone into labour shortly after Scotty had gone off to fetch his brother, leaving Peralta no alternative but to assist Sir David in birthing the child where they were.

To the great delight of all, the delivery had gone off without a hitch.

"Well, that was definitely interesting," said Peralta, leaving the room with Sir David at his side. "Can't say I'll ever forget that…"

"Blessed be that little boy," said the old bishop, peering into the room. "He is most probably the first to be born into the new age of the Christ Consciousness, and just like the baby Jesus, he too was born in a secret cave on Christmas!"

Peralta shook his head in resignation.

"It won't be a secret cave for long," he rasped. "The military will be taking possession of it soon enough, and I'll be going to jail for good."

The others all looked at the rumpled scientist, realizing for the first time what the discloser of the submarine port meant. Peralta had broken many laws in occupying the military bay. He would surely pay for his crimes. It was as they contemplated these facts that the medics emerged bearing Anita on a stretcher. She asked them to stop so that she could have a word with Peralta.

"Thank you, Captain," she said in earnest, taking Peralta's hand. "You saved my life, and the life of my baby."

Peralta smiled genuinely.

"The pleasure was all mine."

Major Roberts emerged from the room carrying a bundle of Anita's things.

"I owe you a great debt, Captain."

"I'm no captain, sir," said Peralta, looking down at his feet. "I'm just an old smuggler on his way to jail."

Roberts put a firm hand on his shoulder.

"I'd sooner lose an entire platoon than lose you, Captain," he said. "I'm going to arrange a full pardon for your past activities. I'm the new governor now, and from this day forward you'll be an honoured officer in the Gibraltar Regiment. That submarine and this entire bay will be officially under your command."

Peralta blinked in surprise, scratching his messy head.

"You'll have a full salary," continued Roberts, liking the idea. "And a pension when you retire. You'll also have a seat of honour in the officer's mess. You're a hero, Captain Peralta, as are all your friends. You'll be received as nothing less!"

Peralta looked at him, speechless.

"There would be one caveat however," added Roberts, bending in closer and lowering his voice. "If you continue to find it necessary to engage in your old trade, do make sure to keep it all underwater, so to speak."

Peralta removed his glasses to wipe the tears from his eyes.

"Those days are over, sir," he stammered. "I would much rather attend to my research and serve Gibraltar in any way I can."

The major took hold of Peralta's hand and shook it enthusiastically.

"Well said, man!"

Everyone applauded when Anita and the baby were carried into the freight elevator. They could never have wished for a happier outcome to their impossible expedition. Being the attending physician, Sir David went with her to complete the required paperwork. Behind were left Peralta, the old bishop, Amir, Bahadur, Scotty, Cassano and a very jovial Shackleton.

"Well then!" said the old bishop. "I do believe we have done it. Humanity is out of the rift and the planet is saved!"

"So far so good," rasped Peralta. "Now it's just up to Gabriel and Natasha to complete their mission."

"They're well on their way," said Amir from the computer banks. "The game's active."

Peralta and the others rushed over to the workstation.

"The website's a flurry of activity," added Amir. "The gnosis from the first two seals has already been released."

Peralta told the bishop and Cassano about the game, and everything else they had learned whilst the two of them had been unconscious.

"And have we had any word from them?" asked the bishop of Gabriel and Natasha.

He was still trying to come to terms with the fact that two hundred years had elapsed in the period of three days.

"Unfortunately, not," said Peralta, pulling up a chair and beginning to tap away at a keyboard. "But something occurred to me while we were delivering the baby. There's a possibility that I could use the game's binaural interface to establish a connection with them."

"How do you plan on doing that?" asked Amir.

Peralta looked up at them.

"I haven't said anything up until now, but I found data paths in the descrambled algorithms that we extracted from the Cube. They're carrying alpha-wave signatures identical to the game's dream simulation interface."

"What the hell's that supposed to mean, mate?" asked Scotty. "Speak in English, God damn it."

Peralta rose to his feet and walked to a different section of the workstation, throwing himself into a chair and beginning to hammer away at a keyboard.

"The reptilians who built the Cube used the binaural interface to enter into its internal architecture. I'm going to do the same thing. I've managed to decrypt their entry codes using the fractal equation that operated the transponder back at the Labyrinth entrance. I have no idea where I'll end up but it's worth a try."

Cassano pushed his way up from the back of the group.

"Are you sure that's a good idea?" he asked. "You're going to be hacking into the most sophisticated piece of technology ever created."

Peralta looked hard at Cassano before responding. The scrawny pirate was right to feel reticent about the plan. The odds of getting lost inside the multi-dimensional artifact were very high. Peralta would be relying on the Cube's intelligence to guide him.

"I just can't shake the feeling that Gabriel and Natasha need our help," he rasped. "It's imperative we establish a connection with them as soon as possible. Going into the Cube is the only way I can think of to do it."

He turned away from Cassano and looked up at the others.

"I've got to put my trust in the Cube."

* * * * * *

Peralta opened his eyes and yawned. He gazed languidly around at his new surroundings as the grogginess left him. He was sitting in a room that he recognized at once, and his heart skipped a beat when his eyes fell on that which lay before him.

There on a worktable was the Compostela Cube, as it had been before Natasha had removed its ornate framework and illuminations.

"My God," he gasped. "Why did it bring me back here?"

He had appeared in Nasrallah's laboratory. The very place where he had been held prisoner. What was more, he could see himself fast asleep on a cot, not four paces away.

I'll be nice and quiet. Waking me up probably wouldn't be a good idea.

Peralta took inventory of the equipment that surrounded him. There was a portable x-ray machine, an old oscilloscope, and a computer monitor filled with x-ray images of the Cube.

"I've definitely come backwards in time," he whispered, amazed. "Back to the night when Nasrallah gave me the artifact to examine…"

Peralta rose to his feet and stood there silently looking around.

"Cassano will be in the dungeons below," he muttered inaudibly. "Nasrallah will be upstairs in his quarters. He didn't come to take the Cube back until midnight. I remember because that old grandfather clock was sounding when he came in and woke me up."

Peralta turned to find the clock and gasped when he saw the time.

Eleven fifty-five!

He looked down and just then noticed a bright orange light shining from the cracks in the Cube's coverings.

"It's active," he muttered, bending over to examine it more closely. "But it's not glowing blue. It must be emitting a different frequency…"

Peralta reached over and switched on the oscilloscope, connecting the Cube to it as quickly as he could.

"Four hundred and seventeen hertz," he said, his brow furrowed. "I know this frequency. Where have I seen it?"

He scratched his messy head and struggled to remember. Something else puzzled him as well. Why had the Cube decided to bring him to Nasrallah's castle to show him this new frequency? Why not some other place in time? Why not back to when he was working with Gabriel in his own laboratory?

It was at that moment he heard the deadbolt outside the chamber being thrown back. Nasrallah was on the verge of entering. The grandfather clock began to chime, and Peralta could see himself stirring on the cot.

My God. I've got to get out of here.

In one swift motion Peralta produced his tablet and terminated the simulation, opening his eyes to find the massive head of Bahadur looking down at him. He was smiling with relief.

"You have been unconscious for almost six hours," he said in his deep basso. "We were beginning to worry, my friend."

CHAPTER 30

In the Labyrinth of Sarras.

Natasha did not like their new surroundings at all. After having spent over two hours navigating the damp worming passages of the Labyrinth, they had crawled into a tiny crevice that had nothing in it but an old well. To make matters worse, the ring of stonework that encased the pit was crusted in bat dung, and the air stank of sewage and rot.

Gabriel dragged himself over to the edge and looked down. An iron ladder had been set into the masonry, disappearing into the murky depths.

"What's that sound?" asked Natasha, crawling up beside him.

The darkness was inky and oppressive here, and there was a dry rattling filtering up from below. It was barely perceptible in the dead air, but Gabriel frowned, nonetheless. An eerie chill was running up his neck and over his scalp. He pushed back his hair.

"I'll go first."

It was not until they had descended a dozen metres that they were able to see the source of the rattling sound. The well had led them into a large, torch lit chamber. They were entering it through the ceiling and the ladder they were on descended all the way to the floor below; a floor that was seething with a carpet of insects.

"Cockroaches," grunted Gabriel, half gagging. "Why did it have to be cockroaches?"

Natasha looked down at him with panic in her eyes. For a long moment they both remained where they were, clinging to the iron ladder but unable to continue downward. It was Gabriel who first broke from the spell.

"We've got to get over there somehow," he said, pointing.

Natasha turned to look. Gutierrez had appeared on a raised area in the corner of the chamber, not twenty paces away. The floor at his feet was curiously free of insects and behind him was the room's only exit: An arched opening leading into a dark corridor. The only way there would be through the cockroaches.

"I'm going to jump down," said Gabriel. "Then you're going to climb on my shoulders. Got it?"

Natasha was shaking her head, her big eyes wide with fear.

"I can't do it, Gabriel."

"Of course you can do it," he said, stepping off the rungs.

He groaned in disgust. The milling nest came up to his knees.

"Get on!" he cried.

He was on the verge of panic. The insects were already in his trousers.

"Now!"

Natasha screamed as she lowered herself onto his shoulders. Gabriel did not waste any time after that. With a grunt of pure repulsion, he moved out into the seething nest, fighting to keep the panic at bay. He forced himself to be deliberate with every step he took. Tripping and falling was not an option.

The repugnant cockroaches were soon crawling all over his body, and to make matters worse, there were also millipedes in the swarm. He used his hands to keep them off his face, but their burning bites were making him feel dizzy and nauseous.

"Hang on!" he cried through clenched teeth.

Natasha could feel the millipedes burrowing through her hair and over her scalp. Dozens of cockroaches were scurrying over her too, no matter how furiously she brushed them away. It was all she could do to remain coherent.

At long last they arrived at the raised area where Gutierrez had stood. He was nowhere to be seen now. They scrambled up a flight of stone steps and proceeded to strip themselves naked, shaking the insects from their clothing and hair.

"That was horrible," said Natasha, wiggling back into her jeans.

Gabriel frowned and buckled his belt.

"Let's not dwell on it," he said, turning to face the tunnel.

Natasha aimed her flashlight into the passage, seeing its light fall onto a thick wall of fog within. There was something unsettling about its density. It was oily and viscous.

"So, what's the next seal?" asked Gabriel, trying to get his mind off the insects.

Natasha cleared her thoughts.

"It belongs to the Islamic side of the Cube," she said. "It centres on the *Jihad bil qalb*; the most difficult of all the greater Jihads of Islam. It's a battle with the devil himself."

"Lovely," said Gabriel, peering into the foggy passageway and then back into the den of cockroaches. "Can't wait for that. Someone in here's hell bent on freaking us out..."

He extended his arm to Natasha.

"Shall we?"

Natasha took it and smiled.

"I thought you'd never ask."

They entered into the fog without hesitation, leaving behind the chamber of insects only to find the passageway infested with hundreds of angry bats. In seconds they were forced to let go of each other to defend themselves. It was only when the onslaught had passed that Natasha reached out for Gabriel and found that he was no longer at her side.

"Gabriel?" she called. "Gabriel!"

She heard him cry out as if from very far away.

"Natasha! Where are you?"

"I'm over here!" she cried, but even as the words left her lips, she knew that Gabriel would never hear them.

The fog was as dense as soup now. It swallowed her voice entirely.

"My God," she whispered, half choking. "What is this?"

She could feel the air growing very warm around her. A second later the fog vanished to reveal an enormous subterranean cavern. She was standing on a stone platform no wider than she was tall. It sat atop a massive fragment of rock that rose from the depths like a jagged finger, surrounded on all sides by a fiery chasm of lava and ash.

"What's going on?" she gasped, and just then a terrible clamor arose from all sides.

It was as if masses of people were crying out in agony. Natasha spun around, looking over the edge to see that there were thousands of figures writhing below. They clung to rocks, or cowered in crevices, their bodies burnt and mutilated by the splashing lava and sulfurous explosions.

If this were not enough, she looked up to see something that amazed her even more. There, on the opposite side of the burning chasm, was an enormous dragon fast asleep on a mountain of golden treasure.

"The fire and brimstone make it clear where I am," she whispered quietly, gawking at the beast. "But why a dragon?"

Natasha spun around on the platform. There was clearly no way off. With a sigh of resignation, she sat down on the hot stone and took a tiny sip of the little water that remained in her canteen.

"*Accidenti,*" she said in Italian gloomily. "Where are you, Gabriel?"

* * * * * *

Gabriel moved forward through the dark fog, fumbling with his radio.

"Natasha," he said. "Can you hear me? Peralta. Are you there? Can anybody hear me?"

He pocketed the device in frustration, only then noticing the fragrant scent in the air. It smelt of hardwood fires on a crisp winter's night, and he breathed it in deeply, his eyes attempting to penetrate a brighter section of fog that was located directly above him.

In moments it thinned into tattered wisps and a full moon materialized in the sky. Snow laden tree boughs formed a canopy above him, and he could see that he was in an olive orchard on a clear wintry night. The ground was covered in a fresh blanket of snow, and jagged moonlit mountains towered in the background.

"Who goes there?" came a haggard voice, and Gabriel spun around to see a robed man approaching.

No sooner had he spotted the *Tree of Life* pendant hanging from his neck than he knew it was Gutierrez. Gabriel watched intently. Gutierrez was carrying a large wooden staff and was using it to help himself plod through the ankle-deep snow.

"It's me," said Gabriel. "Natasha and I just got separated."

The alchemist came up to him and threw back his cowl. It was only then that Gabriel noticed how old Gutierrez had become. His black beard was now long and white, as was his hair and eyebrows.

Gabriel was amazed. The minutes that had passed for him had been decades for Gutierrez. It was only after a long moment that the old man recognized him.

"Hero of God!" he proclaimed suddenly. "Long has it been since I gazed upon your noble face, my King!"

He lowered himself reverently to a knee and would have been unable to get up again had Gabriel not helped him.

"Do you remember when we last met?" asked Gabriel.

Gutierrez smiled and nodded.

"We parted ways in the Labyrinth," he said, his brow furrowing as he remembered. "We had arrived at the dragon's lair."

The dragon's lair?

Gabriel cocked an eyebrow but decided not to comment. Instead, he looked around, noticing only then the snow-covered village that lay behind them. It was medieval in style, and warm firelight was coming from the windows of its inn.

"You wouldn't know where Natasha was, by any chance," he asked, watching a pair of drunken men staggering out onto the cobbled streets.

Gutierrez moved to Gabriel's side.

"She is in the den of the dragon *Ialdabaôth*," he said, frowning. "To rescue her you must learn the ways of the *Mujahid.*"

Gabriel nodded slowly.

"The Holy Warrior."

"Yes," said Gutierrez, motioning towards the inn. "Come with me, my Liege. We must begin your training at once."

CHAPTER 31

Gibraltar.

Peralta opened his eyes and looked around. He was in the secret submarine port, sitting at his workstation by the dark, lapping waters.

"Bahadur," he rasped, rising to his feet and stretching. "Where are you hiding?"

Peralta could distinctly remember having seen the brown giant when he had awoken but realized that he must have drifted off again without knowing it.

"Shackleton!" he called out. "Are you here?"

He scanned the submarine port. There was not a soul in sight.

"They must have gone up top," he muttered with a shrug. "I might as well get started on the communications array."

He opened a nearby drawer and produced the glowing sample of *blue goo* that he had taken from the Labyrinth entrance. It was the size of his fist, and still covered in the tangled circuitry he had connected it to.

Thinking back on his recent adventure, Peralta recalled why the Cube's new frequency had seemed so familiar to him. It belonged to the *Solfeggio Scale*; a set of seven mysterious notes originating from ancient India and adopted in medieval times by Gregorian monks in their chants.

Apart from the scale's professed powers of spiritual enlightenment, the sequence of notes had been found to contain inexplicable properties. Amazingly enough, biochemists were using the scale's third frequency to repair human DNA.

"If these notes can fix damaged cells then there's a good chance they can at least stimulate the goo."

Peralta bent over an adjacent computer and launched a program that would generate the special sine wave needed for his experiment.

"Four hundred and seventeen hertz is the second frequency in the scale," he muttered, entering in the data. "Let's see what happens..."

He plugged in his headphones and placed them carefully over the reptilian-made substance, turning the volume to its maximum setting. No sooner had he initiated the sine wave than the blue-glowing sample began to glow in a rich hue of orange.

"Yes!" cried Peralta, rubbing his hands together. "It's matched the Cube's new frequency! This ought to work now!"

"Gabriel!" he said into his radio. "Natasha! Can either of you hear me?"

The response came almost instantly.

"You son of a gun!" cried Gabriel. "You couldn't have had better timing!"

Gabriel checked his voice, noticing only then that he was drawing attention to himself. He was sitting in the inn's common room, and although masked for the most part by the drunken din of merriment, those at a neighbouring table had heard Peralta's tinny voice coming from his radio and were looking over at him suspiciously.

Gabriel lowered the volume and brought the radio closer to his ear.

"How's everybody doing?" he asked. "Give me an update."

"Everybody's fine!" came Peralta's reply. "The world was unconscious for a total of ninety-one hours. Everyone woke up when you and Natasha opened the first seal. Anita had her baby about ten minutes after that. Oh yeah, I almost forgot. We popped out of the rift two hundred years in the future."

"What?" exclaimed Gabriel, and then lowering his voice he added:

"How the hell did that happen?"

"Severe time dilation," said Peralta. "But it's a good thing. All the radiation's gone now. A game appeared on the website. I think it's an extension of the Labyrinth, complete with seals that have to be traversed. It works on a binaural dream simulation interface. How's Natasha?"

"She's great," said Gabriel, turning his back on his inquisitive neighbours. "But we got separated about an hour ago. We've been encountering some pretty surreal stuff. Right now I'm sitting in a ninth century pub while Natasha is being held prisoner by a dragon."

"Are you being serious?"

"Very," said Gabriel.

Peralta scrubbed at his head.

"Well, I wouldn't take things too literally if I were you. I'm pretty sure the Labyrinth is like the game. It's a dream simulation that interfaces with the Cube. I wouldn't be surprised if you could actually shape events if you tried. My guess is that your physical bodies are still in the sarcophagi."

"They are," said Gabriel. "And they're being buried alive as we speak."

"The sarcophagi would have been specifically designed for that purpose," said Peralta. "I'm sure your bodies will be safe in them."

"I hope you're right," said Gabriel. "Now how can I get a hold of Natasha?"

"You'll have to wait until she turns her radio on," said Peralta. "The Cube's emitting a different frequency now. The blue goo I used to link our radios is now orange goo. I'll be keeping an eye on our connection from this end."

"It'll be changing colours every time we pass through a new seal," said Gabriel, seeing only then that three ruffians were approaching his table.

"I've got to go," he said. "I've got company. Stay in touch."

"Will do," rasped Peralta. "And good luck!"

Peralta severed the connection but left his radio on standby. Seeing that his work was done, he decided to visit the upper galleries and search for his friends.

It was not until the elevator door opened that Peralta noticed things were not as they should be.

"This looks like something straight out of Star Trek," he muttered.

The tunnel walls were glowing with light, and the floor appeared to be made of glass.

"Coolmaster!" said a voice, and Peralta turned to see a young man approaching. "Welcome! The oracles be blessed! I must have missed their announcement of your coming!"

Peralta looked at the boy in confusion.

"The oracles?" he rasped, cocking an eyebrow. "And who are the oracles?"

The boy nodded as though Peralta had said something very profound.

"It is true, Coolmaster," he said respectfully. "They are only people. The same as you and I. We are all divine."

Peralta was going to respond, but a group of children engulfed him before he could do so. They could barely contain their excitement. Peralta made the connections. The young man who had spoken to him was obviously their teacher. He could hear some of the children whispering behind his back.

"Look at his old skin!" said a little girl.

"...And his white hair!" said another.

In moments the children had taken hold of Peralta's hands and were guiding him down the passage, crying out in happy voices.

"A Coolmaster has come! A Coolmaster has come!"

Peralta let himself be herded along until a large door opened before them. On the other side was Gibraltar's main street, crowded with people. A regular stream of flying cars was passing by overhead, but other than that, the place seemed unchanged. The air was fresh and clean.

"My God!" gasped Peralta, looking down at the children who surrounded him. "What year is this?"

They all laughed at his question, their eyes alight with joy.

"Yes, we know!" they cried. "Tonight is New Year's Eve! That's why you've come, isn't it, Coolmaster?"

Peralta decided to play along.

"Of course," he rasped. "And what year will it be tomorrow?"

"One thousand of the New Era!" they cried in unison.

Peralta looked around at his surroundings, amazed that he was seeing his hometown ten centuries in the future. The original structures of Gibraltar had been perfectly preserved. He breathed in the fresh sea air, reveling in its cleanliness.

"I like what you've done with the place," he said, nodding in approval. "Is there still a governor in Gibraltar?"

The children laughed at his question as though it were silly.

"Can you take me to him?" he asked.

"We would be delighted, Coolmaster," said the young teacher approaching.

CHAPTER 32

In the Labyrinth of Sarras.

Gabriel turned to see that Gutierrez was making his way towards him through the inn's crowded common room. He took a sip from his mug and leaned back in his chair. Three ruffians approached him as the old priest arrived.

"This is the knight of whom I spoke," said Gutierrez, gesturing towards Gabriel. "He requires sparring partners, but it must be with naked steel. You will all be paid, but the man who brings him down will receive this prize."

He held up a small leather pouch and emptied its contents onto the palm of his hand. Twenty pieces of gold. The eyes of the men lit up at the sight. Gabriel rose to his feet.

"Now hang on a second," he said, looking at Gutierrez with shocked anger. "I'll be having no quarrel with anyone in this place."

Gabriel sized up the burly men, taking special note of the heavy swords that hung from their belts.

"Least of all with these good gentlemen," he added, flashing the most charming smile he could muster.

The men frowned and turned their attention back to the gold coins.

"If you kill him, you shall have double," said Gutierrez.

Gabriel tore his eyes from the ruffians and turned to face the priest.

"Are you crazy?" he whispered. "What are you saying?"

Gutierrez ignored him entirely.

"Do you accept my offer, gentlemen?"

The three ruffians grunted in unison and moved off to wait outside. Gabriel was going to speak but Gutierrez held up a hand.

"Come with me, my Liege," he said. "I have arranged so that you might be dressed and armed."

* * * * * *

Gabriel walked through the common room with Gutierrez at his side, surprised by how unencumbered he felt in his chainmail armour. He put a hand on the broadsword that hung from his belt, his fingers running over three slots in its pummel. It seemed odd that they should be there. A circle, a square, and a triangle.

"You do realize I have no idea how to use this," he said, looking hard at Gutierrez while motioning to the sword.

"Is that so," said alchemist. "Are you sure of that, my King?"

They left the inn and made their way into a snow covered square in the centre of the night enshrouded hamlet. Gabriel could see the three men Gutierrez had hired, accompanied by a drunken mob of spectators, all lit by the flickering light of torches that had been set around the courtyard.

No sooner had they laid eyes on Gabriel than the crowd began to place bets, and in no time a clamor of excitement had infected everyone. More and more people were emerging from the inn as word of the spectacle spread. Gutierrez paid them no heed.

"If you are to slay the dragon and open the third seal," he said, shuffling forward through the snow, "you must learn the ways of the *Mujahid*. The time has come to reawaken your Inner Warrior, my King."

Gabriel looked over at Gutierrez.

"And how exactly am I supposed to do that?"

"You must establish a connection with him."

Gabriel watched the brutes begin to spar with one another.

"And exactly who is this inner warrior I'm supposed to connect with?"

"He is the greatest of all warriors," said Gutierrez. "He is the Kristos."

Gabriel turned to face Gutierrez.

"Jesus Christ?" he asked, his hands on his hips. "Are you crazy? I think I'll need to connect with someone a little more assertive than a hundred-pound weakling in sandals."

Gabriel noted the force with which the sparring blows were being dealt and looked back at the old alchemist.

"I think someone like Conan the Barbarian would be much more suitable, given the circumstances."

Gutierrez frowned.

"I will have you know that Jesus was not the emasculated man that the Vatican invented, my Liege," he said soberly. "He was neither poor, weak, celibate, nor timid. He achieved the highest possible state of body and mind that a man can achieve, and he did this by connecting fully with the inner Christ Consciousness."

"He connected with himself?"

"Indeed, he did," said Gutierrez. "And so can we all. The Christ Consciousness resides at the core of every human being. It has been called many names over the ages, but it has always been one with our higher-self, and one with the Creator himself. Jesus was simply the first man to establish a full and unobstructed connection to it."

"And that made him a warrior?"

"Many and powerful were the demons who fought to prevent this connection from taking place," said Gutierrez. "They attacked him viciously and incessantly, in both physical and psychic ways. He defeated them all. Jesus Christ was, and is, the greatest warrior in existence, my Liege. He was the first Mujahid. He is the Kristos."

Gabriel looked at Gutierrez, trying to understand.

"And you say he wasn't celibate?"

Gutierrez shook his head.

"Contrary to what the blasphemous Vatican might have you believe, my King, sexual union is not a bestial sin. It is a great and wonderful blessing that draws us ever towards unity consciousness."

Gabriel considered what he was being told.

"Your Jesus seems a lot more real than the one I've always heard about," he said. "He actually sounds human. How do I make contact with him?"

"To connect with the Inner-Christ, you must allow yourself to feel his love for you."

Gabriel groaned.

"Couldn't we just leave out that whole *Jesus loves you* part?"

Gutierrez gave him a puzzled look.

"It is the only way to shed the hidden contempt that you have for yourself, my Liege. There is not a human being alive who does not house this self-contempt, whether he or she is conscious of it or not. Unless you allow yourself to feel the Christ's unconditional love for you, you will never feel worthy of merging with so great a force as he."

Gabriel considered what the old alchemist was saying. It aligned perfectly with the gnosis of the last two seals. He turned and saw that his opponents were now waiting to engage. The crowd was growing impatient.

"You cannot defeat Ialdabaôth if you are not Mujahid," said Gutierrez. "And you cannot be Mujahid if you cannot experience *Tawhid*, or true Oneness with God. Jesus Christ was the first to accomplish this state, and having done so, he opened the way for others to follow."

Gabriel nodded with understanding.

"He injected his ability to connect with the Inner-Kristos into the collective consciousness," he said. "That's what Natasha and I are supposed to be doing with the gnosis as we open the seals."

"In the three days that passed between his death and symbolic resurrection," said Gutierrez, "Jesus Christ gathered his archangels and led a war against the hosts of Lucifer in Hades. He was victorious, and he opened the Seventh Seal of Ostium Sanctus; the gateway to the higher spheres. Your task is to help the world make their way through that seal."

Gabriel looked at Gutierrez, understanding at last why the seventh seal required no divine action to open. Jesus Christ had unlocked it two thousand years earlier. Gutierrez sensed Gabriel's new understanding and smiled.

"Do not forget who you truly are, my Liege," he said. "In your ancient incarnation you already established a full connection with the greatest warrior of all time. Make a silent prayer to the Inner-Kristos and ask him with humility to help you remember how to do battle. The rest will come naturally."

Gabriel nodded and moved forward, reminding himself of what Peralta had only just confirmed. The truth was that he was in a dream simulation, a virtual reality. Everything here was symbolic. He would be able to control events if he could establish the correct mindset. At the same time, he recalled what Gutierrez had told him when they had first met. He could still die in this dream.

"All right," he said. "Here goes nothing."

Gabriel met his opponents in the centre of the square, drawing his sword and thrusting it into the ground. He bent on a knee before it.

"Jesus," he prayed. "I'm seriously and humbly asking for your help. I've had my doubts that you exist, but if you really are who Gutierrez says you are, you'll understand. Please help me remember my connection to the Inner-Kristos. I need to make this sword work."

Gabriel rose to his feet, but before he could think he had already acted on a strong gut feeling, spinning around to deflect an overhead blow that would have cut him in two.

The battled that ensued was nothing short of miraculous, with Gabriel showing a proficiency that was unmatched by anything the spectators had ever seen. Not only did he defeat his opponents, but he did so without inflicting any mortal wounds. They were soon lying in the snow, either groaning in pain, or completely unconscious.

"Well done, my Liege," said Gutierrez, shuffling past Gabriel as he stood there panting. "Come along now. We have a dragon to slay."

* * * * * *

It seemed to Natasha that she would surely die in this heat. Across from her the dragon still slept on its mound of treasure, oblivious to the incessant wailing of the damned. The beast had broken from its slumber only once, opening one of its emerald eyes to lazily spy on her just before turning over and falling asleep again.

It was only then that Natasha remembered her radio, and she reached into her pack to retrieve it, switching it on.

How could I have been such a dummy?

"Gabriel, are you there? Can you hear me?"

"Natasha!" came Gabriel's crackling voice. "Yes, I'm here. I've been waiting for you to turn your damn radio on!"

"I completely forgot about it," she said apologetically. "Oh, thank God."

"Are you all right?"

"Yes, but it's really hard to breathe down here," she said. "I'm trapped on a rock shelf, surrounded by a fiery chasm. It's filled with screaming people, Gabriel. Can you hear them? It's straight out of Dante's Inferno. There's something else here too. Something that doesn't really belong…"

"What?" asked Gabriel with concern. "What is it?"

"There's a dragon," she said. "It's sleeping on a big pile of gold."

"I know."

"You do?"

"Gutierrez told me all about it."

"Well then get me out of here!" she cried. "What's taking you so long?"

CHAPTER 33

Gabriel looked over his shoulder, taking in the expansive moonlit view. He and Gutierrez were high in altitude now, on horseback and picking their way along a narrow, frigid trail. It stretched out before them, making its way to the top of a jagged, snow-covered mountain. The little hamlet could still be seen far below. It was shrouded in blue, with gossamer threads of moonlit smoke emerging from its chimneys.

Gabriel drew his pelt around him and looked ahead at Gutierrez. He too was wrapped in furs, and for all his years was managing his horse like the best of equestrians.

Gabriel inhaled the mountain air. The cold was intense and there was not a breath of wind. Above him the stars glowed, twinkling through waves of heat that appeared to be rising from the mountain itself.

"We have arrived at the entrance," said Gutierrez over his shoulder. "We now can dismount."

They led their horses into a sheltered area, finding the ground littered with crumbled masonry. Warm, sulfurous gusts were rushing from the mouth of a cave.

"Looks like the villagers tried to shut him in," said Gabriel, surveying the decimated fortifications.

"Ialdabaôth cannot be locked away and forgotten," said Gutierrez. "He will always break free, no matter how fervently one denies him."

It was not long before they were making their way through round, fire scorched lava tubes. Even after having stripped themselves of all their furs, they were still sweating profusely, and for the first time Gabriel was feeling the weight of his chainmail and sword.

He stopped before a fork in the passage as Gutierrez came up beside him.

"To the left lies the easiest way to the lair, but it is sure folly to travel that route. We will take the right-hand path, which is the more difficult of the two. It will take you where you want to go, but it will bring hardships."

"Why doesn't that surprise me?" muttered Gabriel, watching as the old priest shuffled off ahead.

They continued onward until they arrived at a deep chasm that split their path. It was only a meter across, but it spanned the entire width of the tunnel. Further ahead they could see a cavernous chamber with three monsters standing motionlessly at its centre. Their disfigured forms were draped in shadow, and each was armed with a massive, two-handed battle axe held point down before it.

On the ground behind the beasts was a circular opening, glowing with the light of unseen lava below. It was enclosed by bars of black iron, and from it came the tortured wailing of the damned. Next to the pit lay a thick length of coiled rope. One of its ends was fastened to a sturdy iron ring anchored into the ground.

"Below lies the lair of Ialdabaôth, my Liege," said Gutierrez. "It is there where you will find both your queen, and the seal."

"And what are *those* things?"

Gutierrez scowled at the shadowy monsters, his mouth contorting with disgust.

"They are the Wormlords, my Liege," he said, turning to face Gabriel. "Insidious demon-kings. They command the many legions of devils and wraiths that prey upon humanity."

"I don't understand."

Gutierrez returned his gaze to the shadowy beasts.

"In the same way that there are angels around us at all times, so too are there demons, my Liege. Those who are close to self-realization can have many demons assigned to them at any given moment. Those who are further from self-realization, and do not pose an immediate threat to Lucifer, will have fewer demons assigned to them."

"And what do these demons do?"

"They attempt to burrow into the human soul substance," said the old alchemist. "Apart from weakening us by feeding on our life force, it is the demon's task to separate us from God, from our fellow man, and from ourselves. They do this by influencing us with mental attitudes that sever our connection to the divine world."

"Why do they look like they're made of earth?"

"Demons are comprised of very dense matter," said Gutierrez. "Much denser than the matter that we are comprised of. It is for this reason that we cannot normally see them. They have a very low energy frequency."

Gutierrez bent closer.

"Demons do everything in their power to distance us from the higher, ethereal states of being. They trick us into believing that the physical world is the only thing that is real. Their presence fills us with confusion, and false rationality, so that it seems that truth does not exist; that it is only a relative concept. This weakens us by undermining our ability to have faith in what we intuitively believe to be true."

Gabriel's eyes opened wide. The old alchemist was slowly dissolving.

"How do I dispel these demons?" he asked urgently.

"By hunting them relentlessly," said Gutierrez. "And by using the positive aggression of the Warrior Christ to vanquish them once they have been found."

"I didn't know there was such a thing as positive aggression," said Gabriel. "I thought aggression was a bad thing."

Gutierrez smiled.

"That is because aggression is most commonly released through destructive means. We fail to see that aggression can also be used for constructive purposes.

"The Mujahid uses it to vanquish the Wormlords, and the many demons that they command. In this way his attitudes remain in alignment with the truth. The demons flee from him. They cannot abide his aggression. It burns them."

"What happens after you dispel a demon? Is it gone for good?"

"Yes," said Gutierrez. "But another might come to take its place if it has the courage. You see, when a demon has been dispelled, it suffers great humiliation in the eyes of its peers. This pain causes it to cry out for God's mercy despite itself, and an upward movement is initiated in the demon's soul.

"For this reason, the Christed Mujahid always strikes without mercy. He knows that by vanquishing a demon, he helps it to evolve, and so furthers the Apocatastasis."

With those words Gutierrez disappeared. Gabriel turned to look across the pit at the demonlords and then brought out his radio.

"Natasha, can you hear me?"

"Yes," came her parched reply, "but please hurry, Gabriel. I don't know how much longer I can stand this heat."

"I'm right above you, baby," he said. "Just look up. Can you see a round opening anywhere?"

She scanned the cavernous ceiling.

"Yes," she said, rising to her feet. "There's one about ten meters above me."

"That's where I'll be coming from," said Gabriel. "There's only one problem. I've got to fight my way past three monsters to get to you. What do we know about this seal?"

Natasha looked over at the sleeping dragon.

"Its alchemical stage is Separation," she said. "Calcination brought out all of our destructive aspects through the fire of introspection. Dissolution dissolved all those faults into a homogenous mass. Separation is the step where the faults are analyzed so as to learn their causes. Truth gets separated from misconception. Read the riddle. I marked the page in the book."

Gabriel sat down on the edge of the chasm, his feet dangling over the side. He opened his pack and brought out the Book of Khalifah, removing it from its watertight bag.

"All right," he said. "My Arabic's nowhere near as good as yours but I'll give this my best shot."

He translated the text as he read it.

At the root of all evil lies the triad of death.

Self-will endeavors to confuse and twist the truth.
Pride limits vision to all but what is apparent.
Fear labours incessantly to separate and divide.

The warrior crosses the threshold and passes into the realm of shadows.
He engages his enemies and so obtains the three keys of purification.

When mother and father are seen in truth,
Religious tradition can be questioned.
Enmity then becomes tolerance,
And tolerance becomes Unity.
After the false god has been slain,
What before seemed impossible, becomes feasible.

Only when the triad is revealed and conquered,
Can there be unity between all nations and creeds.

Gabriel put down the book and picked up his radio.

"What do you think?"

"I remember reading something about self-will, pride, and fear in your father's journal," said Natasha. "You need to find that entry, Gabriel. It was somewhere near the middle of the book."

Gabriel produced the diary and located the page.

"My father's saying that nobody's entirely free of self-will, pride, and fear," he said, scanning the text. "While one might be more prevalent than the other two, all three are always present at the same time. He says they're the sole cause of all our suffering, both individually and collectively."

Gabriel read the rest of the entry aloud.

Self-will is not to be confused with free will. Self-will comes from the desires of the little ego. It strives to get what it wants at any cost, regardless of the harm it does along the way. Self-will resides mostly in the unconscious mind, and conflicts with the good intentions of the conscious mind.

Pride means that our little ego is more important than the other person's; that we desire advantages for ourselves, and that we have vanity. If we feel the humiliation of another person less than our own humiliation, then we have pride. Only by detaching ourselves from our vanity, can we have the same reactions for ourselves as we do for others.

Fear that our pride will be hurt, and fear that the desires of our self-will will not be obtained, makes us cling to self-will out of pride, and to pride out of self-will. This is what the ancients referred to as the triad of death; a vicious circle linking the three destructive attributes. The triad can only be broken by observing its mechanisms in the depths of our own unconscious mind.

Gabriel closed the book.

"The three Wormlords have got to be the enemies in the riddle," he said. "They represent the triad."

"If that's the case," said Natasha, "then they also embody confusion, materialism, and separation. The demon of confusion makes truth appear to be untrue, and untruth appear to be true."

Gabriel nodded.

"Confusion is also linked to self-will in the riddle," he said. "Mixing up truth and lies is always great for rationalizing destructive acts and manipulating people."

Gabriel scratched his head.

"What about the second element of the triad?"

Natasha wiped the perspiration from her face and tried to ignore the incessant wailing around her. She was feeling a deep wisdom rising up from within her. She was remembering.

"The second element is materialism," she said. "It denies the existence of anything other than the surface appearance of things. It negates the invisible world of spirit, and as a result, the true meaning and purpose of life. Materialism is linked to pride because it takes humility to accept that there are spiritual laws that must be obeyed."

"And the third?" asked Gabriel.

"Fear," she said, concentrating inwardly. "It's the central instrument of the left-hand path. It divides and conquers wherever it's present. Fear keeps us isolated from everything, and from everyone, including ourselves."

"Done," said Gabriel. "There's a chasm directly in front of me. That's got to be the threshold to the realm of shadows that the riddle speaks of."

"The unconscious mind…" said Natasha.

Gabriel nodded. He too was remembering.

"The unconscious mind is where our real enemies exist," he said. "I can see them standing on the other side of the chasm. They'll hold the three keys of purification that the riddle speaks of."

"But what about the false god in the riddle?" asked Natasha.

"It's Ialdabaôth," said Gabriel, packing away the books and rising to his feet. "He's the dragon."

"Of course," said Natasha. "Ialdabaôth was humanity's first monotheistic god. He's false because he's obsolete. I still don't understand Ialdabaôth's connection to the triad though."

"Give it some thought while I take these Wormlords down," said Gabriel, drawing his sword and stepping across the chasm.

"Be careful!"

"Don't worry about me," he said, swinging his sword with expert proficiently. "I seem to have developed some very useful skills of late."

Gabriel made his way into the chamber, watching as the three Wormlords gathered in front of the opening in the ground. He could see that its bars were held fast by three golden padlocks. He said a quiet prayer to Jesus Christ, requesting his assistance again, and then moved forward, grunting with disgust.

In the light that came from the opening, he could at last make out the repugnant forms of his adversaries. Although similar to the other demons he had encountered, these were crawling with pale maggots. They stank of decay and putrescence.

"I believe that you gentlemen are in possession of keys to that pit," he said, fighting back an urge to vomit. "Why don't you make this easy for all of us and just give them to me?"

Gabriel received an answer to his question in the form of a powerful attack from the middle beast. At the last second, he dodged aside as its massive axe hissed by. Another attack came from the next fiend immediately afterwards, followed by a stabbing thrust from the third.

In a matter of seconds Gabriel was engaged with all three demons, emptying his mind of all thoughts so as to follow every signal that came to him through his newfound intuition. The result was a fluid dance of sorts, each movement placing his sword in the perfect position to parry the incoming blows.

With a decisive thrust Gabriel sunk his sword deep into one of the beasts. The Wormlord imploded with a sickening crunch as the blade found home, and it did not take long before Gabriel had felled the others in similar fashion. In the end they laid in dead heaps on the ground, the seething worms and maggots already beginning to break apart their corpses.

Gabriel moved to study the padlocks, finding that they each contained a differently shaped slot, identical to those in the pummel of his sword. One was square, one circular, and the other triangular. Embedded into the soles of each of the monster's feet, Gabriel found three shining gemstones bearing the exact same shapes. He used them to open the padlocks and then stuffed them into his pocket, pulling out his radio.

"Natasha," he said, poking his head down through the opening. "Look up."

Natasha's expression transformed with relief.

"I can't tell you how good it is to see your face, Gabriel."

She squinted through the rising waves of heat and brought the radio closer to her mouth.

"Are you wearing armour?"

"Chain mail," replied Gabriel proudly.

He picked up the rope and threw it down.

"I'll be right there."

No sooner had Gabriel set foot onto the stone platform than Natasha threw herself into his arms. He handed her his canteen and watched as she drank. In an effort to lessen the heat, Natasha had ripped the hem from her blouse, and used it to tie up her hair. It fell in thick ringlets around her face.

Gabriel's eyes found the dragon. Natasha had not been exaggerating. From head to tail it must have measured a hundred feet. He shifted his gaze to the throngs of writhing bodies that filled the cavern. They were steeped in lava and ash and wailing in agony.

"I can see why people have always listened to angry priests…" he said, shaking his head.

Gabriel produced the gemstones and fit them into the pummel of his sword. They began to glow as soon as they were embedded in their slots. He looked over at Natasha and held out his hand.

"Are you coming?"

"Where?"

Gabriel feigned surprise. No sooner had she taken his hand than he pulled her over the precipice with him. In that instant they were swallowed by an eruption of smoke and ash, only to find themselves standing face to face with the dragon when the air cleared. Natasha snapped her jaw shut.

"How did you know that would happen?"

The dragon reared up and spread its wings. It was enormous.

"I didn't," said Gabriel, craning his neck to look up at the beast. "I just followed my gut."

Natasha was eyeing the dragon as well.

"Does your gut know a way to stop this thing from burning us to a crisp?"

Gabriel gave her a wink and held up his sword. Its blade was shimmering with the light of its three glowing gemstones.

"It sure does…"

The dragon was by now in a furious rage, and the fire that spewed from its mouth was blanketing the cavernous ceiling in a wash of rippling flames. Around them the damned were screaming in terror, but Gabriel was unaffected. He simply scrambled up the mound of golden treasure until he was directly below the beast, and then thrust his sword up into its belly.

The dragon roared and collapsed backwards, shaking the ground as it fell. The wailing of the damned ended shortly after. Gabriel turned to look down at Natasha.

"That was impressive," she said, arching an eyebrow. "A bit anticlimactic but impressive…"

Gabriel gave a knightly bow, his face a mask of relief. On his way back down the treasure shifted under his boots, exposing the third golden seal in the ground before them.

"This is the symbol for the *Manipura* chakra," said Natasha, bending over the seal. "It's a ten-petaled lotus flower; the energy centre for willpower and achievement. It's located where we have the scars on our upper abdomens."

Gabriel squatted down next to her, producing the Cube from his pack. It was still glowing bright orange.

"Willpower fits this seal perfectly," he said, inserting the artifact into its slot. "This gnosis is all about positive aggression, and not taking any bullshit."

Natasha brought her hands to her head as the new alpha-wave link was established.

"I'll never get used to that," she said. "It really hurts!"

Both watched as the Cube transformed in colour, this time becoming bright yellow. Gabriel pulled it out of its slot and packed it away. He brought out the Book of Khalifah again and handed it to her, laying himself back onto the mound of golden treasure.

"All right then," he said, stretching himself. "All we have to do now is figure out the rest of the riddle."

Natasha leafed through the ancient pages.

"Tell me about the glowing stones in the handle of your sword."

Gabriel held the pummel out to better study it.

"I took one from each of the Wormlords," he said lazily. "They opened three padlocks in a gate that barred the hole I came down through."

Natasha chewed her lip as she considered.

"So symbolically speaking, your victory over self-will, pride, and fear not only allowed you to gain entry to the place where the dragon of the false god exists in your unconscious mind, but it also gave you the means to kill it."

"It would appear so," said Gabriel, impressed by Natasha's insight.

"Ialdabaôth," she muttered, continuing to study the book. "This was the name the gnostic priests had for Yahweh. He fizzled out two thousand years ago, but subconsciously we all still try to appease him, hoping he won't destroy our lives."

"What do you mean?" asked Gabriel, propping himself up on an elbow.

Natasha looked over at him.

"Most of us have a completely distorted view of what God is," she said. "That's why so many people reject God's existence.

"Take Yahweh for example. He was a primitive god for a primitive people. When he came onto the scene three thousand years ago, humanity was much less evolved than it is now. We needed fear to make us obey the law, and a terrible father figure to enforce it. Yahweh was perfect. He was monotheistic, which was a great step forward from polytheism, but he was not at all the way God really is."

"And how is God, really?" asked Gabriel.

Before Natasha could answer, Gutierrez appeared from behind the dead dragon.

"God is the substance that makes up all things, physical and metaphysical," he said, studying the remains of the dragon. "He comprises the laws of nature and of being. He is truth and love. He is beyond good and evil. In short, the true ineffable God is infinitely more than a vengeful old man who lives up in the sky."

"So God's impersonal then," said Gabriel. "Kind of like a powerful super-computer."

"Certainly," said Natasha, giving Gutierrez a warm smile, and noting how much older he was. "But he's also *everything*, so that makes him personal too. He's out there, and in here, all at the same time."

"People often think of God as being on one side, and the devil on the other," added Gutierrez. "This is not the case at all. Even Lucifer must abide by God's laws, for no matter how far away he goes from God, Lucifer is always surrounded by God, made up of God, whether he likes it or not."

"We all are," said Natasha. "It's kind of like living in God soup. We're all soaked in it; permeated by it. Anything that can possibly be, is made of God. Even our thoughts and emotions are made of God."

"Humanity's concept of the Creator evolves as humanity evolves," said Gutierrez. "Religious conflict occurs when we do not allow our concepts to change; when we rigidly defend the views handed down to us by our forebears. This always comes about as a result of pride, self-will, and fear."

"So when Jesus came to the Jews with a new concept of a loving, all forgiving God," said Gabriel, "they didn't accept him because of their pride, self-will, and fear?"

Natasha considered.

"I think that people would have accepted Jesus if their corrupt religious leaders had helped them accept him," she said. "The Jews were ready and eager to take the next spiritual step."

"Contrary to the Vatican's inflammatory dogma," said Gutierrez, "it was not the Jews who killed Jesus at all."

Natasha nodded in agreement.

"It was the Romans," she said. "Herod was a Roman, and the Sadducees were his political puppets. Jesus was an upstart that threatened the Roman system, so they killed him. The Sadducees were not the only ones who held on to the outdated Yahweh, though. The Roman fathers of the Christian church found him very useful too."

"Yahweh instills fear in the people," said Gutierrez, "and fear is power. This is why such a contradiction exists between the God of the Old Testament, and the God described in the New Testament and in the Koran. The fathers of the church could hardly deny the true version of God that Jesus and Muhammad brought, but they kept the old version to help them manipulate and control."

"Of course," said Gabriel. "The new version of God, or Allah, was merciful and all forgiving; a much more evolved concept of God than the one that followed the ancient Jews around, killing people and tearing down cities."

"Yahweh, or Ialdabaôth, is the god of the ego," said Gutierrez. "And like the ego, he behaves like a selfish little child who thinks itself omnipotent. The child demands complete obedience, loyalty and servitude, and if it does not get these things, it becomes angry, jealous, and punishing.

"But as humanity evolves, Yahweh's threats become empty. Eternal hell is seen for the lie it is; a deception devised by the same religious authorities that have led humanity astray for so many centuries."

"They altered the gospels," said Natasha. "They turned Jesus into a meek and passive figure that preached poverty and submission. It's all nonsense, Gabriel. The real Jesus was not like that at all. His teachings were about achieving abundance and self-empowerment."

"You're absolutely right," said Gabriel, recalling his recent experiences in battle. "What Christians need to do is separate the truth from the lies. Jews and Muslims need to do the same, just as all the people from every religion in the world.

"As it stands, most of humanity is throwing the baby out with the bathwater. We're either rebelling and dumping religion entirely, truths and falsities alike, or we're submitting and making ourselves swallow everything that our religious leaders tell us to believe."

Gutierrez held up a finger.

"We fear that if one thing in the doctrine is untrue, then it must all be untrue. Our pride does not want to admit that our ancestors could have been mistaken about some things. Our self-will works to resist change in any way it can. It always does this by denying the truth of the matter. Namely, that religions are both right and wrong at the same time."

"This is what the riddle means when it talks about questioning religious tradition," said Natasha, "and seeing our parents, or forebears for what they really were: Human beings prone to error and misconception."

"We've all been lied to by our leaders in one way or another," said Gabriel. "It's a matter of separating the truth from those lies."

"And separation is the third alchemical stage," said Natasha.

Gabriel sat up, thinking of the final three lines in the riddle.

"With this new frame of mind, something that always seemed impossible suddenly becomes feasible…"

"The fusing of the six world religions," gasped Natasha with sudden realization. "One of the primary purposes of the Cube. When the six fragments of truth contained in each of the six religions are brought back together again, the original gnosis will be re-established. What was broken will be made whole again…"

All watched as the golden seal dissolved, revealing yet another passage leading down into the Labyrinth.

"Well, that solves that," said Gabriel, rising to his feet and pulling up Natasha. "Slowly but surely, we're getting through this maze. Let's see what this next seal has to offer."

CHAPTER 34

Gibraltar.

Peralta looked out of the window, watching the rocky terrain pass below. He and the governor were in the back seat of a self-driving flying car, the luxurious interior oddly simple, and reminiscent of the styles popular in the nineteen-forties. He peered out the forward-facing window to see their destination come into view. It was a small observatory, built on the Rock's topmost peak.

"Don't you find it even a little incredible that I've come from the past?" he asked, turning to face the governor.

"Not in the least," replied the latter. "We were expecting you."

Peralta had met the governor the moment he arrived at the Convent. The bureaucrat was exceedingly young for his position, appearing to be in his thirties, but he showed the confidence and wisdom of a man twice his age.

Peralta had told him who he was, and where he had come from, and had been very surprised at how readily the governor had accepted his farfetched story. The fact that he had travelled through time had not fazed the bureaucrat in the least.

"I'm afraid the world is once again in a bit of a crisis, Mr. Peralta," said the governor as the car began to decelerate.

"What kind of crisis?"

"Your friend will tell you everything."

"My friend?" asked Peralta, watching as the car navigated its way into the observatory's loading bay. "Who?"

The governor pointed outside.

"The oldest Coolmaster on Earth."

Peralta turned to look just as the car came to a stop. Standing beside them was a well-preserved senior citizen in a nicely tailored suit. He had perfectly groomed, snow-white dreadlocks.

"Amir?" exclaimed Peralta through the glass. "What the hell are you doing here?"

* * * * * *

Peralta moved to the centre of the planetarium, taking in the nebulous expanse that had been projected onto the domed surface above. It was a three-dimensional representation, and as his line of vision followed Amir's pointing finger, he could see what looked to be a planet.

"That's Niburu X," said Amir.

His voice was that of an old man's, but his demeanor was identical to what it had always been.

"The earth's under imminent attack, my friend. The hosts of Satan are on that planet."

"What?" exclaimed Peralta, turning to look at Amir. "That's ridiculous. Niburu X is an internet myth. It doesn't exist."

"I'm afraid it does…"

Peralta had to force his jaw shut. Niburu X was the central theme of one of the most ludicrous conspiracy theories he had ever encountered. It stated that there existed a planet whose orbit crossed with the Earth's once every ten thousand years. Discovered and named by the ancient astronomers of Sumer, Niburu X was said to be home to an evil race of beings that would usurp the earth at the next planetary conjunction.

"The Nephilim of Niburu X," said Peralta, shaking his head incredulously. "The ancient race of giants that were said to have once ruled earth…"

The governor came to their side.

"Astronomers all over the world have been monitoring its approach for the past twenty-four hours," he said. "The planet came out of nowhere and is approaching very quickly. We will cross paths with it in precisely twelve hours and forty-three minutes. We really don't know what to expect. Its velocity is tremendous."

Peralta turned to look at the man.

"And is the world armed and ready?"

The governor trained his eyes on Peralta.

"The Earth has not possessed military forces for over six hundred years," he said. "There has been no need even for police."

"No military," said Peralta aghast, and then turning to Amir he asked:

"How do you know that Satan is even on that planet? Doesn't that sound a little superstitious and paranoid?"

"It's in the Book of Revelations," said Amir, his white eyebrows gathering. "There would be one thousand years of peace after the second coming of Christ. After that, Satan would return for his final battle."

"The second coming of Christ?"

"Of course," said Amir matter-of-factly. "It occurred when Gabriel and Natasha activated the Cube. That's what that feeling of euphoria was when we made the crossing. It was the mass induction of the Christ Consciousness into the Collective Consciousness."

"I see," said Peralta, adjusting his glasses, "It wasn't a literal second coming… And the thousand years of peace are up tonight at midnight…"

"They are indeed," said the governor.

"But I would have thought the opening of the seals would have negated that part of the prophecy," said Peralta.

"And you would have been correct, my friend," said the governor, "if all the seals had in fact been opened."

"I don't understand."

Amir put an old hand on Peralta's shoulder.

"Gabriel and Natasha never succeeded in opening the sixth and final seal," he said. "Humanity's been waiting a thousand years for them to finish their mission."

"But what are you saying?" exclaimed Peralta. "That would mean that Gabriel and Natasha are still trapped in the Labyrinth!"

"Most certainly," said Amir, "but as I'm sure you know, time has no meaning in the Dark Rift. To them, thousands of years could pass in a few hours."

Peralta nodded slowly. He knew well of the time-warping characteristics of the galactic plane. When considered from this perspective, Amir's words did not seem so farfetched.

"What the hell is going on here, Amir?" asked Peralta, fully awakening to the situation. "How did you know I'd be popping up in the future? And what the hell are you still doing alive?"

* * * * * *

It was only when they had seated themselves in the observatory's small pub that Amir and the governor agreed to answer Peralta's questions. A young waitress arrived with their pints.

"God bless you, girl," said Amir. "Talking's a parched business without a nice bit of stout to sooth the throat."

Peralta took a sip and wiped the froth from his mustache. He looked at Amir and the governor in turn.

"It's good to see that the Irish are still getting the planet into trouble."

He put down his glass.

"Now if you'll please be so kind," he rasped, directing his attention at Amir. "You don't look a day over eighty. How did you manage to live for a thousand years? And what the hell is a Coolmaster? Why did the children think I was one?"

"Because of your white hair," said Amir, putting his glass down pensively. "If you haven't noticed, people here don't age past thirty-three."

Peralta looked over at the governor and found that it was true. He had not seen a single elderly person since he had arrived in the future.

"Thirty-three's the maximum age of genetic development in humans," said the governor, sipping his beer. "We stop ageing once we've reached it."

Peralta was going to say something, but Amir spoke first.

"It was no advancement in science that made people stop aging," he said. "It happened as a result of slow and steady spiritual evolution. You see, the more a person embraces the gnosis, the longer he lives and the happier he becomes."

"Then why do you look so old?" asked Peralta.

"Because I was born before the crossing," he said. "Most of us have died. The ones that still live are what you might call holy men and holy women. We're called Coolmasters."

"And why are you called Coolmasters?" asked Peralta.

Amir took a long, slow draught from his stout.

"It was observed that the more one advanced on the spiritual path of Illac Domus, the cooler one became."

"How so?" asked Peralta.

"People on the path become very laid back," said Amir with a shrug. "They're self-confident, relaxed, non-judgmental, easy-going, loving, considerate, or in other words, cool.

"If you really think about it, cool people have always been around. They rarely say brainless things. They rarely do things that aren't cool, like forcing their will on other people, or committing destructive acts. They never need to impress anyone. They don't have hang ups about sex or letting loose and having a good time. But they're also extremely responsible, dependable, and fearless. They live life in a rich, full, and spontaneous way. That's what it means to be cool."

Peralta considered what his friend was saying.

"I never thought about it that way before," he said, thinking. "Cool people are spiritually evolved people, even if they don't consider themselves to be spiritual at all..."

"They rarely consider themselves to be anything," said Amir. "They just *are,* and that's what makes them cool. Of course there have also been the poser types; those who try to act cool by being detached and aloof, but it's all just an act, and they're often more insecure than anyone else."

Peralta watched in muted shock as Amir produced his chillum pipe along with an old-fashioned box of matches. It was the same pipe he had always seen him with; an ancient, carrot-shaped artifact covered in Sanskrit texts.

"And what kind of a holy man drinks beer and smokes hash, for God's sake?" said Peralta, watching in disbelief as Amir stoked the pipe to life.

"A true holy man," he said, exhaling a great cloud of very pleasant-smelling smoke. "One who's not pretending to be anything he's not."

He smiled happily and leaned back in his chair.

"Genetically modified marijuana kief," he said, admiring the pipe. "It's quite good for you. The smoke vapor is comprised of antioxidants, coupled with a variety of vitamins and minerals. It actually scrubs your body of toxins as you smoke it."

He took a long sip of stout and looked at Peralta over the rim of his pint glass.

"It's got a crazy buzz too," he said, tilting his dreads to the side and taking another haul from the chillum. "Way more mind-expanding than the old stuff."

He proffered the pipe to Peralta, but the latter just looked at it and shook his head in disbelief.

"You're no holy man," he rasped. "You're a bloody fraud! A one-thousand-year-old fraud!"

Amir only winked happily.

"A very strange thing happened after the crossing."

"What?" rasped Peralta irately.

"All stress, everywhere, just vanished. Within a few weeks the whole planet had become so calm you wouldn't have even recognized the place. It was incredible. It happened to everyone, in every country. Hatred and fear just dissolved."

Peralta seemed genuinely surprised.

"How's that?"

Amir shrugged.

"Hatred and fear belonged to the world before the cataclysm," he said, leaning back. "After the crossing, there was nothing it could latch onto anymore. Everything lost its severity. Anxiety disappeared."

"I've been feeling that way since I arrived..." said Peralta, realizing it only then. "I feel like I haven't got a problem in the world."

"And you don't."

"But how can you even begin to say that?" exclaimed Peralta. "Satan is about to attack the planet with a race of evil giants from the planet Niburu X! This is serious shit, man!"

Amir smiled affectionately.

"I missed you, old friend," he said, waving the waitress over. "You've got to try and understand the universal laws. Nothing can happen in the outer world that isn't a reflection of the inner world. This applies to individuals, and to humanity as a whole.

"Consider the shadow government that tried to take over the world at the time of the crossing. It was just a reflection of the shadowy self that resided in every individual, vying for control. Once that lower self was exposed and vanquished, shadow governments couldn't exist anymore."

Peralta struggled to understand.

"So World War Three was just a reflection of an internal war?"

Amir nodded.

"Absolutely. That's why it was called Armageddon; the final battle between the higher-self and the lower-self; between good and evil. It was being waged in every heart a long time before it manifested in the outer world."

Peralta understood at last.

"So then climate change was just a reflection of the changes happening in the collective consciousness. The outer world has always been a product of our inner state of mind. It's a quantum projection... Collectively and individually..."

Amir gave a nod and just then the waitress arrived.

"We'll have another round, my little Venus," he said flirtatiously.

To Peralta's surprise, the girl smiled and gave Amir a sultry look. When she left, he leaned closer and spoke in a low voice.

"A Coolmaster's longevity is partly due to his heightened sex drive."

"At your age?" said Peralta in shock. "You should be ashamed!"

Amir shot him a mischievous wink.

"The young ones always come looking for me."

Peralta turned to the governor for support but found the bureaucrat nodding knowingly.

"It's very true," he said. "Quite incredible, really."

"All right," rasped Peralta, waving his hands. "I've heard enough. Tell me what else has happened to this crazy planet."

Amir sat back in his chair.

"Things altered rapidly after the cataclysm," he said, nodding as he remembered. "People began to question everything they thought they knew. There came about massive changes in politics, education, and religion. The truth about our place in the universe, coupled with the knowledge of the true meaning of life, altered the way we looked at ourselves. It also altered the way we looked at each other, and at life in general. You see we'd moved into the next higher sphere without even knowing it. Society was transformed."

Peralta leaned forward in his chair.

"In what ways?"

"No more money for one thing," said Amir, looking over at the governor.

"No more war," added the bureaucrat. "Transparent direct democracies everywhere. No more hunger."

"How could there be no money?"

Amir shrugged again.

"Seven centuries ago, the publicly owned and operated Cube Corporation bought out the last of the private corporations, and took over the United Nations, forming a single world government that was democratically run by the citizens of the planet. Profits were spread evenly throughout the entire population."

"A tipping point was also reached in the collective consciousness at that time," added the governor.

Amir nodded in agreement.

"Everyone was playing a lot of Apocatastasis," he said. "They really began to understand the gnosis as a result of that game. It became easier and easier for them to apply what they learned in the game to their lives."

"But what about the global financial system?" asked Peralta.

"All the money anybody needed came from their Cube Corp dividends," said the governor. "As such, people started giving products and services away."

Amir took another haul from his chillum.

"Currency became less and less necessary," he said. "Until it was finally phased out entirely."

"So who does all the work around here?" asked Peralta. "If there's no need to earn money, then there's no need for anyone to work."

"People go to work because they want to give," said Amir, glancing over at the young waitress. "They do what they feel most inclined to do, and for this reason, people generally love their jobs. The jobs that nobody wants to do are done by humanoid robots."

"One of the biggest lessons humanity has learned is that a person's happiness is directly related to giving," explained the governor. "If you give to your maximum potential, you can't help but be happy."

"It's all about giving, old friend," said Amir. "And receiving is just another form of giving."

Peralta struggled to understand.

"How's that?"

Amir shrugged.

"You give someone a gift when you accept what they want to give you. It works the same with the universe. God wants us to have everything we desire, so you give him a gift when you let yourself receive universal abundance."

"Weren't there any problems at all?"

"Growing pains," said Amir. "Over the years, the population continued to increase, albeit at a much slower rate than before. As third world nations were transformed, their birth rates naturally fell. Even still, when we reached nine billion, we began to dedicate our collective attention to developing space travel and terra-forming technology.

"Interplanetary colonization became an obsession for many people, and science made an exponential leap shortly after that. The knowledge given to us by the reptilians, combined with the spiritually inspired minds of our scientists, gave birth to an entirely new technology."

"Could you be more specific?" asked Peralta, his professional interest peaking. "What kind of technology?"

"The long-awaited unification of physics and metaphysics," said Amir. "Through it we learned how to isolate gravitons and dark matter. Our scientists used them for everything from free energy to inter-galactic space travel. They opened up new worlds that could rapidly be terra-formed and populated. Human colonies can now be found all over this galaxy. The earth is no longer overcrowded."

"I can't believe it," said Peralta. "Gravitons. Dark matter. Incredible. What's next then? Where is humanity headed?"

"Inward," said Amir. "There's nowhere to go but *in*. There never was."

"But what about Niburu X?" said Peralta, feeling a sudden wave of sleepiness begin to take hold of him.

"Niburu X is a test," said Amir. "Like everything else in the outer world, this invasion is simply a reflection of our inner state of mind. It comes as a result of the upward spiral movement of spiritual evolution."

"Resistances have to be revisited before they can completely be dissolved," explained the governor. "Niburu X will be humanity's last encounter with the echo of fear it once had. This will be like a final exam."

"I didn't know we were in school."

"That's precisely where we are," said the governor.

"Ever since the crossing," explained Amir, "we've learned that every event and occurrence in life has a lesson behind it. Everything is symbolic, no matter how meaningless it appears to be. If you stub your toe, or drop something, try to remember what you were thinking of when it happened, and you'll see the symbolic connection."

"Sure," said Peralta, yawning, "but you could look at anything that way, and come up with a million symbolic interpretations."

"Most certainly," said Amir, "and isn't it amazing that out of all the interpretations you could have possibly chosen, you chose the one you did?"

"I see your point..."

The governor leaned forward in his chair.

"You'll find that if you empty your mind, the first interpretation that pops up will always be the true one. If you follow your intuition, life will always reveal a lesson in every event you're experiencing."

"It's the only way to advance on the path of Illac Domus," said Amir. "This kind of observing has to be done constantly. It's a lot of fun. It turns life into the mystery-solving game it was always meant to be."

Peralta rubbed his face in an effort to wake himself up. The Cube's dream interface was on the verge of taking him. Amir produced a little canister from his pocket and emptied a blue pill onto the table.

"What's this for?" asked Peralta, picking it up.

"It'll help you find answers once you get back into the Cube's central interface," he said. "Take it."

Peralta looked at Amir and then swallowed the pill, washing it down with a gulp of stout.

"I still feel sleepy as hell," he said.

Amir smiled.

"As you should, old friend. I want you to relay a message to Gabriel and Natasha for me."

"What shall I tell them?" asked Peralta, yawning.

The governor bent forward and looked at Amir.

"He really doesn't know, does he..."

Amir shook his head.

"He hasn't a clue."

"Know what?" asked Peralta, struggling to keep his eyes open.

Amir put a hand on his forearm.

"You'll learn all you need to know when you're in the central interface," he said. "But there's also something you've got to figure out for yourself. Think of the *Tree of Life*. Think of the structure of the Cube and compare it to the structure of the universe. Think of the dream interface and compare it to waking life. When you find the answers, you'll understand."

"But what am I supposed to tell Gabriel and Natasha?" asked Peralta, barely managing to remain awake.

"You've got to make them see the truth, and you can only do that if you know the truth yourself. It's not the same if we tell you, but I can give you some clues. There are four dimensions in this universe. There is length, width, height, and depth.

"Think! Where is depth? How is it connected to the other three dimensions, and to the gravitational singularity? Use that messy head of yours. Find the answers and apply them. If you can't make Gabriel and Natasha understand the truth, they'll never make it through the last seal, and the Nephilim of Niburu X will destroy Earth. We're all depending on you, old friend."

Peralta wanted to ask another question, but the pull of sleep was too strong. He struggled to open an eye, but instead fell headlong into slumber.

CHAPTER 35

In the Labyrinth of Sarras.

After what seemed like hours spent traversing the winding passages of the Labyrinth, Gabriel and Natasha came at last to a cavernous chamber, its jagged low ceiling lit by dozens of oil lamps.

The golden seal could be seen in plain view here, adorning the ground below what appeared to be a prehistoric cave painting. It depicted a crude target or sorts; a large round dot surrounded by a circular ring.

Gabriel wasted no time. He bent over the seal and inserted the Cube into its slot. After the customary jolt of pain, he and Natasha watched as its colour changed from yellow into a rich hue of emerald green. Natasha explained that this was the colour of the fourth *Anahata* chakra, the energy centre located in the centre of the chest, just above the heart.

"A dot within a circle," she said, looking up at the crude painting on the wall. "This is the alchemical symbol for gold, but it's also a circumpunct, an ancient symbol for the higher-self."

Gabriel examined the painting.

"There's a second outer circle here," he said, running his hand over its surface. "It's very faint."

Gabriel opened his duffel bag and produced the Book of Khalifah, handing it to Natasha. She read the fourth riddle aloud.

The Two look inward to the divine core,
But first come to the walls that enclose it.
One is of deception.
The other of misconception.

There is a fragment here that never sleeps.
To transcend it one must be relentless.
If the child is to mature,
The teacher must be patient.
Only then can the apprentice become the master.

"I'm completely lost," said Gabriel. "What's the alchemical stage for this seal anyway?"

"Conjunction," said Natasha, putting the book down on a nearby boulder and moving closer to the painting. "The bringing together of two parts to make a single element."

Gabriel rubbed the stubble on his face as he considered.

"And what's this seal's divine action?"

Natasha was examining the painting's surface.

"*Atma-Jnana*," she said. "It's the Hindu contribution to the gnosis. It means self-realization, which is the experience of the true self, and its oneness with *Brahman* or God."

Gabriel nodded.

"So the riddle and the cave painting are both referring to the same thing: The higher-self."

"Yes, but it's not just a cave painting," said Natasha, turning to face him. "It's a mandala; a meditative symbol. The central dot represents our divine core. The outer circles represent our lower-self."

"So the outer circles are the walls that the riddle talks about," said Gabriel. "The ones that prevent us from reaching our divine core. One circle symbolizes deception, and the other circle symbolizes misconception. Which is which?"

"The outer circle is definitely deception," said Natasha, pausing for only a moment before continuing. "It represents our mask-self."

"The person we pretend to be," said Gabriel, thinking.

Natasha went back to where she had laid the Book of Khalifah and began to search through its pages.

"This is starting to make sense, Gabriel," she said, finding the passage. "Listen to these lines. I remembered having seen them in the cleric's letter to the Umayyad Caliph of Cordoba."

She translated from the Arabic as she read.

"Know, oh prince, that the divine core is hidden like an emerald in a cake of muddy clay. Only when the mind's eye unites with this core can the mud be washed away, and the inner child exposed and re-educated. In this way the lower shall be raised to the higher, and the two conjoined at last."

Natasha looked up from the book.

"The lower-self is the inner ring in the mandala," she said. "It's being likened to an ignorant child full of misconceptions. The child can be re-educated only if the teacher is patient, and that's where the love from the heart chakra is taken into account. It's not a question of destroying the lower-self, it's a matter of helping it to grow up. After that, the inner child sees things clearly, and it merges with the divine core, or the higher-self."

Gabriel went to investigate a shadowy area of the chamber and soon found a rough bench carved into the rock.

"I think I might have just found that *mind's eye* you were reading about," he said, directing the beam of his flashlight to a crude image on the ground.

Natasha came up next to him. At the foot of the bench was the painted image of an eye.

"This bench symbolizes the objective point of view," she said, sitting down upon it.

She patted the space beside her and smiled. Gabriel sat down too. From their new position they could see that the oil lamps in the room had in fact been strategically positioned. Their light was reacting with a reflective material in the paint and giving the mandala a magical glow.

"Mandalas are meant to be meditated upon," said Natasha. "Try to concentrate on the symbol and think about the knowledge it's relating to you."

Gabriel did as he was told, emptying his mind of all other thoughts. Natasha continued.

"The alchemists believed that the human personality was comprised of three basic components," she said. "The mask-self, the lower-self, and the higher-self. Once the mask-self is dissolved, the lower-self can begin to be integrated into the higher-self."

"Conjunction," said Gabriel. "The fourth stage of alchemy."

"Yes," said Natasha, "and when it's accomplished, one becomes the *Jivanmukta*."

"What's that?" asked Gabriel, looking over at her.

"It's Sanskrit for a person who has experienced the state of Atma-Jnana and attained *Moksha*."

"Which is…?"

"Liberation from the cycle of death and re-birth," said Natasha, turning to look back at Gabriel. "Ascension to the higher spheres. Moksha is the reason why we incarnate on Earth."

Gabriel returned his gaze to the glowing mandala.

"Tell me more about this mask-self," he said. "Why is the ring that represents it in the mandala so hard to see?"

"Because the mask-self doesn't really exist," said Natasha. "It's a fabrication."

"A psychological image?" asked Gabriel.

"Yes. A master image. It comes into being during childhood. It's designed to bring us happiness, but it brings the exact opposite."

"How so?"

"It's basic psychology," said Natasha. "When a child misbehaves, the parents usually take away their love as punishment. This is the most traumatic thing a child can experience. On the other hand, when the child is good, the parents reward him with even more love. The basic image the child formulates is that he must be good and saintly and avoid being bad at all costs."

"So the child tries to be good," said Gabriel with a shrug. "What's the damage in that?"

"He ends up creating a mask-self," said Natasha. "One that's always good. The trouble is, the child knows he's nowhere near as good as his mask-self is. It's just an act, and he can sense there's something really dishonest about it. Because of that guilt, the whole construct eventually gets buried in his unconscious mind, but the feeling of being a fraud never entirely disappears."

"I get it," said Gabriel. "And as we grow up, we start to identify with our mask-self, instead of with our true, imperfect self."

"Yes," said Natasha. "And as we can never live up to the mask-self's ridiculously high standards, we begin to hate ourselves, or feel we're failures. Either way, we put more and more energy into maintaining our mask-self, thinking that if we pretend hard enough, we'll eventually become that person.

"Of course we can't do this because that person's been a lie from the start, but the more we try, the more separated we become from our real self. We can't bear to look at our lower-self attributes, because admitting we have them would mean we're not who we think we are."

"And that's when things start getting messy," said Gabriel. "If we can't see our faults, we can never grow out of them. That's what the first and second seals were all about."

Natasha nodded, her eyes trained on the mandala.

"The mask-self can be found in almost everyone," she said. "At least to some degree. It's hard to uncover it because in one respect, it seems like the right thing to do. After all, how could it be wrong to be decent and loving, and never get angry or envious; to always try to be perfect?"

"You're right," said Gabriel, nodding. "But in the meantime, the unconscious fear of getting found out as a fraud rots you from the inside, even if you can't put a finger on it."

"That's why the mask-self has to be uncovered and dissolved before anything else can happen," said Natasha. "It's not hard to do once you've seen it in action and understand the damage it causes on so many different levels."

Gabriel crossed his arms.

"The initiate has to learn how to become perfectly imperfect..."

As he said these words, the outer ring of the mandala began to slowly disappear, leaving only one ring around the central circle.

"Well, there you go," said Gabriel. "We just dissolved the mask-self. All we have to do now is make that outer ring merge with the inner circle and we'll be through this seal. What about the *fragment that never sleeps*. What's that all about?"

Natasha concentrated on the riddle's fifth line but drew a blank. It was only then that Gutierrez appeared suddenly behind them.

"The lower-self and the inner-child comprise what is often referred to as the ego," he said. "They are one and the same thing."

"Hey!" said Gabriel, turning in his seat. "Where do you keep wandering off to?"

Gutierrez shrugged and then gave a courteous bow.

"You were both doing so well that I did not want to disturb," he said. "But here I must interject and remind you both that the human ego must be considered as a part of this mandala. The ego's transcendence is directly related to Atma-Jnana."

Natasha looked at Gabriel and then back to the priest.

"Of course it is," she said. "Please continue."

"The ego is comprised of two parts, my Queen," said the old alchemist. "The higher ego, and the lower ego. The higher ego is the mind's eye that the riddle speaks of. It can look at the entire personality objectively and can ask the divine core to take over, so that the ego might begin to transcend itself. The lower ego wants no part of this and works incessantly to prevent any of this from happening."

"So the lower ego is the *Fragment that never sleeps,*" said Gabriel.

"It is," said Gutierrez. "The lower ego is but a small fragment of a person's entire consciousness. It is the initiate's task to re-educate this aspect of himself so he might expand his field of operations. His awareness. His capacity to create.

"The trouble is that to the limited ego, expansion of this kind is synonymous with annihilation. The lower ego says, 'If my higher-self takes over, then I will cease to exist.' This, of course, is not at all the case.

"The ego is a divine aspect of the whole personality. It has its place in life. All that is required is that it allow the divine core to take control. Its resistance to do so must be overcome, again and again, until this is accomplished."

"And the initiate has to be relentless in order to make this happen," said Natasha, thinking of the riddle.

"Yes," said Gutierrez. "The lower ego uses pride, self-will, and fear to trick us into believing that the ego is all we are. Its attitude is always, *I versus you*. This is pride. The ego's defiance and rigidity comprise its self-will. It is always stubborn and spiteful. It says, "I will stay as I am." Finally, the ego uses fear to make free expansion seem like a mortal threat. Life is always growing and changing, but the ego wants no part of this."

Gabriel understood at last.

"And almost everyone alive is living in this fragmented ego state," he said. "Cut off from our divine core and everything that we truly are and can become."

Natasha smiled. She knew that they had solved the riddle.

"But the more we identify with our higher ego and use it to ask our divine core for assistance, the more we obtain the wisdom we need to teach our lower ego the truth about things; so that it can step down, and let the higher-self take over."

"*Only then can the apprentice become the master,*" said Gabriel, quoting the riddle.

In that instant the cave painting transformed into a single circle, exploding with light as the seal beneath it dissolved.

"Done," said Gabriel, rising to his feet and holding out his hand for Natasha. "Come on. Just two more to go and we can get the hell out of this place."

CHAPTER 36

Gibraltar.

Peralta opened his eyes to once again find the massive head of Bahadur looking down at him. The reflected light of the submarine port's waters was animating his bear-like features, accentuating the depth of his frown.

"You have been unconscious for almost six hours, my friend," he said in his deep basso. "We were beginning to worry."

Peralta rose groggily from his chair and rubbed his face.

Didn't he say that already?

He leaned on the worktable beside him, his eyes finding Shackleton. He was sitting erectly on his haunches, staring intently at him, as though waiting for an explanation.

"What was it that you experienced?" asked Bahadur.

Peralta stared back at the giant.

"I need caffeine," he rasped. "I need a lot of caffeine…"

By the time Peralta had finished his third cup of coffee, Scotty, Amir, Cassano, and Bishop Marcus had also joined them.

"Very well, my son," said the old bishop. "You have now most certainly had enough time to wake up."

"Spit it out, man," said Amir, putting a heavy hand on Peralta's shoulder. "Let's hear it. What happened?"

Peralta looked at them all in turn. He scrubbed at his messy head again, furrowing his brow in an effort to gather his thoughts.

"The Cube took me into the past, and into the future."

Amir cocked an eyebrow.

"In the game, you mean to say," he said. "In Apocatastasis, the dream simulation."

Peralta did not respond. He looked at Amir, still seeing him as an old man. He struggled to find a place to begin his story.

"Do you remember the symbol that Sir David and his knights had on their shields and tunics?"

"The Tree of Life," said Bahadur. "It was also carved into the doors that led into the City of Sarras."

Bishop Marcus pulled up a chair and sat down.

"The Tree of Life is an ancient analogy, my son," he said, adjusting his travelworn vestments. "Why do you bring it up now?"

Peralta held his gaze.

"Because it isn't just an analogy," he said. "It's also a map."

They heard a match flare and glanced over to see Scotty Roberts lighting up one his cigarillos. He pushed aside some clutter on a nearby workbench and sat himself down.

"A map of what, mate?" he asked offhand.

"A map of spacetime," said Peralta. "A map of the multiverse…"

Everyone looked at the unkempt engineer, waiting for an explanation.

"Einstein's theory of relativity states that past, present, and future, all exist simultaneously," he rasped. "They coincide in a block of what he called spacetime."

"What the hell are you blabbering on about now?" said Scotty, spitting out a shred of tobacco.

Peralta adjusted his glasses.

"I'm talking about the illusion behind our perception of time," he said carefully. "Think of a movie reel. It's made up of thousands of still images. When the images are projected one after the other, we get the illusion that they're moving, but they're not moving at all. They're just a collection of still images."

Amir was as lost as Scotty.

"So?"

"So, our perception of time is no different," said Peralta. "Think of every moment in time as being frozen, just like a single frame in a movie reel. All those frozen moments are contained inside the spacetime block, just like all those individual frames are contained in the movie reel."

Amir frowned as he considered the concept.

"So every moment in time, from the distant past, to the present, to the distant future, is a stationary moment frozen in the spacetime block?"

"Precisely!" cried Peralta. "Time isn't what moves. *We're* what moves. Our consciousness moves through the spacetime block. That's what gives us the illusion that time is passing. Time doesn't really exist. Einstein called it a stubbornly persistent illusion."

"And how does the Tree of Life fit into this, my son?" asked the bishop.

Peralta thought for a moment, and then opened a nearby drawer. He produced a deck of cards and tossed it into the air.

"I could do that a million times," he said as the cards fluttered to the ground, "and each time, the cards would fall in a slightly different pattern. As far as spacetime is concerned, all those millions of patterns happened simultaneously just now, even though we only experience one of them. The same thing happens with absolutely every event that could possibly take place. All variations occur simultaneously."

"I'm afraid I do not understand..." said the old bishop. "If all those other possibilities exist, then where are they?"

"They exist in physical universes that are adjacent to our own. The whole structure is called the multiverse. If you could map them, they would take the form of a tree."

"But with so many different universes being created at every moment, the cosmos would be impossibly huge," said Amir. "Each variation would create an infinite number of other variations that would stem from it, and each of those variations would do the same."

Peralta nodded.

"Absolutely," he said. "The size and complexity of the Tree of Life is so vast that it's beyond human comprehension."

"And you're saying we live in this tree," said Scotty.

"Yes," said Peralta. "We make our way through it much like a character makes his way through a video game. Any event we could possibly encounter, already exists within the program, or in our case, within the Tree of Life.

"Anything is possible because everything that's possible already exists in spacetime. Achieving your goals in life is just a matter of correctly navigating your way through the tree. It's all about cause and effect; making the right decisions and doing the right actions so as to move along the right branches."

"And how does the Cube play into all of this?" asked Amir, a cinnamon toothpick in his mouth as he spoke.

Peralta paused to gather his thoughts.

"The Cube appears to be directly synced to this tree," he said, frowning. "I still don't know exactly to what extent, but what I do know is that the reptilian king and queen used the Cube to travel back to the birth of spacetime; to the root of the tree."

"Why?" asked Amir.

"To build the Labyrinth," said Peralta.

"But why the beginning of time, my son?" asked the old bishop.

Peralta gave him a nod of gratitude. It was a good question.

"The purpose of the Labyrinth is to disseminate the gnosis," he said. "That gnosis has to filter up through the

Tree of Life. If they'd built the Labyrinth any time after the birth of the universe, there'd be branches of spacetime that the knowledge could never reach.

"Any fallen angels inhabiting those branches wouldn't be able to access the gnosis and would be lost forever. In order for the Apocatastasis to occur, every fallen angel has to return to the higher spheres; even Lucifer, but he'll be the last to ascend, because he was the first to fall."

"Incredible," said the old bishop.

"It gets even crazier," said Peralta. "Building the Labyrinth was a suicide mission. It would need to be built in the lowest level of Hades, and the king and queen knew there'd be no way to get out after they'd finished. They'd be forced to go through another two hundred and fifty-million-year cycle of evolution, even though they'd already reached enlightenment, and could have ascended to the higher spheres if they'd chosen to."

"This was an inconceivable sacrifice they made…" said Bahadur.

"I'd say," said Peralta.

"But why didn't they ascend and then incarnate as humans to build the Labyrinth?" asked Amir. "Why did they have to do it as reptilians?"

"Because of two factors," said Peralta. "Energy requirements and the wormhole. To build the Labyrinth would require an inordinate supply of energy. The universe is powered by gravity. It's the strongest of all the forces, even though it appears to be the weakest because of its dispersion through the infinite dimensions of the multiverse.

"The only place to access the kind of gravitational force needed to build the Labyrinth was in the galactic plane. They needed one pass through it to harvest the energy required to build the Labyrinth, and another pass through it to activate the Cube."

Amir nodded.

"The galactic plane is a flattened-out black hole. It has an incredibly strong gravitational field…"

"Yes," said Peralta, rising to his feet and beginning to pace. "That's why we were thrown forward in time when we came out of it, and that's why Gabriel and Natasha are racing towards the future the longer they remain in it."

Peralta seemed deeply troubled.

"What is the matter, my son?" asked Bishop Marcus.

"There's something about the Cube that I can't seem to make any sense of, and it's driving me crazy."

"Tell us," said the bishop, leaning forward. "It will ease your mind."

Peralta turned to face the old man.

"All the reptilian technology is based in biomimicry," he said, pointing to a bank of monitors that were blinking with streaming reptilian data. "They copied the way nature works. The Cube is a perfect replica of the multiverse. It's so precise, that I don't know where it ends, and where our present universe begins. It's as though the two were quantumly entangled."

"Back to your bloody blabbering again," said Scotty, lighting a second cigarillo. "Speak in English, mate!"

Peralta resumed his pacing and proceeded to relate all the events that had befallen him while in the Cube's dream interface. He told them of how he had visited the governor of Gibraltar and found Amir one thousand years in the future. He related all the strange things he had seen, telling them of the planet Niburu X, and what he had learned after taking the blue pill that Amir had given him.

"But none of that was real," said Amir. "I wasn't real. It was all just a simulation, can't you see? It was a dream."

Peralta stopped and turned to face him.

"Was it?" he asked. "And what exactly is a dream, my friend? The exact same number of neurons fire in your brain when you're dreaming as they do when you're awake. To our brains, there's no difference whatsoever between being awake and dreaming."

Peralta turned to look at the submarine. It sat in the centre of the cave, the black water lapping around its dark hull.

"In the future," he said at length, "Amir and the governor knew something I didn't know. They said they couldn't tell me what it was; that I had to figure it out for myself..."

Bahadur came to his side.

"To transcend the Cube is to see it in all things," he quoted. "Perhaps the answer to your mystery is contained in those words."

Peralta turned and looked up at the giant, his face transforming as a thought occurred to him.

"But that would mean that all this time..."

"What are you thinking?" asked Amir, rising to his feet.

Peralta rubbed his face.

"How could I have been so stupid?" he said, understanding at last. "It's not a matter of the Cube and our universe being tangled up. It's a matter of the Cube and our universe being one and the same thing!"

He returned to the computers and tapped away at a keyboard, watching as a new series of exponents ran across the screen. He shook his head incredulously as the mathematical proof was offered up to him, and then turned to face the others.

"I've just initiated a computer simulation to confirm the data, so I won't know all the facts for at least another few hours, but this much I can tell you. We, my friends, have been squeezed into a three-dimensional, cube-shaped multiverse for the past 14.6 billion years. Ever since we fell!"

"What do you mean?" asked Amir.

"I mean this whole world; the one we think is so real, is in actual fact a simulation! It's no different to the Cube's dream interface. It came into existence when Lucifer opened up the Einstein-Rosen Bridge that we call the Portal of Ahreimanius. Lucifer made some promises, and we followed him into it, despite all the warnings that we'd been given. As it stands, the only way out of this prison we're in, is to dream our way out!"

"But surely this is just a theory," said Bahadur.

Peralta shook his head.

"Math doesn't lie. The fractal equation that the reptilians used in their axiomatic decryption code is a constant in the fabric of spacetime. It's the bloody mathematical recipe of creation! We're living in a dream simulation. We always have been!"

"What the hell is a fractal equation?" asked Scotty.

Amir answered the question for Peralta.

"It's a mathematical pattern," he said, still contemplating the magnitude of what Peralta had just said. "It's the same on all scales, no matter how big or small it gets."

Scotty exhaled a mass of cigar smoke and Amir pointed to it.

"Clouds are a great example," he said. "If you zoom into them, the shapes you see are identical to the shapes you were just looking at. If you zoom out, the shapes you see are the same too, even if they're in a nebula that measures millions of light years in diameter.

"Fractals go on forever in both directions. They're like algorithms that nature's built on. They govern everything from the way a blood vessel grows to the way a galaxy forms."

"The micro is in essence the macro," said Peralta. "And vice versa. For this reason, everything can be seen within everything else. *To transcend the Cube is to see it in all things.* The reptilians mimicked this characteristic of the universe to create the Cube, and in the same way, the Cube has mimicked the characteristics of life to create the game."

"How so?" asked Amir.

"The game's a metaphor of life," rasped Peralta. "It performs the same function as a myth."

"And how the hell does it do that?" asked Scotty.

Peralta turned back to the monitors and spoke as he studied the data that was coming up.

"Myths have always had to relate sublime universal concepts in terms that primitive people could understand," he said, scanning a line of code. "That's why they always sound so primitive. A shaman would delve into the unknown depths of his psyche, uncover profound universal truths, and then try to relate what he'd found by coming up with stories that his villagers could understand."

"And?" asked Scotty.

Peralta turned away from the monitors to look at him.

"And that's exactly what the reptilians have done," he rasped, taking off his glasses to wipe them. "Only they had it a lot easier than the shaman did. The reptilians knew that people would be a lot less dumb in the future.

"Instead of the meaning of life having to be likened to a hero cutting his way out of the belly of a whale, the reptilians are telling us that the meaning of life is like a hero making his way through a video game, so that he can *escape* from the video game!"

Amir shook his head incredulously. Peralta was making perfect sense. He removed the toothpick from his mouth and used it as a kind of talking stick.

"In the Cube's game," he said. "You incarnate as an avatar and collect experience points by getting past barriers and going through good times and bad times. You assimilate knowledge and move up in levels until you eventually ascend as a god. It's just like life. The only difference is that the Cube's world isn't real. It's a myth. It's true, and not true, all at the same time."

"Every myth is true!" exclaimed Peralta, moving away from the monitors to where he had placed his electrode-covered sample of reptilian goo. "Even the most primitive ones. They all point at the same existential facts. I tell you, our universe is like the Matrix, but unlike the movie, it's our souls that are plugged into it, not our bodies."

"But what's outside of the Cube?" asked Amir. "That's the real question."

Peralta had a look of awe about him as he replied.

"Countless inhabitable dimensions that we are totally incapable of experiencing in our current state of awareness..."

"What dimensions?" said Scotty, unimpressed.

Peralta glanced over at him, still lost in amazement.

"Take for example our three dimensions," he said. "There's length, width, and height. They're easy for us to understand, right? Well, when Amir was an old man in the future, he told me that there was also a fourth dimension to our world. He called it *depth.*"

"But depth is just another way to describe length," said Bahadur. "The depth of the ocean can be measured."

"Old man Amir wasn't referring to that kind of depth," said Peralta. "Think of depth in terms of feelings and emotions. It's hard to grasp, but you can easily sense it if you try. Depth can be felt within you. It goes into a place that can't be measured with a ruler. That place is an inner world. It's every bit as real as the outer world we live in, but it's sitting in a different dimension."

"So what's your point?" asked Scotty.

"My point is that if it's hard for us to grasp a dimension like depth, imagine how impossible it would be for us to imagine other dimensions that are completely foreign to us?"

"Yet they're every bit as real as our four dimensions..." said Cassano, assisting Peralta with the wiring.

"Exactly," said Peralta. "We're like fish trapped in an aquarium. The first step out of the tank is to know that we're *in* the tank. The real world is much bigger than our limited little universe. If we could get out of this Cube, we'd be able to experience it."

"What on earth are you up to now?" asked Scotty, watching as Peralta placed a set of headphones over the orange glowing goo.

"When I was in the future, Amir told me that it was imperative that we make contact with Gabriel and Natasha. He said the fate of humanity depended on it. Gabriel and Natasha need to know the truth. Without it, they'll never be able to open the sixth seal."

"What truth, mate?" asked Scotty.

Peralta turned away from his work and looked back at the smuggler, his expression dumbfounded.

"Have you been asleep this entire time?" he asked, amazed. "We're in the bloody Cube, man! Humanity is, and has always been, trapped inside a holographic simulation! Knowing that kind of changes our perception of things a little, don't you think?"

Scotty Roberts only shrugged and produced yet another cigarillo.

"Keep your bleeding shirt on, mate," he said, striking a match. "If life's just a video game, then there's no point getting stressed about it now is there? Bloody hell…"

CHAPTER 37

In the Labyrinth of Sarras.

Natasha looked over at Gabriel. They were still squeezing their way through the worming passages, burrowing deeper and deeper into the Labyrinth. For quite some time now a sound similar to that of the ocean had been getting progressively louder.

"Can you smell that?" she asked.

Gabriel inhaled and nodded.

"It smells like the sea."

In that moment a briny gust engulfed them both, and Natasha grabbed Gabriel's hand, tugging him forward.

"This is the first fresh air I've breathed in what feels like months. Come on!"

It was not long before the constricting tunnel opened onto an expansive ocean, its untamed waters crashing on giant rocks below. A full and waxing moon lit the scene, and they could see that they were at the outermost point of a promontory, at the base of a towering cliff. Below them, a sturdy breakwater made its way out into the pounding surf.

"My God," said Natasha, her hair blowing in the wind. "This is so beautiful…"

Gabriel scanned the moonlit cliff face that they had emerged from. It looked to be over six hundred feet high and was comprised of glossy wet granite. At its top was an old Roman watchtower, crumbling and overgrown.

Gabriel turned back to find that Natasha had made her way down the rocky crags to the water. She was sitting down on a narrow shelf overlooking the pier, her legs dangling over the side and swinging contentedly.

"Come down!" she cried over the crashing waves. "It is wonderful here!"

Gabriel sauntered down the craggy steps, awestruck by the unbridled power of the ocean. The waves looked to be over fifty feet high and were crashing with such force that they shook the bedrock.

"This has got to be Finisterre!" he hollered over the pounding surf.

He sat down next to Natasha and put an arm around her, pulling her close.

"*La Costa de la Muerte*," he said into her ear. "The druids called this Land's End."

"What do you think that is?" asked Natasha, pointing to the end of the jetty.

Gabriel frowned and rose to his feet to get a better look.

"I have no idea…" he cried, squinting into the wind. "It looks like a crate…"

He offered Natasha his hand.

"Shall we investigate, pretty girl?"

Natasha let Gabriel pull her up and then fell into his arms, giving him a passionate kiss that ended with a beaming smile. She was glad to be with him, and out of those horrible tunnels. She took Gabriel's hand and led him down to the jetty.

At the end of the pier the two of them came upon an antique, iron-shod trunk. It was battered by the elements and slick with ocean spray.

"It's an old sea chest!" hollered Gabriel over the howling wind.

He opened its latch and within found a Viking's blowing horn, ornately carved with Nordic runes. Gabriel produced his flashlight to better study the thing.

"This is weird!" he cried, pointing to a string of text engraved around the horn's open end. "There's a Latin inscription."

"*Manifestabo Desideriis Renuntians Eos.*" cried Natasha, reading the text. "Manifest your desires by renouncing them."

"In other words," shouted Gabriel, handing Natasha the horn and rising to his feet. "Make your dreams come true by giving them up. I thought we were supposed to hold on to our dreams!"

He turned to look out over the raging surf, only to find that Gutierrez was standing beside him. Strangely enough, the roaring of the ocean and the howling of the wind lessened just then. It was as though the old alchemist had cast a spell.

"Well?" asked Gabriel, welcoming the reprieve. "Got anything to offer up on this one?"

Gutierrez scanned the ocean, the silent wind billowing through his robes.

"Desire is like sculptor's clay, my Liege," he said. "One must learn how to work it, or one will always make a botch of things."

Natasha came up on the other side of the alchemist, amazed by the sudden silence. It lent a surreal quality to the turbulent scene that surrounded them.

"Eastern philosophy claims that true happiness can only be attained when all desire is eliminated," she said. "They believe that desire is a hindrance."

"This is only partly true, my Queen," said Gutierrez, with a bow. "It is untrue in the sense that it is impossible to be motivated to create anything if desire is absent, even if what you want to create is desirelessness. Desire in itself is neither right nor wrong. Its creativeness or destructiveness is a direct result of its expression. It is a vital force, even if it has been feared and repressed throughout the ages."

"If desire's so important," asked Gabriel, "why would we want to renounce it?"

Natasha answered before Gutierrez could.

"Because if you can't give a desire up," she said, "it was never a desire in the first place. It was a demand; a product of self-will, not love."

Gutierrez nodded.

"Whatever your demands create will never fulfill you," he said. "Only the life force can manifest what you truly long for, but the life force can never be threatened or coerced. It must be induced with a patient and harmonious soul movement."

"And what exactly is a soul movement?" asked Gabriel.

"A soul movement is comprised of the feelings and attitudes that are connected to any desire you might have," said Gutierrez. "The movement can be healthy or unhealthy."

"I don't understand," said Natasha.

Gutierrez turned to her.

"If you observe how a particular desire makes you feel as you contemplate it, my Queen," he said, "you will easily discern the nature of the soul movement behind it. A disharmonious soul movement will feel tight and urgent, while a harmonious one will feel soft and flowing. For a desire to be truly fulfilled, no urgency can be attached to it. You must be so content and fulfilled in your present situation that the desire need not even be realised."

"But that would mean that it wasn't even a desire anymore..." said Gabriel, suddenly realizing that this was what renouncing a desire meant.

Gutierrez took the horn from Natasha and handed it to him.

"You must be able to say of your desire, *My life is already full, and as such, I can live without it. I can go through the pain of not having it.* In this state of mind, you allow the life force to make that desire become manifest.

"Tell me, my King, what is it that you most desire at this moment?"

Gabriel looked at Natasha.

"To get past these last two seals and get the hell out of this labyrinth."

"Very well," said the alchemist. "Relate this desire to your innermost being and then sound the horn. But be sure to keep everything that I have said in mind as you do so."

Gabriel reached over and took Natasha's hand, pulling her towards him.

"Any last suggestions?"

Natasha smiled.

"I think you're the kind of man who usually gets what he wants. Just do what you normally do. I'm sure it'll work."

Gabriel looked over at Gutierrez and held up the horn.

"What I normally do is not let myself give a shit."

The old alchemist gave a single nod.

"That is what is more reverently known as *Holy Indifference*, my Liege."

Gabriel shrugged and then blew into the horn with all his might. In an instant a loud note sounded, and no sooner had it done so than the pounding surf became suddenly calm.

Gabriel lowered the horn, amazed. The raging ocean had turned into a sea of glass.

"Look," said Natasha. "There's a boat on the horizon."

It was not long before the craft arrived, and they saw that it was a medieval bark, with a high prow and stern, and a single mast holding aloft a tattered, square sail. It had no pilot, and inlaid into its otherwise empty deck was a shining, golden disc.

"That's got to be the fifth seal," said Gabriel as the boat pulled up to the peer.

Gutierrez drew their attention to a sign that was affixed to its hull.

BE WARNED, ANY WHO WOULDST SET FOOT
IN ME, THAT THOU BE STRONG OF FAITH AND
PURE OF SOUL, FOR I AM NAUGHT BUT LOVE
AND TRUTH, AND I WILL CAST DOWN ANY WHO
SPEAK THE POISONED WORD AGAINST ME.

Gabriel looked over at Gutierrez.

"Well that's definitely something to keep in mind before going aboard."

Natasha hopped onto the boat without a second thought.

"Wait!" cried Gabriel. "What are you doing?"

"Do you really think we would have made it this far if we weren't strong of faith and pure of soul?"

She knelt down beside the seal.

"Really, Gabriel. I'm surprised at you."

Gabriel looked back at Gutierrez only to find that the old alchemist had vanished.

"I was just playing it safe..." he said, hopping aboard.

"This is the *Vishuddha* chakra," said Natasha, studying the symbol on the seal. "It's located in the throat region, but it governs hearing."

Gabriel's fingers found the scar on his neck.

"Hearing..." he pondered, pacing the deck. "Wasn't the Divine Action for this seal, *Logos*, or *The Word?*"

Natasha looked up and nodded.

"It's the Christian contribution," she said. "Logos is at the root of all creation. *In the beginning was the Word, and the Word was with God, and the Word was God.*"

"The first lines in the Gospel of St. John..." said Gabriel, looking around. "Tell me, is there anything familiar to you about this boat?"

Natasha scanned the bark.

"Not really," she said. "Should there be?"

"Of course there should be," said Gabriel. "It's straight out of *The Quest For The Holy Grail.* Don't you remember the chapter about the boat that King Solomon built to serve the last of his bloodline?"

Natasha made the connection at once.

"It had a similar warning attached to its hull," she said. "It took Galahad and the Maiden to the heavenly City of Sarras, where they healed the Fisher King."

Gabriel smiled and nodded.

"That boat was the method of transport between the earth and the higher realms," he said. "If that boat is *this* boat, then we're standing on our ticket out of this labyrinth."

"Sarras was Holy Jerusalem," whispered Natasha in awe. "The City of God in heaven. If the legend is being mirrored, the king would have to be healed before we could get there. How are we supposed to do that?"

Gabriel produced the glowing Cube and turned it in his hands. Its rich emerald light was breathtakingly beautiful.

"The infirmed Fisher King wasn't just a guy," he said, looking into the Cube. "You yourself said it. He was a metaphor for the corrupt Catholic Church, and all the world's corrupted religions for that matter. We heal him by unlocking the gnosis and plugging that knowledge into the collective consciousness with the Cube."

He held up the shimmering artifact.

"You're absolutely right, Gabriel," said Natasha, amazed.

"Once that's done," he continued, "all the screwed up religious beliefs in the world will begin to get set straight, and just like in the legend, the land will be restored. Remember what my father said? The Cube is the Holy Grail, Natasha. It always was."

Natasha was shaking her head in astonishment.

"It also makes sense if you draw a comparison between us and the characters in the Grail legend. Brother Bernardo said that we're both Rex Angelus; direct descendants of Jesus Christ. In the story, it was hinted that Galahad and the Maiden were as well.

"Think about it. We've arrived at Finisterre, or at the End of the World, and now we're on the legendary boat that Solomon built for us. It's clear that we're going to be taken to Sarras, which is basically where this whole thing began. Sarras is heaven, or the higher spheres. It's our true home; the home we all left long ago."

Gabriel squatted down beside the disc and looked deeply into Natasha's eyes.

"What's the alchemical stage connected to this seal?"

"Fermentation," said Natasha, suddenly realizing how close they were to completing their mission.

"Fermentation in what sense?"

"In the sense of allowing all the knowledge we've unlocked so far to merge and ferment."

"So that it can be applied to a single purpose," said Gabriel. "So that it can be applied to Logos; to speaking the Word of Creation."

Natasha removed the Book of Khalifah from his pack.

"I'm getting the feeling that we're about to unlock something really big..."

She read the fifth translation aloud.

In the soil of the Earth there exists a power that brings forth life,
Yet it cannot be seen.
In the depths of the ocean there exists a power that sustains the world,
Yet it cannot be seen.
In wind, and in fire, there exists a power that governs all existence,
Yet it cannot be seen.

Therefore, that which is invisible is the true power,
And that which can be seen is the result of it.
Earth, water, wind, and fire are servants of the Master.
The Two speak the Word and are obeyed.

Mighty is he who knows the invisible.

The power of powers will be his to command.
Cursed is he who is blind to the invisible.
His struggle will only cease when the poison has been revealed.

Wealth cannot come from poverty.
Abundance cannot be born from lack.
Therefore, the Master finds the great richness within.
He sees what he desires and possesses it in faith.
He tempers his will and waits patiently for the arrival.
In this way he brings heaven to the earth.

"All right," said Gabriel, holding the Cube over the seal. "Are you ready?"

Natasha watched as he inserted it into its slot. No sooner had he done so than they felt the familiar jolt of pain in their heads and saw the Cube change from green to a deep purple.

"That is so beautiful…" whispered Natasha.

Gabriel was equally enthralled. The colour seemed to be of the same frequency as black light. He looked out over the becalmed ocean, noticing only then that the bark was taking them out to sea.

"You know, there's no way this boat could have brought the seal to us if the waves hadn't died down."

"A symbolic event," said Natasha, watching the jetty grow smaller and smaller as they slipped away. "The turbulent ocean was like a turbulent mind. It became still because your soul movement was healthy and harmonious when you made your wish."

"And what about the sign on the hull?" pondered Gabriel. "It says that the boat will cast down anyone who speaks the poisoned word."

Natasha scanned the bark.

"This boat must represent the life force," she said. "It'll take you to what you want, but only if you're pure of soul and strong of faith. If you're not, and you're speaking a poisoned word, it'll give you what you need, which might mean going down, before you can go up again."

Gabriel pushed back his hair and ran the riddle over in his mind.

"If Logos is the *Power of Powers*, then Logos must be invisible to us, like the things in our unconscious mind…"

Natasha nodded slowly.

"And if we harbour negative unconscious thoughts, we're going to create negative events. Remember what Uncle Marcus was talking about at the picnic. The physical universe is made up of malleable stuff. We literally shape it with our thoughts. That's what the riddle's saying when it states that the four elements are the servants of the master. They serve us by becoming what we tell them to become."

"And that's why making the Word visible is the key," said Gabriel, amazed by his sudden comprehension. "The Word is nothing but an unconscious thought that tells the life force what to create. The life force doesn't differentiate between good or bad. It just makes what you tell it to make. To take control of the creative process, the initiate has to find the screwed-up words that he's unconsciously speaking and then exchange them for healthy words."

"That's the divine action of Logos," said Natasha.

"You know," said Gabriel, thinking. "There's probably not a single person out there, including myself, who's wanted something so bad and gone through all the effort of working towards it, only to watch it all fall apart when it was just about to happen."

"There can only be two reasons for a failure like that," said Natasha. "A poisoned unconscious word, or an urgent, disharmonious soul movement behind the desire. In most cases it'll be a combination of the two."

Gabriel frowned.

"I guess the big question is, what does a poisoned word sound like, and how do you change it up for a healthy word?"

"I don't think that Logos is just about the words that are being spoken unconsciously," said Natasha. "It's also got to be about the general intentions and motives behind those words. Maybe there are fears or hidden agendas there, or negative things that we're only half aware of.

"Do you want the thing you desire for the sake of having it, or do you want it so that you can appear to be better than other people, or have power over them? That kind of thing…"

"The Triad of Death," said Gabriel, rising to his feet and beginning to pace again. "If what you want is in any way connected to self-will, pride, or fear, then your inner word will always be poisoned. This is precisely why the alchemical stage for this seal is fermentation. Everything the initiate has learned up to now has to be combined if he's ever going to find the unconscious poison that screws up his life."

Natasha nodded in agreement.

"In other words, we teach ourselves how to create good things in our lives by fully understanding how we've unconsciously created the bad things in our lives."

Gabriel smiled. Natasha had summed it up nicely.

"And that means not putting the blame on anything outside of ourselves when things don't go the way we want them to go," he said. "It means accepting that it was us who sabotaged our success, and no one else. There are no victims of chance here. There's only complete self-responsibility."

Natasha looked at Gabriel but said nothing. A deep understanding was pouring into them both. Logos truly was the secret of secrets. With this knowledge people could create anything they desired.

"I think that deep inside most of us feel we don't deserve the desires that continue to elude us," said Natasha. "We're scared of what might happen if we were to get them. The child in us thinks that maybe we'll be punished somehow, or we'll not be able to live up to the expectations and responsibilities connected to the desires. Maybe we feel guilty…"

"There could be a million reasons," said Gabriel, "but the bottom line is if you're not getting something you want in life, it can only mean that somewhere inside you're speaking a poisoned word against that thing."

He moved to the boat's railing and looked down at the water as it rushed past. He could feel the gnosis flooding into him. He was remembering. He looked over his shoulder at Natasha.

"The easiest way to prove you're speaking a poisoned word is to visualize actually having the thing you want, but can't seem to get, and listening into yourself as you do it. If you're ruthlessly honest with yourself, chances are you'll find a voice in you that says no to your desire, or maybe you won't even be able to make yourself visualize the desire in the first place. You'll put off doing it, or your thoughts will drift when you try. Either way it'll be pretty clear there's a blockage in you."

Natasha came to his side.

"In the same way," she said, "if you think about the wishes you've had in the past that have come true, you'll find there's no blockage in you with regard to those particular issues. There's only a deep inner yes that says you can have them; that you deserve them."

Gabriel bent to pick up the Book of Khalifah and read the last lines of the riddle aloud.

Wealth cannot come from poverty.
Abundance cannot be born from lack.
Therefore, the Master finds the great richness within.
He sees what he desires, and already possesses it in faith.
He tempers his will and waits patiently for the arrival.
In this way he brings heaven to the earth.

"The last three lines remind me of Mark 11:24," said Natasha. "*What things so ever ye desire, when ye pray, believe that ye receive them, and ye shall have them.*"

"What about the first three lines?" asked Gabriel. "And how does, *The master finds the great richness within* fit into any of this?"

Natasha sat down with her back against the railing and chewed her lip. She was stumped by the question. The fact that wealth and abundance could not be born from poverty and lack was obvious. The rich always tended to become richer, while the poor seemed to always grow poorer. But this inner richness that the riddle spoke of… What was it?

It was only after Gabriel had sat himself down next to Natasha, and they had both pondered the riddle for some time, that Gutierrez appeared before them.

"My dear King and Queen," he said with a formal bow. "What can a rich man do that a poor man cannot?"

Gabriel looked at Natasha before responding.

"He can spread his wealth."

Gutierrez nodded.

"And what if the rich man was to give away all of his wealth? Would he still be rich?"

"What are you getting at?" asked Natasha.

Gabriel answered before the old alchemist could.

"He's saying that a rich man can have nothing and still be rich, because inside he knows that his true nature is abundance. He can give away his entire fortune and never feel poor because he knows he already possesses everything. He can acquire another worldly fortune whenever he wants."

Natasha understood at once.

"There's no urgency in his desire to get rich again; no poisoned unconscious word that stops him. He always reacquires his fortune because being rich is his natural inner state, regardless of his current life situation."

"I guess that's what being truly rich means," said Gabriel. "It's got nothing to do with what you've got in your bank account, and everything to do with what you know you've already got right now."

Natasha's eyes lit up.

"So finding our inner richness means realizing our higher-self is just like the rich man. It's only our poisoned words that make us think otherwise."

"The fact of the matter is that no one is ever poor, my Queen," said Gutierrez, smiling kindly. "Even the most wretched of us is a very wealthy person. They just fail to realize this fact."

"At worst we're just broke," said Gabriel. "But there's a huge difference between being broke and being poor. One's a temporary state that we'll eventually evolve out of. The other is a lie."

"There goes the seal!" cried Natasha. "Gabriel, we're through!"

CHAPTER 38

A long minute passed before Gabriel or Natasha were able to voice their astonishment. After the seal had vanished, they had passed through the opening and descended a short ladder into the bark's lower cabin, only to find the most sumptuous room imaginable.

"This is incredible..." muttered Gabriel, stooping under the low ceiling.

Natasha remained silent. Her eyes were wide with wonder. Before them, under the golden light of many shimmering oil lamps, was a spacious canopied bed, laid out in deep crimson damask. It sat within a structure that was comprised entirely of polished tree boughs, their tangled branches strangely beautiful, and serving to hold aloft a veil of intricately embroidered silk.

At their feet were plush rugs, their rich hues merging with the dark wood that made up the cabin's walls and ceilings.

"This is the bed that Chrétien de Troyes wrote about in the Grail Quest," said Natasha, still in awe. "The one that King Solomon's wife built using boughs from the Tree of Life."

"You're absolutely right," said Gabriel, making his way to the bedside. "I never could figure out why the only thing that Chrétien de Troyes put on the boat was a bed. It seemed like such an odd thing to do."

He drew aside the diaphanous veil, seeing only then the silken sheets and sumptuous pillows that bordered the mattress on all sides.

"It's like a little world in there," said Natasha, peering over his shoulder. "It smells so fresh..."

Gabriel ran his hands over the strange boughs and then moved away to inspect the rest of the cabin. He looked back to see that Natasha had already climbed onto the mattress. She was luxuriating on it, a happy smile on her face.

"You're not going to find anything out there, you know," she said, her eyebrow arched suggestively.

Gabriel looked at her with a puzzled expression and then continued with his inspection of the room, walking around the bed to look for anything that might be relevant to the seal.

Not fifteen seconds had passed before he began to find it extremely difficult to ignore Natasha. As she had said, the cabin was empty, and he found himself increasingly engulfed by a very strong desire to lie with her. He turned in her direction.

"See what I mean?" she said from behind the veil. "This cabin's all about the bed. Come and see for yourself."

Gabriel watched as Natasha stretched her slender, ballerina's body out over the pillows, writhing with pleasure. He swallowed hard.

"I'll be right there."

No sooner had Gabriel spoken however, than Peralta's raspy voice sounded over his radio, the harsh static shattering the mood entirely.

"Are you guys receiving this?" rasped the engineer. "Can you hear me?"

Gabriel looked down at the device on his belt and hesitated.

"Gabriel Parker," said Natasha soberly.

He looked up to see that she was now on her knees, her hands clasping the polished boughs as she strained to look through the embroidered veil. Gabriel groaned and then pressed the speaker button.

"This had better be good."

"I've got them!" cried Peralta to the others before continuing. "Wow, you guys are really moving! At the sixth seal already! I had to reconfigure this goo three times before establishing this link! We've pretty well gone through the whole Solfeggio scale!"

Gabriel climbed into the bed not knowing what the quaky engineer was talking about. He drew the veil behind him as he entered.

"Hello? Hello!" rasped Peralta's voice. "Are you receiving?"

"Affirmative, Captain," said Gabriel, watching Natasha's fingers as they unhooked his armour. "How's everything on your end?"

"All is well, my son!" exclaimed the old bishop unexpectedly. "Did we catch you at a bad time?"

"Uncle Marcus!" cried Natasha, her words cut short by a loud bark on the other end of the line. "Shackleton! I'm right here!"

"I hate to cut this short," said Peralta, "but we can't waste any time with pleasantries. The goo's losing power fast, and this connection's already beginning to decay. I learned some important stuff when I hacked into the Cube's dream interface. I need to tell you about it."

"You hacked into the Cube?" asked Gabriel, cocking an eyebrow. "What did you dig up?"

"For starters, both of you are the same person."

"Say again?" asked Gabriel, exchanging a confused glance with Natasha.

"You guys were a single angel before the universe happened," said Peralta. "You *fell* on purpose, and you were split into two halves as a result."

"Why would we fall on purpose?" asked Gabriel.

"It was the only way you could help the other fallen angels get back to the higher spheres," said Peralta. "But there's no time to explain. What's important is that you understand that you're not two people. You're one."

Gabriel looked at Natasha and nodded.

"What else?"

"Waking life and the Cube's dream interface are essentially the same thing," continued Peralta. "One's just a reflection of the other. Simply put, humanity's been living in a holographic dream simulation since the beginning of time. We're all trapped in a three-dimensional Cube. The higher spheres are the innumerable dimensions that lie outside of the Cube. In short, life as we know it is a kind of super-high-tech video game."

"Like the Matrix?" asked Natasha.

"Yes," rasped Peralta. "But it's not our bodies that are plugged into the machine, it's our souls. The Cube is part of that machine. It's directly linked to a massive CPU that runs every aspect of the simulation. The CPU is alive and conscious, and extremely intelligent. You might call it God, or at least an aspect of God… There's only one catch, and I just figured it out about three minutes ago when the results of a simulation I've been running came in. The CPU only has one user slot!"

"Are you saying that only one person can interact with the dream interface at any given time?" asked Gabriel.

"I'm saying that there is only one person *in* the dream interface. Period."

"What are you talking about?" asked Gabriel. "That can't be right. There are close to eight billion people on this planet. They've all got to be in the interface too."

"I don't know how all this works," said Peralta. "Everything about the Cube and this universe is a paradox. The only thing that's important right now is that we get you out of that Labyrinth, out of this Cube, and into the higher spheres. The fact that there's only one user slot completely changes the game."

"How so?"

"If there's only one person plugged into the simulation, then only one person can be unplugged from it. It can't work any other way. You guys are going to have to be that person if you want to get back to the higher spheres. But you can't be that person until you become the *SAME* person."

"The alchemical marriage," said Natasha, looking over at Gabriel. "The unification of male and female aspects. Its metaphorical expression would be a man and a woman fusing into a single entity. Remember what the old gypsy woman said? We need to transcend duality and become like the divine androgyne…"

Gabriel nodded.

"Like Isis and Osiris in the pre-Egyptian myth. We need to become like Atum."

"Atum!" exclaimed Peralta, remembering. "Yes, that's right!"

Gabriel scratched his head.

"Natasha and I weren't the only angel that split into two halves after the Fall," he said. "Every angel got split. Nobody can get back into the higher spheres until they've merged with their other half and become a single entity again."

"And how the hell are we supposed to find our other half, mate?" came Scotty's voice. "I know for damn certain that it ain't the bloody witch I've got waiting for me at home."

"The universe takes care of the details," said Natasha, struggling not to laugh. "The two halves are brought together when they are both ready, and not a moment before. It can happen in this lifetime or in a future incarnation."

"But what about the single user slot thing?" came Amir's voice, the static growing increasingly louder. "If you guys end up being the person in the higher spheres who's wired up to the Cube, or the multiverse, or whatever it is, and this is your simulation, then who the hell is everyone else?

"We must all be computer generated simulants," said Peralta, disappointedly. "It's the only possible explanation. None of us exist outside the Cube."

"You're very mistaken, Mr. Peralta," said Natasha. "The ancient wisdoms state that we are all One."

"Like in the Beatle's song," came Amir's crackling voice. "*I am he, as you are he, and you are me, and we are all together.*"

"Exactly," said Natasha. "If there's only one user slot in the Cube, it's because there's only one person who can be plugged into it, and we're all that person."

It was only then that the connection at last began to fail.

"Guys!" cried Gabriel, picking up the radio. "Can you hear us?"

He looked at Natasha. It sounded like Peralta was speaking.

"The goo... losing... temporal coherence... need to say goodbye..."

Natasha spoke into the radio urgently.

"We love you all so much!" she said. "Thank you for all of your help! Thank you!"

The bishop's voice could be heard coming through the interference.

"God speed, my children. We shall meet on the other side!"

The connection terminated. Gabriel put down the radio and shrugged.

"Well, I guess that's that."

He looked up and saw that Natasha was crying.

"Now why on Earth are you doing that?"

"We'll not be seeing them again for a long time, Gabriel. They can't come where we're going. They're not ready yet..."

Gabriel touched her cheek and bent closer to her.

"You don't know that," he said gently. "And chances are you're wrong. I'll bet we see them all again, and very soon. Time doesn't exist in the higher spheres, remember?"

Natasha smiled and kissed Gabriel. He could taste the salt from her tears.

"You always have the right answers..."

"Always," said Gabriel, smiling.

He turned to hang his sword on the headboard only to notice a symbol carved into its surface. It was of a single eye at the centre of a square, with the image of a boat just above it.

"Now what could that mean?" he asked.

Natasha wiped away her tears and smiled radiantly. She pulled open the veil and looked under the bed, turning to face Gabriel with shining eyes.

"Give me the Cube."

Gabriel shot her a puzzled glance and produced the artifact from his pack. Natasha snatched it out of his hands.

"Ready for a little pain?" she asked.

Gabriel leaned over the side of the mattress to watch Natasha crawl under the bed and lie next to the sixth seal. It sat directly beneath the mattress. He watched her insert the Cube into its golden slot and felt the familiar pang of pain as the new alpha-wave link was established.

Both watched as the Cube changed back to its original hue of iridescent blue. Seconds later, Natasha was back atop the bed, leafing through the Book of Khalifah.

"How'd you figure out where the seal was?" asked Gabriel, still amazed.

"It was easy," she said. "The eye on the headboard is the same eye that we've seen depicted at the centre of every labyrinth symbol we've come across. It's the *All-Seeing Eye*. It represents enlightenment, or the Seventh Seal.

"The square in the carving represents the Cube, and the boat on top of it is where we are. We're literally right outside the Sacred Chamber, Gabriel. There was only one place where the seal could be. Directly beneath us."

Gabriel shook his head in amazement.

"Nice job," he said. "I couldn't have done it better myself."

"Here it is," said Natasha suddenly, placing the Book of Khalifah between them so that he could see it as well. She read the sixth riddle aloud.

The gateway to heaven is the mother of All.
It resides at the centre of the universe.
In this place the many souls are but one,
And the ten thousand places the same.
To transcend the Cube is to see it in all things.

Gabriel rubbed the stubble on his face.

"What's the alchemical stage for this seal?"

"Distillation," said Natasha. "What was fermented in the last stage is now distilled into an entirely new substance with no impurities in it."

"And the seventh stage?"

"Coagulation," said Natasha, looking deeply into Gabriel's eyes. "It's the final stage of the transmutation of the soul. If you think of the lead into gold analogy, the liquid gold that was distilled in the sixth stage is allowed to cool and gather itself into a solid metal."

"And what about the sixth chakra?" asked Gabriel, "The one that's related to this seal?"

"It is called *Ajna*, and it signifies the end of duality. Its seed syllable is the mantra, *OM*. You must have heard of this word before."

"I have," said Gabriel. "It's supposedly the name of God, and when properly uttered, it duplicates the natural frequency that the universe resonates at."

Natasha looked at Gabriel in surprise.

"I can't believe that you knew that!"

"I'm not as crude as I look," said Gabriel, frowning in mock offense. "I took a yoga class once."

"Well then you must know that the Ajna chakra is where the third eye is located."

Gabriel reached over and passed his thumb over the faint scar on Natasha's forehead, his eyes scanning her pretty face.

"What exactly does the third eye do, anyway?" he said softly.

"It's what we look through to see non-physical things," said Natasha, gazing deeply into his eyes. "It's the *mind's eye* from the fourth seal; the *mystical eye; the inner eye*. They say that to see through it is to be in harmony with the mind of the Kristos, or the Christ Consciousness."

"And how does all this tie in with the sixth divine action?"

"It ties in seamlessly," said Natasha, shaking her head in astonishment. "To see through the third eye is to temporarily transcend duality and experience things in their true, unified state.

"Transcending duality is what the sixth divine action is all about. It's called *Binah-Chokhmah*; the Judaic contribution to the gnosis. The Ajna chakra is directly attributed to it. The whole spiritual concept is referred to as *Unity Consciousness*."

"Binah-Chokhmah," repeated Gabriel. "What does it mean?"

"In the Jewish Kabbalah, the Tree of Life is made up of ten *Sephirot*, or enumerations, through which the Infinite reveals itself to mankind. Binah and Chokhmah are the two topmost sephirot. Only the sephirot *Keter* is above them."

"And what's Keter?"

"The ineffable mind of God," said Natasha. "Something we can't possibly experience with our normal consciousness. The seventh chakra, the crown chakra, is directly related to it. It's called *Sahasrara;* the thousand-petaled lotus."

"Then Keter must be the state of mind that allows you to inhabit those multiple extra-dimensions that Peralta was talking about," said Gabriel. "The ones that exist outside of our three-dimensional world; outside of the Cube…"

"The higher spheres," said Natasha, her eyes alight.

"And how do we attain this mental state of Keter?"

"Binah and Chokhmah have to become one," said Natasha. "Binah represents Understanding, which is the supreme feminine trait. Chokhmah signifies Wisdom, which is the supreme masculine trait. The sixth divine action fuses the two and opens the way to the seventh seal."

"The end of our journey..." said Gabriel. "The Labyrinth's exit."

Natasha nodded and pointed to the carving on the headboard.

"The *Ostium Sanctus* is located directly below us," she said. "But the only way to it is through Mithuna. We need to become *one*."

Gabriel understood at once.

"That's why Chrétien de Troyes put a bed on the boat," he said. "It's for Mithuna. He even made it from the boughs of the Tree of Life. It was a direct reference to Jewish mysticism."

Natasha reached over and resumed her task of unbuckling Gabriel's armour.

"It certainly seems that way," she said, smiling excitedly. "But there's only one way to find out..."

CHAPTER 39

Gabriel and Natasha's entangled bodies were moving in a slow, tantric dance. Their skin was bathed in the ship's warm lamplight, glistening with the sweat of hours of lovemaking. It was not long after they had been joined in Mithuna that they had begun to experience the mysterious, transcendental effects brought on by the ancient sexual positions.

All was fueled by the enigmatic Kundalini energy the professor had written of. It was a mystical force that rose and circulated through them with the power of a small sun. In this ancient ritual, two distinct individuals could occupy a single mind and body, bathed, as it were, in the golden light of the purest love imaginable.

Natasha was immersed in joy and bliss, her big eyes heavy with ecstasy. The cyclical pattern of their lovemaking was carrying her and Gabriel along a truly magical trajectory. What had begun as a slow, almost sleepy cadence, was gradually increasing in pace and intensity. Their physical surroundings were transforming as well, and soon their interwoven bodies had left the bedchamber entirely. They were hurtling through what could only be described as a rushing tunnel of plasma light.

A potent current of orgasmic pleasure was coursing up through Natasha's body now. It felt like cool, slippery water, and from her heart and breasts it passed into Gabriel's chest, transforming there into a molten flow of desire that descended through his torso to gush from his penis.

In Natasha's vagina, his fire was quenched, only to rise up through her body again, cool and shimmering, to begin the rapturous Kundalini cycle yet again. This was the fabled *Circle of Light* that Gutierrez had written of, and its radiant energy was carrying the two lovers into uncharted regions of body, mind, and spirit.

At ever-increasing intensity, they soared forward and inward simultaneously. The tunnel of plasma light was rushing past them at impossible speeds now, until even it could withstand the flight no longer. They had arrived at a critical velocity, where their passion could no longer be retained and controlled.

In a sudden bursting flash of sublime existentiality, the Circle of Light detonated like a sun in supernova. It stole the breath from their lungs and left them spinning slowly and weightlessly in a formless void of light and love.

The result of this culmination was pure ecstasy, and as the effects of the transcendent orgasm began to slowly ebb away, Gabriel and Natasha fell into a deep state of peace and relaxation. They were fully out-of-body now, and their consciousness floated unhindered in a vast and infinite cosmic landscape.

Gabriel... It's so beautiful...

As before, they had once again astral travelled to a distant star constellation; one that was easily recognizable to Gabriel by the shape of the giant nebula that lay before them. It resembled a proud eagle, light years across, and it was breathtakingly beautiful in its enormity.

Natasha could hear Gabriel's thoughts as if they were her own.

We're in the Serpens Constellation. The wormhole's taken us to the Eagle Nebula.

Natasha recognized it at once from the famous photo taken by the Hubble Space Telescope.

The Pillars of Creation...

It was only then that the effects of their trance began to wear off, and they quickly found themselves in the bark's bed chamber once again, lying in each other's arms.

Natasha wiped the perspiration from Gabriel's forehead, giving him a deep and passionate kiss.

"That was incredible," she cooed. "I think I'll keep you around."

She pushed herself off Gabriel and bent over the side of the mattress to look under the bed.

"Well?" asked Gabriel, propping himself up on an elbow.

Natasha returned to his side.

"The seal's still there…" she said with a pout. "Shouldn't it have opened by now?"

"We're missing something," said Gabriel. "We've got to figure out the riddle. I don't think we're going to be able to just shag our way through this seal."

Natasha nodded; her face still flushed from their lovemaking. She opened the Book of Khalifah.

"This shouldn't be so hard," she said. "It's only five lines long."

She read it aloud again.

The gateway to heaven is the Mother of All,
It resides at the centre of the universe.
In this place the many people are but one,
And the ten thousand places the same.
To transcend the Cube is to see it in all things.

Gabriel sat up.

"The *gateway to heaven* has got to be the seventh seal, Natasha. I think it's being called the *Mother of All* because it's the user slot Peralta was talking about."

"I don't understand."

"If a user slot existed, it would be the *mother* of the entire simulation."

"Why?" asked Natasha.

Gabriel collected his thoughts.

"If life's a simulation being created by the Cube, then anything on this side of the user slot is part of that simulation, and anything on the other side of the user slot is the real, multi-dimensional world where the user, or the *player,* lives. The higher spheres."

Natasha made the connection.

"That's why the final line of the riddle says that in order to transcend the Cube, it has to be seen in all things. If the Cube can be seen in everything, it's only because everything here is being generated by the Cube."

"Exactly," said Gabriel. "Our bodies are like characters in a video game. They're part of the game's software, and so is anything you can see, hear, smell, touch, taste, and even think. Everyone and everything is part of the Cube's software."

Natasha shook her head in amazement.

"Anything we can experience is made of *Cube stuff...*"

They were both silent for a while, thinking.

"That would put the Seventh Seal at the centre of our cosmos..." said Natasha at length.

Gabriel was confused.

"How's that?"

"If the Seventh Seal is what's projecting our three-dimensional universe," she said, "then it would have to be at the centre of that projection, right?"

"That could be the reason why we've been astral travelling while in Mithuna..." said Gabriel. "We've been trying to find the centre of the universe."

He passed a hand over the stubble on his face.

"The first time we ended up in the Crab Nebula in the Taurus Constellation," he said, thinking. "And we just came back from the Eagle Nebula in the Serpens Constellation. The two are over fourteen thousand light years apart. We've certainly been looking for something."

They fell into silence once again, thinking. Gabriel was first to speak.

"I still can't get my head around everybody being the same person," he said. "Even if we are all part of the same software program. How can everyone be the same person if we're different people? It just doesn't make sense..."

"Maybe we just think we're different people," said Natasha. "I've always found it amazing that we all feel the same emotions. They're like energy currents that each of us moves in and out of. If I feel sadness, it's not some unique emotion that only I can experience. It's the exact same emotion of sadness that people have been feeling for hundreds of thousands of years. It's like that with all our emotions. So really, how different can we be?"

Gabriel's expression suddenly changed. Natasha's words had struck a chord. He closed the Book of Khalifah with a thump.

"Let's suppose that I was the single player in the simulation's only user slot," he said. "According to what we've learned, I'd be creating the world I live in, right?"

"Always," said Natasha. "Thoughts create things and events."

"All right," said Gabriel, holding up his hands in a gesture of patience. "Now what if the world's population was made up of elements from my own unconscious mind?"

"What are you saying?" asked Natasha, confused.

Gabriel groaned in frustration.

"What if the person in the Cube's only user slot was a schizophrenic with eight billion alternate personalities?"

Natasha's eyes lit up with understanding.

"That would make everyone on this planet elements of a single, very confused, mind!"

Gabriel shrugged.

"What do you think?"

"I think you're on to something," said Natasha. "The only way a schizophrenic can truly be healed is when the impermeable barriers that separate his personalities are made permeable again."

"So the only way humanity can be healed," said Gabriel, "is for everyone to realize that we're all unique aspects of the same mind, and as such, we're all essentially the same person."

Natasha shook her head in amazement.

"The billions of people on this planet are nothing more than individual fragments of a consciousness that fell and exploded into this three-dimensional, dualistic multiverse."

"Everyone alive is the single user," said Gabriel. "It's kind of like how the entirety of a hologram is contained in each of its parts..."

"How's that?" asked Natasha.

"It's got to do with the way holography records light wave interference patterns," he said. "In our case, the entirety of the original mind would be contained in each of its fragments."

Natasha smiled.

"A mystic would say that an entire ocean is contained in every drop of seawater."

"All, truly, is One..." said Gabriel in stupefaction. "All the angels that fell... We all came from the same consciousness..."

He paused for a moment.

"But who's consciousness was it?" he asked. "Who's plugged into the user slot?"

Gabriel looked up at Natasha, his eyes wide with wonder.

"It's God, Natasha," he whispered. "There's only one consciousness, and that consciousness is God. It got fragmented after the fall, but it never stopped being God. We're all God. Everything is God."

Natasha bent over the edge of the bed again but saw that the seal was still intact.

"There must be something else, Gabriel," she said. "Something we're missing..."

"I know what it is, baby," he said, taking her hands into his. "Let me take you there."

* * * * * *

The nebula that stretched out before them was beautiful beyond description. Its form took the shape of a great golden eye with an iris of translucent blue.

"The Helix Nebula. It's also been called the Eye of God."

It was Gabriel's thought that came to Natasha's mind. The effects of their orgasm had still not fully dissipated in her, and she felt drunk with the beauty she was experiencing.

"We made it, Gabriel. We're here."

Gabriel's response came almost immediately.

"The nebula's not the centre of the universe, Natasha... This is."

Natasha felt a tingling sensation in her solar plexus.

"Look around," came Gabriel's thought. *"What do you see in every direction?"*

Natasha did as she was asked, her eyes wide with rapture.

"I see infinity…"

"Exactly, and that puts you directly at the centre of the universe."

"I don't understand."

"It's called triangulation. It's simple math. If you're surrounded by infinity in every direction, you can't be anywhere else but at the centre of the universe."

Natasha gazed into the Nebula.

"So then the Eye of God is at the centre of the universe."

"Yes and no," came Gabriel's thought. *"We were surrounded by infinity back in the Serpens Constellation too. That place was the centre of the universe as well, even though it's six and a half thousand light years from where we are right now."*

"I don't get it," said Natasha. *"How can the centre of the universe be in two places that are so far away from each other?"*

"It can't be," said Gabriel. *"The centre of the universe is always in the same place. It's right here."*

Natasha felt the tingling in her solar plexus again, and this time she understood why.

"*So, no matter who you are, or where you go,*" she said, "*no matter how many thousands of light years you may travel, you're always going to be surrounded by infinity in every direction. That puts you at the centre of the universe wherever you happen to be...*"

Gabriel looked deeply into the nebula, the enormity of the cosmic landscape filling him with unbounded awe.

"*Each and every one of us is the source of the projection, Natasha.*"

She was silent for a moment before responding.

"*That can only mean one thing, Gabriel. The Seventh Seal is directly within us...*"

In the blink of an eye they found themselves back in the bedchamber again, but this time everything, including their own entwined bodies, seemed to be in a state of dematerialization.

Below them, through the dissolving bed, they could see the golden seal and the Cube. Moments later everything was melting into nothingness, leaving a black and lightless void looming beneath them.

Natasha began to feel a deep fear overcoming her.

"Gabriel... I can't go in there..."

At that very moment the voice of Gutierrez came to them both.

"Do not be frightened, my King and Queen," he said. "Have faith in faith. Trust in trust. Fear is an illusion, a ghost without substance. It is easily dispelled. Love is the only true reality!"

And just then a radiant light seemed to ignite deep within Gabriel and Natasha, and it filled them with courage. Their ascension into Mithuna had fused them, body, mind, and spirit, and now, as one, they took the great plunge, letting themselves be taken by the black void that had engulfed the chamber.

In the blink of an eye a golden light returned to encapsulate them again, only this time with unparalleled splendour. They began to feel themselves dissolving into its radiance, but there was no more fear or dread, only joy. Tremendous joy.

Back in their sarcophagi, Gabriel and Natasha's physical bodies were breaking down into their base components of energy and information. It felt to them like a buzzing, orgasmic tingling, and it was profoundly comforting; like being lowered into a cradle, or a warm and cozy womb. The frequency was comprised of the purest essence of love imaginable, and it pulled them into a deep and blissful sleep.

"Praise be to God in the highest!" came Gutierrez' radiant call. "We are victorious!"

* * * * * *

Gabriel opened his eyes to see that he was lying in a clearing in the woods, surrounded by a circle of standing stones. Natasha was fast asleep in his arms, and he knew that he himself would not be able to stay awake much longer. The pull of sleep was far too potent.

He could vaguely recall having visited this place a long, long time ago, in a previous incarnation. He and Natasha had been children during the time of the druids then. They had unwittingly been drawn into the Portal of Ahreimanius, so as to fulfill certain requirements of their mission.

But whereas then the stones had been the source of a tremendous evil, they were now indescribably beautiful, and exuded a feeling of such tranquil peace that Gabriel was instantly filled with bliss.

It's so wonderful, but I don't understand...

It seemed that everything around him was veiled in a tingling, fragrant mist. It was only when sleep began to take him that he saw two diaphanous figures approaching. Their bodies were emitting light, and as they drew nearer, he recognized them at once.

"Suora? Fra?" he managed to utter. "What are you guys doing here?"

"Dear, Gabriel," said Suora, smiling tenderly. "Sleep, my child. You have been through a great ordeal. We have only come to take you home."

Gabriel felt a great happiness and tried to smile, but the urge to sleep was far too encompassing. A moment later he had slipped back into a deep and blissful slumber.

CHAPTER 40

Gibraltar.

The old bishop helped himself to another slab of prime rib roast, drowning both it and his Yorkshire pudding in thick, rich gravy. He was in the Royal Convent's officer's mess, seated at the bottom of a table laden with food and drink, and surrounded on all sides by his dearest friends. Each was dressed in his finest and flanked by his own personal waiter.

Directly across from Bishop Marcus, at the head of the festive table, lay the empty ceremonial armchair traditionally reserved for the Prince of Wales. In his jovial state, Scotty Roberts was in the process of dropping a generous slab of roast beef onto the prince's golden plate. Everyone was laughing merrily.

"It's time for an official toast!" said Major Roberts, standing up and raising his glass of wine. "I call upon our worthy bishop to do the honours!"

"And I second that motion, mate!" cried Scotty, rising alongside his brother.

All came to their feet, their faces bright and proud. The old bishop, preparing himself to rise, saw the heroic company of men standing at attention before him and his heart was joyful beyond description.

To his right was Captain Peralta, and beside him Amir, and the noble giant Bahadur. To his left was Sir David, wearing the elegant cloak that bore the seal of his order, along with Cassano, Scotty and the handsome major, in full uniform.

"My dearest friends!" said Marcus, coming to his feet.

His old eyes shone proudly.

"We have at last come to the end of our great adventure! The world has been saved, and humanity has happily entered into a new age of enlightenment. Let this toast be to Gabriel and Natasha, for without them, our victory would not have been possible!"

"To Gabriel and Natasha!" cried all in unison, and just then they turned their heads to see what the astonished bishop was pointing at.

In the time they had been toasting, Shackleton, who had been residing under the table, had climbed into the Prince of Wales's armchair, and sat himself stiffly upon his haunches, as though he too were partaking in the toast.

He was looking proudly back at the congregation, a puzzled expression on his handsome canine face. There could be no doubt that the dog was questioning their sudden interest in him.

"To Sir Shackleton!" cried Amir, raising his glass.

The resounding reply came from all those present.

"To Sir Shackleton!"

"And long live the new Prince of Wales!" bellowed Scotty drunkenly.

And as all returned merrily to their meals, so too did Shackleton begin his, bending over his plate of solid gold to gobble down all the meat that Scotty Roberts could heap upon it.

CHAPTER 41

When Gabriel at last awoke he found himself lying alone in what looked to be a hospital room. A soft, golden light was filtering in through the open window, and the bright chirping of birds outside told him it must be morning.

He had no sooner sat up in bed than Natasha entered, more beautiful than ever. She was wearing a glowing white summer dress, and her dark chestnut hair fell in thick ringlets over her bare shoulders. Love and happiness were shining from her eyes.

"Well, look who's up!" she said, stopping in her tracks and putting her hands on her hips. "It's about time!"

Suora and Fra entered the room just behind her. Gabriel could see that they were much younger now, just as they had been when he was a boy. He rubbed his eyes and then broke into a broad smile.

"You two," he said groggily, rising to his feet and embracing them both. "I thought I dreamed the whole thing…"

He put an arm around Natasha and drew her close, kissing the side of her head.

"And you!" he added affectionately. "Fancy not waking me up sooner."

Natasha only shrugged and motioned to Fra.

"I must confess that it was under my strict orders that she did not," he said. "Now is a time for rest. You must both be fully restored before you can proceed."

Gabriel went back to his bed and sat down. He was still feeling drained.

"Proceed?" he asked, looking around. "What is this place? I thought the spirit world was multi-dimensional and unlike anything I could imagine. This place looks pretty damn normal to me."

"We're on a hospital island," said Natasha, sitting down beside him. "It's a place where people come to rest before they proceed."

Gabriel looked at her incredulously.

"You're telling me that there are hospitals in the spirit world?"

Suora chuckled knowingly.

"Most definitely, my child," she said. "Everything on the Earth-sphere is an imitation of what has always existed in the spirit world. Here we have hospitals, schools, theatres, golf courses… Absolutely everything that can be found on Earth, and much, much more."

"And everybody who dies comes to this hospital island first?" asked Gabriel, amazed by what he was hearing.

"Not everyone, my son," said Fra. "Only those who have suffered traumatic deaths or endured rigorous ordeals leading up to their transition. From this island are portals that lead into all the various spheres of the spirit world.

"An entity's level of spiritual purification will dictate through which portals he or she may pass. Most will go to spheres where they can be reunited with loved ones and begin the process of planning their next incarnation on the Earth-sphere."

"We plan our lives on Earth ahead of time?"

"Most definitely, my son!" said Fra. "There are special advisors who assist people in this task. It is a lengthy process. Recent incarnations are evaluated and compared with previous ones. It is similar to watching a movie of your life. You can see where you succeeded in satisfying the life plan goals you set out to accomplish, and where you still need improvement."

"What kind of goals?"

"Goals of spiritual purification," said Natasha. "If you still have problems with self-will, for example, your advisor will help you to create a life plan that will focus on bringing out those faults so you can become aware of them and fix them."

Suora elaborated.

"Any impurities that are preventing you from entering into the next higher sphere will be focused on, my child. One does have to be patient though. You do not want to bite off more than you can chew in a single incarnation. People with very trying lives are usually people who have been very aggressive in their life plan."

Gabriel was amazed by what he was hearing.

"And how do these advisors make life plans happen?" he asked. "Is everyone's life pre-destined?"

"Not at all, my son," said Fra. "Life incarnations are predetermined by who an entity incarnates with, and in what historical period they take place. The actual events of a life incarnation are never planned, but factors are chosen that will direct universal laws to make a specific life plan manifest itself."

"Parents and other authority figures will be specially chosen for the person to be incarnated," said Suora. "Their faults and virtues will help him or her to evolve, just as he or she will help them to evolve as well. The geographic and political conditions that he or she lives in are also chosen for the same reason. Everything works seamlessly, my child. The Earth-sphere is a vast training ground."

Gabriel was shaking his head in amazement.

"A virtual school projected inside a cosmic, three-dimensional Cube…"

Suora put a reassuring hand on Gabriel's shoulder.

"You and Natasha are no longer required to incarnate on Earth anymore. You are sufficiently purified to move to the next higher spheres. The resistance of matter, and all the hardships it brings, are no longer necessary for your purification."

"And how many more spheres are there before we reach the top?"

"We are not moving to the top, Gabriel," said Fra, smiling kindly. "We are moving to the *Centre;* to the *One.* This place is called *The House of God.* It cannot be measured or quantified. It is indivisible. We will arrive when we arrive."

"Try not to dwell on any of this now, my child," said Suora. "You will understand soon enough. For now, you must rest. Think of this island as a kind of holiday resort. Anything you could possibly want can be had here. All you need to do is visualize it and it will immediately materialize before you."

Gabriel rose and walked to the window, astounded by what he was hearing.

"Now ain't that something," he said, gazing out onto the lush, tropical grounds. "We've been teleported to Fantasy Island for God's sake..."

He turned to face the others.

"Will we be having dinner with Mr. Roarke and Tattoo this evening?"

Natasha clapped her hands and laughed aloud.

"Yes!" she exclaimed. "We can definitely make that happen!"

* * * * * *

Gabriel sat at the wheel of his sportscar, its tuned exhaust note rising and falling rapidly as he revved the engine. They had been on the island for over a month now, and while it had been a wonderful stay, they were both anxious to move on.

He looked over at Natasha. She was sitting in the passenger seat, her face lit by a sun that was setting over a beautiful tropical ocean. The sky was ablaze with orange and crimson light.

"It kind of looks like a star gate," said Gabriel, studying the portal that lay directly ahead of them. "You know…? Like the ones from the TV show *Stargate*…?"

Natasha rolled her eyes.

"You're such a nerd."

Gabriel shot her a sidelong glance and returned his attention to the portal. It sat at the end of a hundred-meter-long stretch of road; a circular disc of what looked to be rippling water. It stood vertically within a golden hoop measuring about ten meters in diameter. Gabriel had caused a stunt ramp to materialize directly before it, and it was at this that the car was pointing.

"We don't have to drive through it you know," said Natasha, looking over at Gabriel. "Every other enlightened person has just walked…"

Gabriel shook his head disapprovingly.

"We're about to enter into a cosmic realm of unlimited possibilities," he said, his heart thumping. "Its dimensions are so vast and so exciting that Suora and Fra couldn't stay on this island for more than a few hours before feeling stifled and claustrophobic. You seriously want to just walk into something like that?"

Natasha shrugged and then smiled excitedly.

"Certainly not!" she said suddenly.

Gabriel revved the engine again.

"Nervous?"

Natasha turned to face him; her eyes alight.

"A little…"

Gabriel gave her a reassuring wink.

"No need to be nervous, my darling," he said, reaching over and giving her knee a squeeze. "I've covered every angle."

He put the car into gear and slipped one of Amir's hot cinnamon toothpicks into his mouth.

Natasha was surprised.

"You told me that you hated those things."

Gabriel only shrugged.

"People change. Now let's go see what all this multi-dimensional hype is about."

With these last words Gabriel released the clutch, launching the car forward, and accelerating to a frightening velocity. In seconds they were at the ramp and then airborne, the car vanishing through the portal without causing so much as a ripple in its surface.

It was only then that the two spectators who had been secretly watching stepped out from their hiding place behind the bushes.

"I thought they'd never leave, boss," said the shorter of the two.

"Neither did I, Tattoo," said Mr. Roarke, rolling his eyes. "Neither did I."

He who had first come to Earth in an ancient incarnation long, long ago, opened his eyes and took in his new surroundings. In his arms lay a sleeping woman of riveting beauty, her tussled blond hair falling over her naked body, accentuating her flawless, golden skin. He took in a breath of her and smiled, his sleepy eyes shining with love as he continued his survey.

They lay in a sun spattered clearing, in the midst of a springtime wood. Around them was a circle of standing stones, their ancient forms seeming to crackle with magical energy. He kissed the woman tenderly.

"Wake up, my love. Wake up."

Her soft eyes opened, and she smiled drowsily. Only then did he see a lone figure approaching. It was bathed in light.

"Brother?" he said, at last recognizing his face. "Is that really you?"

"It is," said the man, smiling. "It's good to see you here, Lucifer. I've come to take you home."

The visitor smiled, struggling to understand why his dead brother had just called him Lucifer. He went over the recent events in his mind. He and his lover had traversed the Great Labyrinth of Sarras and had assimilated each of the six stages of gnosis. They had transcended duality, passed through the Seventh Seal, and then arrived here.

"Why do you call me Lucifer?" he asked sleepily, struggling to remain awake.

"Because that's who you are," said his brother with a casual shrug. "You're the *Bringer of Light*, and your crazy stunt only confirms it. The Kingdom of God is fulfilled because of you. This might sound strange, but you are a hero here; truly the *Morning Star.*"

"I don't understand," he said, gazing down to see that his lover was fast asleep again. "If I truly am Lucifer, how could I possibly be a hero? Lucifer caused the Fall. One third of heaven has suffered in agony for aeons because of him."

"All that's water under the bridge," said his brother, smiling affectionately. "All's well that ends well."

It was at that moment that memories of the man's many past life incarnations flooded back into him. He realized that the person who stood before him was none other than his older brother Jesus, and that he himself truly was Lucifer; the first angel to fall, and the last angel to ascend.

With his arrival the apocatastasis had at last come to its fruition. Every fallen angel had now returned home, and Hades had been vanquished forever. The Kingdom of God had been restored at last.

"But a hero?" asked Lucifer, laying his head back.

The urge to sleep was overpowering. Jesus bent down next to him and put a hand on his shoulder.

"*The end of all our exploring will be to arrive where we started, and know the place for the first time,*" he said, quoting T.S. Eliot. "You unwittingly gave us a priceless gift, brother. You showed us all what home really is."

Lucifer looked sleepily into his brother's eyes, and in that moment knew that all the horrible acts he had committed were completely forgiven. A great happiness spread over him, coupled with the peace that only true redemption can bring.

"*And the Spirit and the bride say, Come,*" said Lucifer, quoting the last lines of the Holy Bible.

Sleep was taking him rapidly now, and it was all he could do to keep his eyes open. Jesus smiled tenderly, continuing the quote.

"*And let him that heareth say, Come. And let him that is athirst come.*"

Lucifer's eyes filled with tears. He knew that he was home now, and that he would never leave this place again.

"And whosoever will," he quoted, as sleep finally took him. *"Let him take the water of life freely."*

THE END

www.ingramcontent.com/pod-product-compliance
Lightning Source LLC
Chambersburg PA
CBHW031337020726
47499CB00005B/1300